This is not convincing :-H

Miss Pym Disposes

Josephine Tey is one of the best known and best loved of all crime writers. She began to write full-time after the successful publication of her first novel, *The Man in the Queue* (1929), which introduced Inspector Grant of Scotland Yard. In 1937 she returned to crime writing with *A Shilling for Candles*, but it wasn't until after the Second World War that the majority of her crime novels were published. Josephine Tey died in 1952, leaving her entire estate to the National Trust.

Praise for Josephine Tey

'A detective story with a very considerable difference. Ingenious, stimulating and very enjoyable' *Sunday Times*

'One of the best mysteries of all time' *New York Times*

'As interesting and enjoyable a book as they will meet in a month of Sundays' *Observer*

'First-rate mystery, ably plotted and beautifully written' *Los Angeles Times*

'Suspense is achieved by unexpected twists and extremely competent storytelling . . . credible and convincing' *Spectator*

'Really first class . . . a continual delight' *Times Literary Supplement*

'Josephine Tey enjoys a category to herself, as a virtuoso in the spurious . . . the nature of the deception on this occasion is too good to give away' *New Statesman*

'Tey's style and her knack for creating bizarre characters are among the best in the field' *New Yorker*

It is unconvincing thus: Mary Innes would not have taken on her shoulder the crime of Beau Innes. There is also the problem of only one part of footstrap. To the Gymnasium - mixture are missing

JOSEPHINE TEY

Miss Pym Disposes

arrow books

Published by Arrow Books 2011

1 3 5 7 9 10 8 6 4 2

First published in Great Britain in 1946 by Peter Davies Ltd

Arrow Books
Random House, 20 Vauxhall Bridge Road
London SW1V 2SA

www.randomhouse.co.uk

Addresses for companies within The Random House Group Limited can be found at:
www.randomhouse.co.uk/offices.htm

The Random House Group Limited Reg. No. 954009

A CIP catalogue record for this book
is available from the British Library

ISBN 9780099556695

The Random House Group Limited supports The Forest Stewardship
Council (FSC®), the leading international forest certification organisation.
Our books carrying the FSC label are printed on FSC® certified paper.
FSC is the only forest certification scheme endorsed by the leading
environmental organisations, including Greenpeace. Our
paper procurement policy can be found at
www.randomhouse.co.uk/environment

MIX
Paper from
responsible sources
FSC® C016897

Printed and bound in Great Britain by Clays Ltd, St Ives PLC

I

A BELL clanged. Brazen, insistent, maddening.

Through the quiet corridors came the din of it, making hideous the peace of the morning. From each of the yawning windows of the little quadrangle the noise poured out on to the still, sunlit garden where the grass was grey yet with dew.

Little Miss Pym stirred, opened one doubtful grey eye, and reached blindly for her watch. There was no watch. She opened the other eye. There seemed to be no bedside table either. No, of course not; now she remembered. There *was* no bedside table; as she had found last night. Her watch had had of necessity to be put under her pillow. She fumbled for it. Good heavens, what a row that bell was making! Obscene. There seemed to be no watch under the pillow. But it must be there! She lifted the pillow bodily, revealing only one small sheer-linen handkerchief in a saucy pattern of blue-and-white. She dropped the pillow and peered down between the bed and the wall. Yes, there was something that looked like a watch. By lying flat on her front and inserting an arm she could just reach it. Carefully she brought it up, lightly caught between the tips of first and second fingers. If she dropped it now she would have to get out of bed and crawl under for it. She turned on her back with a sigh of relief, holding the watch triumphantly above her.

Half-past five, said the watch.

Half-past five!

Miss Pym stopped breathing and stared in unbelieving fascination. No, really, did any college, however physical and hearty, begin the day at *half-past five*! Anything was possible, of course, in a community which had use for neither bedside tables nor bedside lamps, but—half-past five! She put the watch to her small pink ear. It ticked faithfully. She squinted round her pillow at the garden which was visible from the window behind her bed. Yes, it certainly was early; the world had that unmoving just-an-apparition look of early morning. Well, well!

Henrietta had said last night, standing large and majestical in the doorway: 'Sleep well. The students enjoyed your lecture, my dear. I shall see you in the morning'; but had not seen fit to mention half-past-five bells.

Oh, well. It wasn't her funeral, thank goodness. Once upon a time she too had lived a life regulated by bells, but that was long ago. Nearly twenty years ago. When a bell rang in Miss Pym's life now it was because she had put a delicately varnished finger-tip on the bell-push. As the clamour died into a complaining whimper and then into silence, she turned over to face the wall, burrowing happily into her pillow. Not her funeral. Dew on the grass, and all that, was for youth: shining resplendent youth; and they could have it. She was having another two hours' sleep.

Very childlike she looked with her round pink face, her neat little button of a nose, and her brown hair rolled in flat invisible-pinned curls all over her head. They had cost her a spiritual struggle last night, those curls. She had been very tired after the train journey, and meeting Henrietta again, and the lecture; and her weaker self had pointed out that she would in all probability be leaving after lunch on the morrow, that her permanent wave was only two months old, and that her hair might very well be left unpinned for one night. But, partly to spite her weaker self with whom she waged a constant and bitter war, partly so that she might do Henrietta justice, she had seen

2

to it that fourteen pins were pressed to their nightly duty. She was remembering her strong-mindedness now (it helped to cancel out any twinge of conscience about her self-indulgence this morning) and marvelling at the survival of that desire to live up to Henrietta. At school, she, the little fourth-form rabbit, had admired the sixth-form Henrietta extravagantly. Henrietta was the born Head Girl. Her talent lay exclusively in seeing that other people employed theirs. That was why, although she had left school to train in secretarial work, she was now Principal of a college of physical culture; a subject of which she knew nothing at all. She had forgotten all about Lucy Pym, just as Lucy had forgotten about her, until Miss Pym had written The Book.

That is how Lucy herself thought of it. The Book.

She was still a little surprised about The Book herself. Her mission in life had been to teach schoolgirls to speak French. But after four years of that her remaining parent had died, leaving her two hundred and fifty pounds a year, and Lucy had dried her eyes with one hand and given in her resignation with the other. The Headmistress had pointed out with envy and all uncharitableness that investments were variable things, and that two hundred and fifty didn't leave much margin for a civilised and cultured existence such as people in Lucy's position were expected to live. But Lucy had resigned all the same, and had taken a very civilised and cultured flat far enough from Camden Town to be nearly Regent's Park. She provided the necessary margin by giving French lessons now and then when gas bills were imminent, and spent all her spare time reading books on psychology.

She read her first book on psychology out of curiosity, because it seemed to her an interesting sort of thing; and she read all the rest to see if they were just as silly. By the time she had read thirty-seven books on the subject, she had evolved ideas of her own on psychology; at variance, of course, with all thirty-seven volumes read to date. In fact, the thirty-seven volumes seemed to her so idiotic and made her so angry that she sat down there and then and wrote reams of refutal. Since one cannot talk about psychology in anything but jargon, there being no English for most of it, the reams of refutal read very learnedly indeed. Not that that would have impressed anyone if Miss Pym had not used the back of a discarded sheet (her typing was not very professional) on which to write:

Dear Mr Stallard,
   I should be *so* grateful if you would not use your wireless after eleven at night. I find it *so* distracting.
                                        Yours sincerely
                                        Lucy Pym

Mr Stallard, whom she did not know (his name was on the card outside his door on the floor below), arrived in person that evening. He was holding her letter open in his hand, which seemed to Lucy very grim indeed, and she swallowed several times before she could make any coherent sound at all. But Mr Stallard wasn't angry about the wireless. He was a publishers' reader, it seemed, and was interested in what she had unconsciously sent him on the back of the paper.

Now in normal times a publisher would have rung for brandy at the mere suggestion of publishing a book on psychology. But the previous year the British public had shaken the publishing world by tiring suddenly of fiction, and developing an interest in abstruse subjects, such as the distance of Sirius from the earth, and the inward meaning of primitive dances in Bechuanaland. Publishers were falling over themselves, therefore, in their effort to supply this strange new thirst for knowledge, and Miss Pym found herself welcomed with open arms. That is to say, she was taken to lunch by the senior partner, and given an agreement to sign. This alone was a piece of luck, but

4

Providence so ordained it that not only had the British public tired of fiction, but the intellectuals had tired of Freud and Company. They were longing for Some New Thing. And Lucy proved to be it. So Lucy woke one morning to find herself not only famous, but a best-seller. She was so shocked that she went out and had three cups of black coffee and sat in the Park looking straight in front of her for the rest of the morning.

She had been a best-seller for several months, and had become quite used to lecturing on 'her subject' to learned societies, when Henrietta's letter had come; reminding her of their schooldays together and asking her to come and stay for a while and address the students. Lucy was a little wearied of addressing people, and the image of Henrietta had grown dim with the years. She was about to write a polite refusal, when she remembered the day on which the fourth form had discovered her christened name to be Laetitia; a shame that Lucy had spent her life concealing. The fourth form had excelled themselves, and Lucy had been wondering whether her mother would mind very much about her suicide, and deciding that anyhow she had brought it on herself by giving her daughter such a highfalutin name. And then Henrietta had waded into the humorists, literally and metaphorically. Her blistering comment had withered humour at the root, so that the word Laetitia had never been heard again, and Lucy had gone home and enjoyed jam roly-poly instead of throwing herself in the river. Lucy sat in her civilised and cultured living-room, and felt the old passionate gratitude to Henrietta run over her in waves. She wrote and said that she would be delighted to stay a night with Henrietta (her native caution was not entirely obliterated by her gratitude) and would with pleasure talk on psychology to her students.

The pleasure had been considerable, she thought, pushing up a hump of sheet to shut out the full brilliance

5

of the daylight. Quite the nicest audience she had ever had. Rows of shining heads, making the bare lecture-room look like a garden. And good hearty applause. After weeks of the polite pattering of learned societies it was pleasant to hear the percussion of hollowed palm on hollowed palm. And their questions had been quite intelligent. Somehow, although psychology was a subject on their timetable, as shown in the common-room, she had not expected intellectual appreciation from young women who presumably spent their days doing things with their muscles. Only a few, of course, had asked questions; so there was still a chance that the rest were morons.

Oh well, tonight she would sleep in her own charming bed, and all this would seem like a dream. Henrietta had pressed her to stay for some days, and for a little she had toyed with the idea. But supper had shaken her. Beans and milk pudding seemed an uninspired sort of meal for a summer evening. Very sustaining and nourishing and all that, she didn't doubt. But not a meal one wanted to repeat. The staff table, Henrietta had said, always had the same food that the students had; and Lucy had hoped that that remark didn't mean that she had looked doubtfully upon the beans. She had tried to look very bright and pleased about the beans; but perhaps it hadn't been a success.

'Tommy! Tom-*mee*! Oh, Tommy, darling, waken up. I'm *des*perate!'

Miss Pym shot into wakefulness. The despairing cries seemed to be in her room. Then she realised that the second window of her room gave on to the courtyard; that the courtyard was small, and conversation from room to room through the gaping windows a natural method of communication. She lay trying to quiet her thumping heart, peering down over the folds of sheet to where, beyond the hump of her toes, the foreshortened oblong of the window framed a small piece of distant wall. But her bed lay in the angle of the room, one window to her right in the wall behind her, and the courtyard window to her left beyond the foot of her bed, and all that was visible from her pillow through the tall thin strip of brightness was half of an open window far down the courtyard.

'Tom-*mee! Tom-mee!*'

A dark head appeared in the window Miss Pym could see.

'For God's sake, someone,' said the head, 'throw something at Thomas and stop Dakers' row.'

'Oh, Greengage, darling, you *are* an unsympathetic beast. I've bust my suspender, and I don't know *what* to do. And Tommy took my *only* safety-pin yesterday to pick the winkles with at Tuppence-ha'penny's party. She simply *must* let me have it back before—*Tommy!* Oh, *Tommy!*'

'Hey, shut up, will you,' said a new voice, in a lowered tone, and there was a pause. A pause, Lucy felt, full of sign language.

'And what does all that semaphoring mean?' asked the dark head.

'Shut up, I tell you. *She*'s there!' This in desperate *sotto voce.*

'Who is?'

'The Pym woman.'

'What *rubbish*, darling'—it was the Dakers voice again, high and unsubdued; the happy voice of a world's darling —'she's sleeping in the front of the house with the rest of the mighty. *Do* you think *she* would have a spare safety-pin if I was to ask her?'

'She looks zip-fastener to me,' a new voice said.

'Oh, will you be quiet! I tell you, she's in Bentley's room!'

There was a real silence this time. Lucy saw the dark head turn sharply towards her window.

7

'How do you know?' someone asked.

'Jolly told me last night when she was giving me late supper.' Miss Joliffe was the housekeeper, Lucy remembered, and appreciated the nickname for so grim a piece of humanity.

'Gawd's truth!' said the 'zip-fastener' voice, with feeling.

Into the silence came a bell. The same urgent clamour that had wakened them. The dark head disappeared at the first sound of it, and Dakers' voice above the row could be heard wailing her desperation like a lost thing. Social gaffes were relegated to their proper unimportance, as the business of the day overwhelmed them. A great wave of sound rose up to meet the sound of the bell. Doors were banged, feet drummed in the corridor, voices called, someone remembered that Thomas was still asleep, and a tattoo was beaten on her locked door when objects flung at her from surrounding windows had failed to waken her, and then there was the sound of running feet on the gravel path that crossed the courtyard grass. And gradually there were more feet on the gravel and fewer on the stairs, and the babble of voices swelled to a climax and faded. When the noises had grown faint with distance or died into lecture-room silence, a single pair of feet pattered in flight across the gravel, a voice saying: 'Damn, damn, damn, damn, damn—' at each footfall. The Thomas who slept, apparently.

Miss Pym felt sympathetic to the unknown Thomas. Bed was a charming place at any time, but if one was so sleepy that neither riotous bell-ringing nor the wails of a colleague made any impression, then getting up must be torture. Welsh, too, probably. All Thomases were Welsh. Celts hated getting up. Poor Thomas. Poor, poor Thomas. She would like to find poor Thomas a job where she would never have to get up before afternoon.

Sleep ran over her in waves, drawing her deeper and

8

deeper under. She wondered if 'looking zip-fastener' was
a compliment. Being a safety-pin person couldn't be
thought exactly admirable, so perhaps——

She fell asleep.

2

SHE was being beaten with knouts by two six-foot Cossacks because she persisted in using the old-fashioned safety-pin when progress decreed a zip-fastener, and the blood had begun to trickle down her back when she woke to the fact that the only thing that was being assaulted was her hearing. The bell was ringing again. She said something that was neither civilised nor cultured, and sat up. No, definitely, not a minute after lunch would she stay. There was a 2.41 from Larborough, and on that 2.41 she would be; her good-byes said, her duty to friendship done, and her soul filled with the beatitude of escape. She would treat herself to a half-pound box of chocolates on the station platform as a sort of outward congratulation. It would show on the bathroom scales at the end of the week, but who cared?

The thought of the scales reminded her of the civilised and cultured necessity of having a bath. Henrietta had been sorry about its being so far to the staff bathrooms; she had been sorry altogether to put a guest into the student block, but Fröken Gustavsen's mother from Sweden was occupying the only staff guest-room, and was going to stay for some weeks until she had seen and criticised the result of her daughter's work when the annual Demonstration would take place at the beginning of the month. Lucy doubted very much whether her bump of locality—a hollow according to her friends—was good enough to take her back to that bathroom. It would be awful to go prowling along those bright empty corridors, arriving perhaps at lecture-rooms unawares. And still more awful to ask in a crowded corridor of up-since-dawners where one could perform one's belated ablutions.

Lucy's mind always worked like that. It wasn't sufficient for it to visualise one horror: it must visualise the opposite one too. She sat so long considering the rival horrors, and enjoying the sensation of doing nothing, that still another bell rang and still another wave of drumming feet and calling voices rose up and swamped the quiet of the morning. Lucy looked at her watch. It was half-past seven.

She had just decided to be uncivilised and uncultured and 'go in her mook' as her daily woman called it—after all, what was this immersion in water but a modern fad, and if Charles the Second could afford to smell a little high, who was she, a mere commoner, to girn at missing a bath?—when there was a knock on her door. Rescue was at hand. Oh, joy, oh, glory, her marooned condition was at an end.

'Come in,' she called in the glad tones of a Crusoe welcoming a landing party. Of course Henrietta would come to say good-morning. How silly of her not to have thought of that. She was still at heart the little rabbit who didn't expect Henrietta to bother about her. Really, she must cultivate a habit of mind more suitable to a Celebrity. Perhaps if she were to do her hair differently, or say over something twenty times a day after the manner of Coué—'Come in!'

But it was not Henrietta. It was a goddess.

A goddess with golden hair, a bright blue linen tunic, sea-blue eyes, and the most enviable pair of legs. Lucy always noticed other women's legs, her own being a sad disappointment to her.

'Oh, I'm sorry,' said the goddess. 'I forgot that you might not be up. In college we keep such odd hours.'

Lucy thought that it was nice of this heavenly being to take the blame for her sloth.

'I do apologise for interrupting your dressing.' The blue eye came to rest on a mule which was lying in the middle of the floor, and stayed there as if fascinated. It was a pale blue satin mule; very feminine, very thriftless, very feathery. A most undeniable piece of nonsense.

'I'm afraid it *is* rather silly,' Lucy said.

'If you only knew, Miss Pym, what it is to see an object that is not strictly utilitarian!' And then, as if recalled to her business by the very temptation of straying from it: 'My name is Nash. I'm the Head Senior. And I came to say that the Senior students would be very honoured if you would come to tea with them tomorrow. On Sundays we take our tea out into the garden. It is a Senior privilege. And it really is very pleasant out there on a summer afternoon, and we really are looking forward to having you.' She smiled with eager benevolence on Miss Pym.

Lucy explained that she would not be there tomorrow; that she was departing this afternoon.

'Oh, no!' protested the Nash girl; and the genuine feeling in her tone caused Lucy a rush of warmth to the heart. 'No, Miss Pym, you mustn't! You really mustn't. You have no idea what a godsend you are to us. It's so seldom that anyone—anyone interesting comes to stay. This place is rather like a convent. We are all so hard-worked that we have no time to think of an outside world; and this is the last term for us Seniors, and everything is very grim and claustrophobic—Final Exams, and the Demonstration, and being found posts, and what not—and we are all feeling like death, and our last scrap of sense of proportion is gone. And then *you* come, a piece of the outside, a civilised being—' She paused; half laughing, half serious. 'You *can't* desert us.'

'But you have an outside lecturer *every* Friday,' Lucy

pointed out. It was the first time in her life she had been a godsend to anyone, and she was determined to take the assertion with a grain of salt. She didn't at all like the gratified feeling that was sniffing round the edge of her emotions.

Miss Nash explained with clarity, point, and no small bitterness that the last three lecturers had been: an octogenarian on Assyrian inscriptions, a Czech on Central Europe, and a bonesetter on scoliosis.

'What is scoliosis?' asked Lucy.

'Curvature of the spine. And if you think that any of them brought sweetness and light into the College atmosphere, you are wrong. These lectures are supposed to keep us in touch with the world, but if I must be both frank and indiscreet'—she was obviously enjoying being both—'the frock you wore last night did us more good than all the lectures we have ever heard.'

Lucy had spent a really shocking sum on that garment when first her book became a best-seller, and it still remained her favourite; she had worn it to impress Henrietta. The gratified feeling came a little nearer.

But not near enough to destroy her common sense. She could still remember the beans. And the lack of bedside lamps. And the lack of any bells to summon service. And the everlasting bells that rang to summon others. No, on the 2.41 from Larborough she would be, though every student of the Leys Physical Training College lay down in her path and wept aloud. She murmured something about engagements—leaving it to be inferred that her diary bulged with pressing and desirable appointments—and suggested that Miss Nash might, meanwhile, direct her to the Staff bathrooms. 'I didn't want to go prowling through the corridors, and I couldn't find a bell to ring.'

Miss Nash, having sympathised with her about the lack

13

of service—'Eliza really should have remembered that there are no bells in the rooms here and come to call you; she's the Staff housemaid'—suggested that, if Miss Pym didn't mind using the students' baths, they were much nearer. 'They are cubicles, of course; I mean, they have walls only part of the way; and the floor is a sort of greenish concrete where the staff have turquoise mosaic with a tasteful design in dolphins, but the water is the same.'

Miss Pym was delighted to use the students' bathroom, and as she gathered her bathing things together the unoccupied half of her mind was busy with Miss Nash's lack of any student-like reverence for the Staff. It reminded her of something. And presently she remembered what it reminded her of. Mary Barharrow. The rest of Mary Barharrow's form had been meek and admiring young labourers in the field of irregular French verbs, but Mary Barharrow, though diligent and amiable, had treated her French mistress as an equal; and that was because Mary Barharrow's father was 'nearly a millionaire'. Miss Pym concluded that in the 'outside'—strange how one already used Klondyke terms about College—Miss Nash, who had so markedly Mary Barharrow's charming air of social ease and equality, had also a father very like Mary Barharrow's. She was to learn later that it was the first thing that anyone remarked on when Nash's name was mentioned. 'Pamela Nash's people are very rich, you know. They have a butler.' They never failed to mention the butler. To the daughters of struggling doctors, lawyers, dentists, business men and farmers, he was as exotic as a negro slave.

'Shouldn't you be at some class or other?" asked Miss Pym, as the quietness of the sunlit corridors proclaimed an absorption elsewhere. 'I take it that if you are wakened at half-past five you work before breakfast.'

'Oh, yes. In the summer we have two periods before

breakfast, one active and one passive. Tennis practice and kinesiology, or something like that.'

'What is kin—whatever-it-is?'

'Kinesiology?' Miss Nash considered for a moment the best way of imparting knowledge to the ignorant, and then spoke in imaginary quotation. 'I take down a jug with a handle from a high shelf; describe the muscle-work involved.' And as Miss Pym's nod showed that she had understood: 'But in winter we get up like anyone else at half-past seven. As for this particular period, it is normally used for taking outside certificates—Public Health, and Red Cross, and what not. But since we have finished with these we are allowed to use it as a prep. hour for our final exams, which begin next week. We have very little prep. time so we are glad of it.'

'Aren't you free after tea, or thereabouts?'

Miss Nash looked amused. 'Oh, no. There is afternoon clinic from four o'clock till six; outside patients, you know. Everything from flat feet to broken thighs. And from half-past six to eight there is dancing. Ballet, not folk. We have folk in the morning; it ranks as exercise, not art. And supper doesn't finish much before half-past eight, so we are very sleepy before we begin our prep. and it is usually a fight between our sleepiness and our ignorance.'

As they turned into the long corridor leading to the stairs, they overtook a small scuttling figure clutching under one arm the head and thorax of a skeleton and the pelvis and legs under the other arm.

'What are you doing with George, Morris?' asked Miss Nash as they drew level.

'Oh, *please* don't stop me, Beau,' panted the startled Junior, hitching her grotesque burden more firmly on to her right hip and continuing to scuttle in front of them, 'and *please* forget that you saw me. I mean that you saw George. I meant to waken early and put him back in the

15

lecture room before the half-past five bell went, but I just slept.'

'Have you been up all night with George?'

'No, only till about two. I——'

'And how did you manage about lights?'

'I pinned my travelling rug over the window, of course,' said the Junior, in the testy tones of one explaining the obvious.

'A nice atmosphere on a June evening!'

'It was hellish,' said Miss Morris, simply. 'But it really *is* the only way I can swot up my insertions, so *please*, Beau, just forget that you saw me. I'll get him back before the Staff come down to breakfast.'

'You'll never do it, you know. You're bound to meet someone or other.'

'Oh, please don't discourage me. I'm terrified enough now. And I really don't know if I can remember how to hook up his middle.' She preceded them down the stairs, and disappeared into the front of the house.

'Positively Through-the-Looking-Glass,' commented Miss Pym, watching her go. 'I always thought insertion was something to do with needlework.'

'Insertions? They're the exact place on a bone where a muscle is attached to it. It's much easier to do it with the skeleton in front of you, than with just a book. That is why Morris abducted George.' She expelled a breath of indulgent laughter. 'Very enterprising of her. I stole odd bones from the drawers in the lecture room when I was a Junior, but I never thought of taking George. It's the dreadful cloud that hangs over a Junior's life, you know. Final Anatomy. It really *is* a Final. You're supposed to know all about the body before you begin practising on it, so Final Anatomy is a Junior exam, not a Senior one like the other finals. The bathrooms are along here. When I was a Junior the long grass at the edge of the cricket field was simply stiff on Sundays with hidden Juniors hugging

16

their Gray. It is strictly forbidden to take books out of College, and on Sundays we are supposed to go all social and go out to tea, or to church, or to the country. But no Junior in the summer term ever did anything on a Sunday except find a quiet spot for herself and Gray. It was quite a business getting Gray out of College. Do you know Gray? About the size of those old family bibles that rested on the parlour table. There was actually a rumour once that half the girls at Leys were pregnant, but it turned out that it was only the odd silhouette that everyone made with Gray stuffed up the front of their Sunday bests.'

Miss Nash stooped to the taps and sent a roar of water rushing into the bath. 'When everyone in College baths three or four times a day, in the matter of minutes, you have to have a Niagara of a tap,' she explained above the row. 'I'm afraid you are going to be very late for breakfast.' And as Miss Pym looked dismayed and oddly small-girlish at the prospect: 'Let me bring up something for you on a tray. No, it won't be any trouble, I'd love to do it. There isn't any need for a guest to appear at eight o'clock breakfast, anyhow. You'd much better have it in peace in your room.' She paused with her hand on the door. 'And do change your mind about staying. It really would give us pleasure. More pleasure than you can imagine.'

She smiled and was gone.

Lucy lay in the warm soft water and thought happily of her breakfast. How pleasant not to have to make conversation among all those chattering voices. How imaginative and kind of that charming girl to carry a tray to her. Perhaps after all it would be nice to spend a day or two among these young——

She nearly leaped from her bath as a bell began its maniacal yelling not a dozen yards from where she lay. That settled it. She sat up and soaped herself. Not a minute later than the 2.41 from Larborough, not one minute later.

As the bell—presumably a five-minute warning before the gong at eight o'clock—died into silence, there was a wild rush in the corridor, the two doors to her left were flung open, and as the water cascaded into the baths a high familiar voice was heard shrieking: 'Oh, darling, I'm going to be *so* late for breakfast, but I'm in a *muck sweat*, my dear. I know I should have sat down quietly and done the composition of plasma, of which I know *ab*-solutely *noth*-ing, my dear, and Final Phys. is on Tuesday. But it *is* such a lovely morning—— Now what *have* I done with my *soap*?'

Lucy's jaw slowly dropped as it was borne in upon her that in a community which began the day at half-past five and ended it at eight in the evening, there were still individuals who had the vitality to work themselves into a muck sweat when they need not.

'Oh, Donnie, *darling*, I've left my soap behind. Do throw me over yours!'

'You'll have to wait till I've soaped myself,' said a placid voice that was in marked contrast to Dakers' high emphasis.

'Well, my angel, *do* be *quick*. I've been late twice this week, and Miss Hodge looked dis*tinct*ly *odd* the last time. I say, Donnie, you *couldn't* by any chance take my "adipose" patient at twelve o'clock clinic, could you?'

'No, I couldn't.'

'She really isn't so heavy as she looks, you know. You have only to——'

'I have a patient of my own.'

'Yes, but only the little boy with the ankle. Lucas could take him along with her "tortis colli" girl——'

'No.'

'No, I was afraid you wouldn't. Oh, dear, I don't know *when* I'm going to do that plasma. As for the coats of the

18

stomach, they simply *baffle* me, my dear. I don't really believe there are four, anyhow. It's just a conspiracy. Miss Lux says look at tripe, but I don't see that tripe proves anything.'

'Soap coming up.'

'Oh, *thank* you, darling. You've saved my life. What a nice *smell*, my dear. *Very* expensive.' In the momentary silence of soaping she became aware that the bath on her right was occupied. 'Who is next door, Donnie?'

'Don't know. Gage, probably.'

'Is that you, Greengage?'

'No,' said Lucy, startled, 'it's Miss Pym.' And hoped it wasn't as prim as it sounded.

'No, but really, who is it?'

'Miss Pym.'

'It's a very good imitation, whoever you are.'

'It's Littlejohn,' suggested the placid voice. 'She does imitations.'

'Is it you, John?'

Miss Pym fell back on a defeated silence.

There was the hurr-oosh of a body lifted suddenly from the water, the spat of a wet foot placed firmly on the edge of the bath, eight wet finger-tips appeared on the edge of the partition, and a face peered over it. It was a long pale face, like an amiable pony's, with the straight fair hair above it screwed up into a knob with a hasty hairpin. An oddly endearing face. Even in that crowded moment, Lucy understood suddenly how Dakers had managed to reach her final term at Leys without being knocked on the head by exasperated colleagues.

First horror, then a wild flush together with a dawning amusement, invaded the face above the partition. It disappeared abruptly. A despairing wail rose from beyond.

'Oh, Miss *Pym*! Oh, *dear* Miss Pym! I *do* apologise. I *abase* myself. It didn't occur to me even to *think* it might be you——'

Lucy could not help feeling that she was enjoying her own enormity.

'I *hope* you're not offended. Not *terribly*, I mean. We are so used to people's skins that—that——'

Lucy understood that she was trying to say that the gaffe was less important in these surroundings than it would have been elsewhere, and since she herself had been decently soaping a big toe at the operative moment, she had no feelings on the subject. She said kindly that it was entirely her own fault for occupying a student's bathroom, and that Miss Dakers was not to worry about it for a moment.

'You know my *name*?'

'Yes. You woke me in the dawn this morning yelling for a safety-pin.'

'Oh, *catastrophe!* Now I shall *never* be able to look you in the face!'

'I expect Miss Pym is taking the first train back to London,' said the voice in the farther bath, in a now-look-what-you've-done tone.

'That is O'Donnell next door,' said Dakers. 'She's from Ireland.'

'Ulster,' said O'Donnell, without heat.

'How d'you do, Miss O'Donnell.'

'You must think this is a mad-house, Miss Pym. But don't judge us by Dakers, please. Some of us are quite grown up. And some of us are even civilised. When you come to tea tomorrow you will see.'

Before Miss Pym could say that she was not coming to tea, a low murmur began to invade the cubicles, rising rapidly into the deep roar of a gong. Into the tumult Dakers' banshee wail rose like the voice of a seagull in a storm. She was going to be *so* late. And she was *so* grateful for the soap, which had saved her life. And *where* was the girdle of her tunic? And if dear Miss Pym would promise to overlook her failings up to date, she would yet show her that she was a sensible female and a civilised adult. And they were *all* looking forward so much to that tea tomorrow.

With a rush and a bang the students fled, leaving Miss Pym alone with the dying pulse of the gong and the throaty protest of bath water running away.

3

AT 2.41, when the afternoon fast train to London was pulling out of Larborough prompt to the minute, Miss Pym sat under the cedar on the lawn wondering whether she was a fool, and not much caring anyhow. It was very pleasant there in the sunlit garden. It was also very quiet, since Saturday afternoon was, it appeared, match afternoon, and College *en masse* was down at the cricket field playing Coombe, a rival establishment from the other side of the county. If they had nothing else, these young creatures, they had versatility. It was a far cry from the lining of the stomach to the placing of a cricket field, but they seemingly took it in their stride. Henrietta, coming into her bedroom after breakfast, had said that if she stayed over the week-end she would at least find it a new experience. 'They are a very varied and lively crowd, and the work is very interesting.' And Henrietta had certainly been right. There was no moment when some new facet of this odd existence was not being presented to her. She had sat through luncheon at the Staff table, eating unidentifiable dishes that were 'balanced' to a dietetic marvel, and making the closer acquaintance of the Staff. Henrietta sat in lonely state at the top of the table and gobbled her food in an abstracted silence. But Miss Lux was talkative. Miss Lux—angular, plain, and clever—was Mistress of Theory, and as befitted a lecturer on theory had not only ideas but opinions. Miss Wragg, on the other hand, the Junior Gymnast—big, bouncing, young, and pink—had apparently no ideas at all and her only opinions were reflections of Madame Lefevre's. Madame

Lefevre, the ballet mistress, spoke seldom, but when she did it was in a voice like dark brown velvet and no one interrupted her. At the bottom of the table, with her mother by her side, sat Fröken Gustavsen, the Senior Gymnast, who talked not at all.

It was to Fröken Gustavsen that Lucy found her eyes going during that lunch. There was a sly amusement in the handsome Swede's clear pale eyes that Lucy found irresistible. The heavy Miss Hodge, the clever Miss Lux, the dumb Miss Wragg, the elegant Madame Lefevre— what did they all look like through the eyes of a tall pale enigma from Sweden?

Now, having spent lunch wondering about a Swede, she was waiting the advent of a South American. 'Desterro doesn't play games,' Henrietta had said, 'so I'll send her to keep you company this afternoon.' Lucy had not wanted anyone to keep her company—she was used to her own company and liked it—but the thought of a South American at an English college of physical training teased her. And when Nash, running into her after lunch, had said: 'I'm afraid you're going to be deserted this afternoon, if you don't care for cricket,' another Senior passing in the crush had said: 'It's all right, Beau, The Nut Tart is going to look after her.' 'Oh, good,' Beau had said, apparently so accustomed to the nickname that it had ceased to have either meaning or oddity for her.

But Lucy looked forward to meeting a Nut Tart, and sitting in the sunlit garden digesting the dietetic marvels she pondered the name. 'Nut' was Brazil, perhaps. It was also the modern slang for 'dippy' or 'daft', she believed. But 'tart'? Surely not!

A Junior, running past her on the way to the bicycle shed, flashed her a smile, and she remembered that they had met in the corridor that morning. 'Did you get George back safely?' she called after her.

'Yes, thank you,' beamed little Miss Morris, pausing to

dance on one toe, 'but I think I'm in a different sort of trouble now. You see, I had my arm round George's waist, sort of steadying him after hanging him up, when Miss Lux came in. I'll never be able to explain away that, I'm afraid.'

'Life is difficult,' agreed Lucy.

'However, I think I really do know my insertions now,' called little Miss Morris, speeding away over the grass.

Nice children, thought Miss Pym. Nice, clean, healthy children. It was really very pleasant here. That smudge on the horizon was the smoke of Larborough. There would be another smudge like that over London. It was much better to sit here where the air was bright with sun and heavy with roses, and be given friendly smiles by friendly young creatures. She pushed her plump little feet a little farther away from her, approved the Georgian bulk of the 'old house' that glowed in the sunlight across the lawn, regretted the modern brick wings that made a 'Mary Ann' back to it, but supposed that as modern blocks go the Leys ensemble was pleasant enough. Charmingly proportioned lecture-rooms in the 'old house', and neat modern little bedrooms in the wings. An ideal arrangement. And the ugly bulk of the gymnasium decently hidden behind all. Before she went away on Monday she must see the Seniors go through their gym. There would be a double pleasure in that for her. The pleasure of watching experts trained to the last fine hair of perfection, and the ineffable pleasure of knowing that never, never as long as she lived, would she herself have to climb a rib-stall again.

Round the corner of the house, as she gazed, came a figure in a flowered silk dress and a plain, wide-brimmed shady hat. It was a slim, graceful figure; and watching it come Lucy realised that she had unconsciously pictured the South American plump and over-ripe. She also realised where the 'tart' came from, and smiled. The outdoor frocks of the austere young students of Leys would not be flowered; neither would they be cut so revealingly; and never, oh never, would their hats be broad-brimmed and shady.

'Good afternoon, Miss Pym. I am Teresa Desterro. I am so sorry that I missed your lecture last night. I had a class in Larborough.' Desterro took off her hat with a leisurely and studied grace, and dropped to the grass by Lucy's side in one continuous smooth movement. Everything about her was smooth and fluid: her voice, her drawling speech, her body, her movements, her dark hair, her honey-brown eyes.

'A class?'

'A dancing class; for shop girls. So earnest; so precise; so very bad. They will give me a box of chocolates next week because it is the last class of the season, and because they like me, and because it is after all the custom; and I shall feel like a crook. It is false pretences. No one could teach them to dance.'

'I expect they enjoy themselves. Is it usual? I mean, for students to take outside classes?'

'But we all do, of course. That is how we get practice. At schools, and convents, and clubs, and that sort of thing. You do not care for cricket?'

Lucy, rousing herself to this swift change of subject, explained that cricket was only possible to her in the company of a bag of cherries. 'How is it that you don't play?'

'I don't play *any* games. To run about after a little ball is supremely ridiculous. I came here for the dancing. It is a very good dancing college.'

But surely, Lucy said, there were ballet schools in London of an infinitely higher standard than anything obtainable at a college of physical training.

'Oh, for that one has to begin young, and to have a *métier*. Me, I have no *métier*, only a liking.'

25

'And will you teach, then, when you go back to—Brazil, is it?'

'Oh, no; I shall get married,' said Miss Desterro simply. 'I came to England because I had an unhappy love affair. He was r-r-ravishing, but qu-ite unsuitable. So I came to England to get over it.'

'Is your mother English, perhaps?'

'No, my mother is French. My grandmother is English. I adore the English. Up to here'—she lifted a graceful hand, wrist properly leading, and laid it edge-wise across her neck—'they are full of romance, and from there up, plain horse sense. I went to my grandmother, and I cried all over her best silk chairs, and I said "What shall I do? What shall I do?" About my lover, you understand. And she said: "You can blow your nose and get out of the country." So I said I would go to Paris and live in a garret and paint pictures of an eye and a seashell sitting on a plate. But she said: "You will not. You will go to England and sweat a bit." So, as I always listen to my grandmother, and since I like dancing and am very good at it, I came here. To Leys. They looked a little sideways on me at first when I said I wanted just to dance——'

This is what Lucy had been wondering. How did the charming 'nut' find a welcome in this earnest English college, this starting-place of careers?

'——but one of the students had broken down in the middle of her training—they often do, and do you wonder?—and that left a vacant place in the scheme, which was not so nice, so they said: "Oh, well, let this crazy woman from Brazil have Kenyon's room and allow her to come to the classes. It will not do any harm and it will keep the books straight".'

'So you began as a Senior?'

'For dancing, yes. I was already a dancer, you understand. But I took Anatomy with the Juniors. I find bones interesting. And to other lectures I went as I pleased. I

26

have listened to all subjects. All but plumbing. I find plumbing indecent.'

Miss Pym took 'plumbing' to be Hygiene. 'And have you enjoyed it all?'

'It has been a li-beral education. They are very naïve, the English girls. They are like little boys of nine.' Noticing the unbelieving smile on Miss Pym's face: there was nothing naïve about Beau Nash. 'Or little girls of eleven. They have "raves". You know what a "rave" is?' Miss Pym nodded. 'They swoon if Madame Lefevre says a kind word to them. I swoon, too, but it is from surprise. They save up their money to buy flowers for Fröken, who thinks of nothing but a Naval Officer in Sweden.'

'How do you know that?' asked Lucy, surprised.

'He is on her table. In her room. His photograph, I mean. And she is Continental. She does not have "raves".'

'The Germans do,' Lucy pointed out. 'They are famous for it.'

'An ill-balanced people,' said Desterro, dismissing the Teutonic race. 'The Swedes are not like that.'

'All the same, I expect she likes the little offerings of flowers.'

'She does not, of course, throw them out of the window But I notice she likes better the ones who do not bring her offerings.'

'Oh? There *are* some who do not have "raves", then?'

'Oh, yes. A few. The Scots, for instance. We have two.' She might have been talking of rabbits. 'They are too busy quarrelling to have any spare emotions.'

'Quarrelling? But I thought the Scots stuck together the world over.'

'Not if they belong to different winds.'

'*Winds*?'

'It is a matter of climate. We see it very much in Brazil. A wind that goes "a-a-a-ah"' she opened her red mouth and expelled a soft insinuating breath 'makes one kind of

27

person. But a wind that goes "s-s-s-s-ss"' she shot the breath viciously out through her teeth 'makes another person altogether. In Brazil it is altitude, in Scotland it is West Coast and East Coast. I observed it in the Easter holidays, and so understood about the Scots. Campbell has a wind that goes "a-a-a-ah" and so she is lazy, and tells lies, and has much charm that is all of it quite synthetic. Stewart has a wind that goes "s-s-s-s-ss", so she is honest, and hardworking, and has a formidable conscience.'

Miss Pym laughed. 'According to you, the east coast of Scotland must be populated entirely by saints.'

'There is also some personal reason for the quarrel, I understand. Something about abused hospitality.'

'You mean that one went home with the other for holidays and—misbehaved?' Visions of vamped lovers, stolen spoons, and cigarette burns on the furniture, ran through Lucy's too vivid imagination.

'Oh, no. It happened more than two hundred years ago. In the deep snow, and there was a massacre.' Desterro did full justice to the word 'massacre'.

At this Lucy really laughed. To think that the Campbells were still engaged in living down Glencoe! A narrow-minded race, the Celts.

She sat so long considering the Celts that The Nut Tart turned to look up at her. 'Have you come to use us as specimens, Miss Pym?'

Lucy explained that she and Miss Hodge were old friends and that her visit was a holiday one. 'In any case,' she said, kindly, 'I doubt whether as a specimen a Physical Training Student is likely to be psychologically interesting.'

'No? Why?'

'Oh, too normal and too nice. Too much of a type.'

A faint amusement crossed Desterro's face; the first expression it had shown so far. Unexpectedly, this stung Lucy; as if she too had been found guilty of being naïve.

'You don't agree?'

'I am trying to think of someone—some Senior—who is normal. It is not easy.'

'Oh, come!'

'You know how they live here. How they work. It would be difficult to go through their years of training here and be quite normal in their last term.'

'Do you suggest that Miss Nash is not normal?'

'Oh, Beau. She is a strong-minded creature, and so has suffered less, perhaps. But would you call her friendship for Innes quite normal? *Nice*, of course,' Desterro added hastily, 'quite irreproachable. But normal, no. That David and Jonathan relationship. It is a very happy one, no doubt, but it'—Desterro waved her arm to summon an appropriate word—'it *excludes* so much. The Disciples are the same, only there are four of them.'

'The Disciples?'

'Mathews, Waymark, Lucas, and Littlejohn. They have come up the College together because of their names. And now, believe me, my dear Miss Pym, they *think* together. They have the four rooms in the roof'—she tilted her head to the four dormer windows in the roof of the wing—'and if you ask any one of them to lend you a pin she says: "We have not got one".'

'Well, there is Miss Dakers. What would you say was wrong with Miss Dakers?'

'Arrested development,' said Miss Desterro dryly.

'Nonsense!' said Lucy, determined to assert herself. 'A happy, simple, uncomplicated human being, enjoying herself and the world. *Quite* normal.'

The Nut Tart smiled suddenly, and her smile was frank and unstudied. 'Very well, Miss Pym, I give you Dakers. But I remind you that it is their last term, this. And so everything is e-norrmously exaggerated. Everyone is just the least little bit insane. No, it is true, I promise you. If a student is frightened by nature, then she is a thousand

29

times more frightened this term. If she is ambitious, then her ambition becomes a passion. *And* so on.' She sat up to deliver herself of her summing-up. 'It is not a normal life they lead. You cannot expect them to be normal.'

4

'You cannot expect them to be normal,' repeated Miss Pym to herself, sitting in the same place on Sunday afternoon and looking at the crowd of happy and excessively normal young faces clustered below her on the grass. Her eye ran over them with pleasure. If none of them was distinguished, at least none of them was mean. Nor was there any trace of morbidity, not even of exhaustion, in their sunburnt alertness. These were the survivors of a gruelling course—that was admitted even by Henrietta—and it seemed to Miss Pym that the rigours might perhaps have been justified if the residue were of such excellence.

She was amused to note that the Disciples, by much living together, had begun to look vaguely alike—as husband and wife often do, however different their features. They all seemed to have the same round face with the same expression of pleased expectancy; it was only later that one noticed differences of build and colouring.

She was also amused to observe that the Thomas who slept was most undeniably Welsh; a small, dark aborigine. And that O'Donnell, who had now materialised from a voice in the bath, was equally unmistakably an Irish-woman; the long lashes, the fine skin, the wide grey eyes. The two Scots—separated by the farthest possible distance that still allowed them to be part of the group—were less obvious. Stewart was the red-haired girl cutting up cake from one of the plates that lay about on the grass. ('It's from Crawford's,' she was saying, in a pleasant Edinburgh voice, 'so you poor creatures who know nothing but

31

Buzzards will have a treat for a change!') Campbell, propped against the bole of the cedar, and consuming bread-and-butter with slow absorption, had pink cheeks and brown hair and a vague prettiness.

Apart from Hasselt, who was the girl with the flat, calm, early-Primitive face and who was South African, the rest of the Seniors were, as Queen Elizabeth said, 'mere English'.

The only face that approached distinction, as opposed to good looks, was that of Mary Innes, Beau Nash's Jonathan. This pleased Miss Pym in an odd fashion. It was fitting, she felt, that Beau should have chosen for friend someone who had quality as well as looks. Not that Innes was particularly good-looking. Her eyebrows, low over her eyes, gave her face an intensity, a brooding expression, that robbed her fine bones of the beauty they might have had. Unlike Beau, who was animated and smiled easily, she was quiet and so far Miss Pym had not seen her smile, although they had had what amounted in this *milieu* to a lengthy conversation. That was last night, when Miss Pym was undressing after having spent the evening in the company of the Staff. There had come a knock on her door, and Beau had said: 'I just came to see if you had everything you want. And to introduce you to your next-door neighbour, Mary Innes. Any time you want to be rescued, Innes will see to it.' And Beau had said good-night and gone away, leaving Innes to finish the interview. Lucy had found her attractive and very intelligent, but just a shade disconcerting. She did not bother to smile if she was not amused, and though friendly and at her ease made no effort to be entertaining. In the academic and literary circles that Lucy had recently frequented this would not have been remarkable, but in the gay over-accented college world it had the effect almost of a rebuff. Almost. There was certainly nothing of rebuff in Innes's interest in her book—The Book—and in herself.

Looking at her now, sitting in the cedar shade, Lucy wondered if it were just that Mary Innes did not find life very amusing. Lucy had long prided herself on her analysis of facial characteristics, and was beginning nowadays to bet rather heavily on them. She had never, for instance, come across eyebrows beginning low over the nose and ending high up at the outer end, without finding that their owner had a scheming, conniving mind. And someone—Jan Gordon, was it?—had observed that of the crowd round a park orator it was the long-nosed people who stayed to listen and the short-nosed people who walked away. So now, looking at Mary Innes's level eyebrows and firm mouth, she wondered whether the concentration of purpose they showed had forbidden any compensating laughter. It was in some way not a contemporary face at all. It was—was what?

An illustration from a history book? A portrait in a gallery?

Not, anyhow, the face of a games mistress at a girls' school. Definitely not. It was round faces like Mary Innes's that history was built.

Of all the faces turning to her so constantly and turning away with chatter and badinage, only two were not immediately likeable. One was Campbell's; too pliant, too soft-mouthed, too ready to be all things to all men. The other belonged to a girl called Rouse; and was freckled, and tight-lipped, and watchful.

Rouse had come late to the tea-party, and her advent had caused an odd momentary silence. Lucy was reminded of the sudden stillness that falls on chattering birds when a hawk hovers. But there was nothing deliberate about the silence; no malice. It was as if they had paused in their talk to note her arrival, but had none of them cared sufficiently to welcome her into their own particular group.

'I'm afraid I'm late,' she had said. And in the momentary quiet Lucy had caught the monosyllabic comment:
'Swot!', and had concluded that Miss Rouse had not
been able to drag herself away from her text-books. Nash
had introduced her, and she had dropped to the grass
with the rest, and the interrupted conversations flowed
on. Lucy, always sympathetic to the odd-man-out, had
caught herself being sorry for the latecomer; but a further
inspection of Miss Rouse's North Country features had
convinced her that she was wasting good emotion. If
Campbell, pink and pretty, was too pliant to be likeable,
then Rouse was her complement. Nothing but a bull-
dozer, Lucy felt, would make an impression on Miss
Rouse.

'Miss Pym, you haven't had any of *my* cake,' said
Dakers, who, quite unabashed, had appropriated Lucy as
an old acquaintance, and was now sitting propped against
her chair, her legs straight out in front of her like a doll's.

'Which is yours?' asked Lucy, eyeing the various tuck-
box products, which stood out from the college bread-and-
butter and 'Sunday' buns like Creed suits at a country fair.

Dakers' contribution, it seemed, was the chocolate
sandwich with the butter icing. Lucy decided that for
friendship's sake (and a little for greed) she would forget
her weight this once.

'Do you always bring your own cakes to Sunday tea?'

'Oh, no, this is in *your* honour.'

Nash, sitting on her other side, laughed. 'What you see
before you, Miss Pym, is a collection of skeletons out of
cupboards. There is no physical training student who is
not a Secret Eater.'

'There has been *no* moment in my *whole* college career,
my dears, when I wasn't *sick* with hunger. Only *shame*
makes me stop eating at breakfast, and half an hour afterwards I'm hungry enough to eat the horse in the gym.'

'That is why our only crime is——' Rouse was

beginning, when Stewart kicked her so hard in the back that she almost fell forward.

'We have spread our dreams under your feet,' mocked Nash, covering Rouse's broken sentence. 'And a fine rich carpet of carbohydrate they are, to be sure.'

'We also had a *solemn* conclave as to whether we ought to *dress* for you,' said Dakers, cutting up chocolate sandwich for the others and unaware that there had been any gaffe in the offing. 'But we decided that you didn't look very particular.' As this raised a laugh, she added hastily, 'In the very *nicest* sense, I mean. We thought you would like us as we are.'

They were wearing all sorts of garments; as the taste of the wearer or the need of the moment dictated. Some were in shorts, some in blue linen games tunics, some in washing-silk dresses of suitably pastel shades. There were no flowered silks; Desterro was taking tea with the nuns of a convent in Larborough.

'Besides,' said Gage, who looked like a Dutch doll and who was the dark head that appeared at a courtyard window at five-thirty yesterday morning and prayed someone to throw something at Thomas and so put a period to the wails of Dakers, 'besides, much as we would like to do you honour, Miss Pym, every moment counts with our finals so oppressively near. Even a quick-change artist like a P.T. Senior needs five full minutes to achieve Sunday-bests, and by accepting us in our rags you have contributed'—she paused to count the gathering and do some mental arithmetic—'you have contributed one hour and twenty minutes to the sum of human knowledge.'

'You can subtract *my* five minutes from that, my dear,' said Dakers, licking a protuberant piece of butter-icing into safety with an expert tongue. 'I've spent the *whole* afternoon doing the cortex of the brain, and the only result is a firm conviction that I personally haven't *got* a cortex.'

'You must have a cortex,' said Campbell, the

literal-minded Scot, in a Glasgow drawl like syrup sliding from a spoon. But no one took any notice of this contribution to the obvious.

'Personally,' said O'Donnell, 'I think the vilest part of physiology are the villi. Imagine drawing cross-sections of something that has seven different parts and is less than a twentieth of an inch high!'

'But do you have to know the human structure in such detail?' asked Lucy.

'On Tuesday morning we do,' said the Thomas who slept. 'After that we can forget it for the rest of our lives.'

Lucy, remembering the Monday morning visit to the gymnasium which she had promised herself, wondered if physical work ceased during Final Examinations week. Oh, no, they assured her. Not with the Dem. only a fortnight ahead. The Demonstration, she was given to understand, ranked only a short head behind Final Examinations as a hazard.

'All our parents come,' said one of the Disciples, 'and——'

'The parents of all of us, she means,' put in a fellow Disciple.

'——and people from rival colleges, and all the——'

'All the civic swells of Larborough,' put in a third. It seemed that when one Disciple burst into speech the others followed automatically.

'And all the County big-wigs,' finished the fourth.

'It's murder,' said the first, simply; summing it up for them.

'I *like* the Dem.,' said Rouse. And again that odd silence fell.

Not inimical. Merely detached. Their eyes went to her, and came away again, expressionlessly. No one commented on what she had said. Their indifference left her marooned in the moment.

'I think it's fun to show people what we can do,' she added, a hint of defence in her tone.

They let that pass too. Never before had Lucy met that negative English silence in its full perfection; in its full cruelty. Her own edges began to curl up in sympathy.

But Rouse was less easily shrivelled. She was eyeing the plates before her, and putting out her hand for something to eat. 'Is there any tea left in the pot?' she asked.

Nash bent forward to the big brown pot, and Stewart took up the talk from where the Disciples had left it.

'What really *is* murder is waiting to see what you pull out of the Post lottery.'

'Post?' said Lucy. 'You mean jobs? But why a lottery? You know what you apply for, surely?'

'Very few of us need to apply,' Nash explained, pouring very black tea. 'There are usually enough applications from schools to go round. Places that have had Leys gymnasts before just write to Miss Hodge when they have a vacancy and ask her to recommend someone. If it happens to be a very senior or responsible post, she may offer it to some Old Student who wants a change. But normally the vacancies are filled from Leaving Students.'

'And a very fine bargain they get,' said a Disciple.

'No one works so hard as a First-Poster does,' said a second.

'For less money,' supplemented a third.

'Or with a better grace,' said a fourth.

'So you see,' Stewart said, 'the most agonising moment of the whole term is when you are summoned to Miss Hodge's room and told what your fate is going to be.'

'Or when your train is pulling out of Larborough and you haven't been summoned at all!' suggested Thomas, who evidently had visions of being engulfed, jobless, by her native mountains again.

Nash sat back on her heels and smiled at Lucy. 'It is not nearly as grim as it sounds. Quite a few of us are

37

provided for already and so are not in the competition at all. Hasselt, for instance, is going back to South Africa to work there. And the Disciples *en masse* have chosen medical work.'

'We are going to start a clinic in Manchester,' explained one.

'A very rheumaticky place.'

'Full of deformities.'

'And brass'—supplemented the other three automatically.

Nash smiled benevolently on them. 'And I am going back to my old school as Games Coach. And the Nut—and Desterro, of course, doesn't want a post. So there aren't so many of us to find places for.'

'I won't even be qualified if I don't go back to the liver pretty soon,' Thomas said, her beady brown eyes blinking in the sun. 'What a way to spend a summer evening.'

They shifted their positions lazily, as if in protest, and fell to chatter again. But the reminder pricked them, and one by one they began to gather up their belongings and depart, trailing slowly across the sunlit grass like disconsolate children. Until presently Lucy found herself alone with the smell of the roses, and the murmur of insects, and the hot shimmer of the sunlit garden.

For half an hour she sat, in great beatitude, watching the slow shadow of the tree creep out from her feet. Then Desterro came back from Larborough; strolling slowly up the drive with a Rue de la Paix elegance that was odd after Lucy's hour of tumbled youth at tea. She saw Miss Pym, and changed her direction.

'Well,' she said, 'did you have a profitable afternoon?'

'I wasn't looking for profit,' said Lucy, faintly tart. 'It was one of the happiest afternoons I have ever spent.'

The Nut Tart stood contemplating her.

'I think you are a *very* nice person,' she said irrelevantly, and moved away, leisurely, to the house.

And Lucy suddenly felt very young, and didn't like the feeling at all. How dared a chit in a flowered frock make her feel inexperienced and foolish!

She rose abruptly and went to find Henrietta and be reminded that she was Lucy Pym, who had written The Book, and lectured to learned societies, and had her name in *Who's Who*, and was a recognised authority on the working of the Human Mind.

5

'WHAT is the college crime?' she asked Henrietta, as they went upstairs after supper. They had paused by the big fan-lighted window on the landing to look down on the little quadrangle, letting the others precede them up to the drawing-room.

'Using the gymnasium as a short cut to the field-path,' Henrietta said promptly.

'No, I mean real crime.'

Henrietta turned to look at her sharply. After a moment she said: 'My dear Lucy, when a human being works as hard as these girls do, it has neither the spare interest to devise a crime nor the energy to undertake it. What made you think of that subject?'

'Something someone said at tea this afternoon. About their "only crime". It was something to do with being perpetually hungry.'

'Oh, that!' Henrietta's brow cleared. 'Food pilfering. Yes, we do now and then have that. In any community of this size there is always someone whose power of resisting temptation is small.'

'Food from the kitchen, you mean?'

'No, food from the students' own rooms. It is a Junior crime, and usually disappears spontaneously. It is not a sign of vice, you know. Merely of a weak will. A student who would not dream of taking money or a trinket can't resist a piece of cake. Especially if it is sweet cake. They use up so much energy that their bodies are crying out for sugar; and though there is no limit to what they may eat at table they are for ever hungry.'

'Yes, they do work very hard. What proportion of any one set finishes the course, would you say?'

'Of this lot'—Henrietta nodded down to where a group of Seniors were strolling out across the courtyard to the lawn—'eighty per cent are finishing. That is about average. Those who fall by the wayside do it in their first term, or perhaps their second.'

'But not all, surely. There must be accidents in a life like this.'

'Oh, yes, there are accidents.' Henrietta turned and began to climb the further flight.

'That girl whose place Teresa Desterro took, was it an accident that overtook her?'

'No,' said Henrietta shortly, 'she had a breakdown.'

Lucy, climbing the shallow steps in the wake of her friend's broad beam, recognised the tone. It was the tone in which Henrietta, the head-girl, used to say: 'And see that no goloshes are left lying about the cloakroom floor.' It did not permit of further discussion.

Henrietta, it was to be understood, did not like to think of her beloved College as a Moloch. College was a bright gateway to the future for deserving youth; and if one or two found the gateway a hazard rather than an opening, then it was unfortunate, but no reflection on the builders of the gateway.

'Like a convent,' Nash had said yesterday morning. 'No time to think of an outside world.' That was true. She had watched a day's routine go by. She had also seen the Students' two daily papers lying unopened in the common-room last night as they went in to supper. But a nunnery, if it was a narrow world, was also a placid one. Uncompetitive. Assured. There was nothing of the nunnery about this over-anxious, wildly strenuous life. Only the self-absorption was the same; the narrowness.

And yet *was* it so narrow, she wondered, considering the gathering in the drawing-room? If this were any other kind of college that gathering would have been homogeneous. If it were a college of science the gathering would consist of scientists; if it were a college of divinity, of theologians. But in this long charming room, with its good 'pieces' and its chintzes, with its tall windows pushed up so that the warm evening flowed in through them full of grass and roses, in this one room many worlds met. Madame Lefevre, reclining in thin elegance on a hard Empire sofa and smoking a yellow cigarette in a green holder, represented a world theatrical; a world of greasepaint, art, and artifice. Miss Lux, sitting upright in a hard chair, represented the academical world; the world of universities, text-books, and discussion. Young Miss Wragg, busy pouring out coffee, was the world of sport; a physical, competitive, unthinking world. And the evening's guest, Dr Enid Knight, one of the 'visiting' Staff, stood for the medical world. The foreign world was not present: Sigrid Gustavsen had retired with her mother, who spoke no English, to her own room where they could chatter together in Swedish.

All these worlds had gone to make the finished article that was a Leaving Student; it was at least not the training that was narrow.

'And what do you think of our students, Miss Pym, now that you have had a whole afternoon with them?' Madame Lefevre asked, turning the battery of her enormous dark eyes on Lucy.

A damn-silly question, thought Lucy; and wondered how a good respectable middle-class English couple had produced anything so like the original serpent as Madame Lefevre. 'I think,' she said, glad to be able to be honest, 'that there is not one of them who is not an advertisement for Leys.' And she saw Henrietta's heavy face light up. College was Henrietta's world. She lived and moved and had her being in the affairs of Leys; it was her father, mother, lover, and child.

'They *are* a nice lot,' agreed Doreen Wragg happily, not yet far removed from her own student days and regarding her pupils with cameraderie.

'They are as the beasts that perish,' said Miss Lux incisively. 'They think that Botticelli is a variety of spaghetti.' She inspected with deep gloom the coffee that Miss Wragg handed to her. 'If it comes to that, they don't know what spaghetti is. It's not long since Dakers stood up in the middle of a Dietetics lecture and accused me of destroying her illusions.'

'It surprises me to know that anything about Miss Dakers is destructible,' observed Madame Lefevre, in her brown velvet drawl.

'What illusion had you destroyed?' the young doctor asked from the window-seat.

'I had just informed them that spaghetti and its relations were made from a paste of flour. That shattered for ever, apparently, Dakers' picture of Italy.'

'How had she pictured it?'

'Fields of waving macaroni, so she said.'

Henrietta turned from putting two lumps of sugar in a very small cup of coffee (*How* nice, thought Lucy wistfully, to have a figure like a sack of flour and not to mind!) and said: 'At least they are free from crime.'

'Crime?' they said, puzzled.

'Miss Pym had just been enquiring about the incidence of crime at Leys. That is what it is to be a psychologist.'

Before Lucy could protest against this version of her simple search for knowledge, Madame Lefevre said: 'Well, let us oblige her. Let us turn out the rag-bag of our shameful past. What crime have we had?'

'Farthing was had up last Christmas term for riding her bike without lights,' volunteered Miss Wragg.

'Crime,' said Madame Lefevre. 'Crime. Not petty misdemeanours.'

'If you mean a plain wrong-un, there was that dreadful

43

creature who was man-crazy and used to spend Saturday evenings hanging round the barrack gate in Larborough.'

'Yes,' said Miss Lux, remembering. 'What became of *her* when we tossed her out, does anyone know?'

'She is doing the catering at a Seamen's Refuge in Plymouth,' Henrietta said, and opened her eyes when they laughed. 'I don't know what is funny about that. The only real crime we have had in ten years, as you very well know, was the watches affair. And even that,' she added, jealous for her beloved institution, 'was a fixation rather than plain theft. She took nothing but watches, and she made no use of them. Kept them all in a drawer of her bureau, quite openly. Nine, there were. A fixation, of course.'

'By precedent, I suppose she is now with the Goldsmiths and Silversmiths,' said Madame Lefevre.

'I don't know,' said Henrietta, seriously. 'I think her people kept her at home. They were quite well-to-do.'

'Well, Miss Pym, the incidence appears to be point-something per cent.' Madame Lefevre waved a thin brown hand. 'We are an unsensational crowd.'

'Too normal by half,' Miss Wragg volunteered. 'A little spot of scandal would be nice now and again. A nice change from hand-stands and upward circlings.'

'I should like to see some hand-stands and upward-circlings,' Lucy said. 'Would it be all right if I came and watched the Seniors tomorrow morning?'

But of course she must see the Seniors, Henrietta said. They were busy with their Demonstration programme, so it would be a private Demonstration all for herself. 'They are one of the best sets we ever had,' she said.

'Can I have first go of the gym. when the Seniors are doing their Final Phys. on Tuesday?' Miss Wragg asked; and they began to discuss time-tables.

Miss Pym moved over to the window-seat and joined Dr Knight.

'Are you responsible for the cross-section of something called the villi?' she asked.

'Oh, no; physiology is an ordinary college subject: Catherine Lux takes that.'

'Then what do you lecture on?'

'Oh, different things at different stages. Public Health. The so-called "social" diseases. The even more so-called Facts of Life. Your subject.'

'Psychology?'

'Yes. Public Health is my job, but psychology is my speciality. I liked your book so much. So common-sensical. I admired that. It is so easy to be highfalutin about an abstract subject.'

Lucy flushed a little. There is no praise so gratifying as that of a colleague.

'And of course I am the College medical adviser,' Dr Knight went on, looking amused. 'A sinecure if ever there was one. They are a disgustingly healthy crowd.'

'But——' Lucy began. It is the outsider, Desterro (she was thinking) who insists on their abnormality. If it is true, then surely this trained observer, also from the outside, must be aware of it.

'They have accidents, of course,' the doctor said, misunderstanding Lucy's 'but'. 'Their life is a long series of minor accidents—bruises, and sprains, and dislocated fingers, and what not—but it is very rarely that anything serious happens. Bentley has been the only instance in my time—the girl whose room you have. She broke a leg, and won't be back till next term.'

'But—it is a strenuous training, a gruelling life; do they never break down under it?'

'Yes. That's not unknown. The last term is particularly trying. A concentration of horrors from the student's point of view. Crit. classes, and——'

'Crit. classes?'

'Yes. They each have to take a gym. and a dancing

class in the presence of the united Staff and their own set, and are judged according to the show they make. Nerve-shattering. These are all over, the crit. classes; but there are still the Finals, and the Demonstration, and being given jobs, and the actual parting from student life, and what not. Yes, it is a strain for them, poor dears. But they are amazingly resilient. No one who wasn't would have survived so long. Let me get you some more coffee. I'm going to have some.'

She took Lucy's cup and went away to the table; and Lucy leaned back in the folds of the curtain and looked at the garden. The sun had set, and the outlines were growing blurred; there was the first hint of dew in the soft air that blew up against her face. Somewhere on the other side of the house (in the students' common-room?) a piano was being played and a girl was singing. It was a charming voice: effortless and pure, without professional tricks and without fashionable dealing in quarter-tones. The song, moreover, was a ballad; old-fashioned and sentimental, but devoid of self-pity and posing. A frank young voice and a frank old song. It shocked Lucy to realise how long it was since she had heard any voice raised in song that was not a product of valves and batteries. In London at this moment the exhausted air was loud with radios; but here, in this cool, scented garden, a girl was singing for the love of it.

I have been too long in London, she thought; I must have a change. Find a hotel on the South Coast, perhaps. Or go abroad. One forgets that the world is young.

'Who is singing?' she asked, as her cup was handed to her again.

'Stewart, I think,' Dr Knight said, not interested. 'Miss Pym, you can save my life if you like to.'

Lucy said that to save a doctor's life would give her immense satisfaction.

'I want to go to a medical conference in London,' Dr

46

Knight said in a conspiratorial undertone. 'It is on Thursday, but that is the day of my psychology lecture. Miss Hodge thinks I am for ever going to conferences, so I can't possibly beg off again. But if you were to take that lecture for me, everything would be grand.'

'But I am going back to London myself tomorrow after lunch.'

'No!' said Dr Knight, much dashed. 'Do you have to?'

'Oddly enough, I was just thinking how much I should hate going back.'

'Then don't go. Stay on for a day or two, and save my life. Do, Miss Pym.'

'And what would Henrietta think of the substitution?'

'That, of course, is sheer affectation, and you ought to be ashamed of yourself. *I*'m not a best-seller, *I*'m not a celebrity, *I*'m not the author of the latest text-book on the subject——'

Lucy made a small gesture acknowledging her fault, but her eyes were on the garden. Why *should* she go back to London yet? What was there to take her back? Nothing and nobody. For the first time that fine, independent, cushioned, celebrated life of hers looked just a little bleak. A little narrow and inhuman. Could it be? Was there, perhaps, a lack of warmth in that existence she had been so content with? Not a lack of human contact, certainly. She had her fill of human contact. But it was a very all-of-a-piece contact, now that she thought of it. Except for Mrs Montmorency from one of the suburbs of Manchester, who was her daily help, and her Aunt Celia down in Walberswick who sometimes had her for week-ends, and the tradespeople, she never talked to anyone who wasn't somehow connected with the publishing or the academic worlds. And though all the ladies and gentlemen belonging to these two worlds were, of course, both intelligent and amusing, there was no denying that their interests were limited. You couldn't, for instance, talk to one and the same person about Social Security, hill-billy songs, and what won the 3.30. They each had their 'subject'. And their subject, she had found to her cost, was only too likely to be royalties. Lucy herself had only the vaguest idea about royalties; especially her own, and could never keep her end up in this sort of conversation.

Besides, none of them was *young*.

At least, not young as these children here were young. Young in years a few of her acquaintances might be, but they were already bowed down with the weight of the world's wrongs and their own importance. It was nice to meet a morning-of-the-world youngness for a change.

And it was nice to be liked.

There was no good in trying to diddle herself about why she wanted to stay a little longer; why she was seriously prepared to forgo the delights of civilisation that had seemed so desirable—so imperatively desirable—only yesterday morning. It *was* nice to be liked.

In the last few years she had been ignored, envied, admired, kowtowed to, and cultivated; but warm, personal liking was something she had not had since the Lower Fourth said good-bye to her, with a home-made pen-wiper and a speech by Gladys Someone-or-other, shortly after her legacy. To stay in this atmosphere of youth, of liking, of warmth, she was willing to overlook for a space the bells, the beans, and the bathrooms.

'Knight,' said young Miss Wragg, raising her voice from the conversation behind them, 'did the Disciples ask you about giving them an introduction to some doctor or other in Manchester?'

'Oh, yes, they asked me. In concert. I said yes, of course. As a matter of fact, I was glad to; I think they will be a great success.'

'Individually, the Disciples are null and void,' Miss Lux said. 'But collectively they have a quadruple ruthlessness that will be very useful in Lancashire. It is the only occasion I have ever come across when nothing multiplied by four became something like six-and-a-half. If nobody wants the *Sunday Times* I shall take it to bed with me.'

No one apparently wanted it. It had been lying unopened in the drawing-room after lunch when Lucy had been the first to look at it, and as far as she had noticed no one except Miss Lux had picked it up since.

'This set of seniors are planting themselves out very nicely. Almost without our help,' Madame Lefevre said. 'There will be less heart-burning than usual.' She did not sound very sorry about the heart-burning; just sardonic.

'It continually surprises me,' said Miss Hodge, not at all sardonic, 'how each year the students slip into their appropriate places in the world's work. The openings come up as the students are ready to fill them. Almost like—like two pieces of the same machine. So surprising and so satisfactory. I don't think we have had a misfit in all my years at Leys. I had a letter from the Cordwainers' School, by the way; in Edinburgh, you know. Mulcaster is getting married and they want someone in her place. You will remember Mulcaster, Marie?' She turned to Madame Lefevre who, except for Henrietta, was the Oldest Inhabitant—and who, incidentally, had been christened plain Mary.

'Of course I remember her. A lump without leaven,' said Madame, who judged everyone by their capacity to execute *rondes de jambes*.

'A nice girl,' Henrietta said placidly. 'I think Cordwainers will be a very good place for Sheena Stewart.'

'Have you told her about it?' Miss Wragg asked.

'No, oh, no; I always like to sleep on things.'

'Hatch them out, you mean,' Madame said. 'You must have heard about Cordwainers before lunch-time yesterday because that was the last post, and it is only now we hear about it.'

'It was not very important,' Henrietta said defensively; and then added with what was nearly a simper: 'But I *have* heard rumours of a "plum", a really wonderful chance for someone.'

'Tell us,' they said.

But Henrietta said no; that no official notice had come, that no official notice or application might come at all, and until it did it was better not to talk about it. But she still looked pleased and mysterious.

'Well, I'm going to bed,' Miss Lux said, picking up the *Times* and turning her back on Henrietta's elephantine coyness. 'You are not going before lunch tomorrow, are you, Miss Pym?'

'Well,' said Lucy, pitchforked of a sudden into decision, 'I wondered if I might stay on for a day or two? You did ask me to, you know,' she reminded Henrietta. 'It has been so nice—So interesting to watch a world so different —And it is so lovely here, so——' Oh, dear, why must she sound so idiotic. Would she never learn to behave like Lucy Pym the Celebrity?

But her stammerings were swamped in the loud wave of their approval. Lucy was touched to note a gleam of pleasure even on the face of Miss Lux.

'Stay on till Thursday and take my Senior Psychology lecture, and let me go to a conference in London,' Dr Knight suggested, as if it had just occurred to her.

'Oh, I don't know whether——' began Lucy, all artistic doubt, and looked at Henrietta.

'Dr Knight is always running away to conferences,' Miss Hodge said, disapproving, but without heat. 'But of course we would be delighted and honoured, Lucy, if you agreed to give the students a second lecture.'

'I should like to. It would be nice to feel myself a temporary member of the staff, instead of a mere guest. I should like to very much.' She turned in rising to wink at Dr Knight, who was squeezing her arm in a rapture of gratitude. 'And now I think I must get back to the student wing.'

She said good-night and went out with Miss Lux.

Lux eyed her sideways as they moved together to the back of the house, but Lucy, catching the glance, thought that there was a friendly gleam in that ice-grey eye.

'Do you really like this menagerie?' Lux asked. 'Or are you just looking for things to stick on cardboard with pins?'

That was what The Nut Tart had asked yesterday afternoon. Have you come looking for specimens? Well, she would make the same answer and see what Lux's reaction would be.

'Oh, I'm staying because I like it. A college of Physical Training wouldn't be a very good place to look for the abnormal, anyhow, would it.' She made it a statement, not a question; and waited.

'Why not?' asked Miss Lux. 'Sweating oneself into a coma may stultify the reason, but it doesn't destroy the emotions.'

'Doesn't it?' Lucy said, surprised. 'If I were dog-tired I'm certain I wouldn't have any feelings about anything but going to sleep quickly.'

'Going to sleep dead tired is all right; normal, and pleasant, and safe. It is when one wakens up dead tired that the trouble begins.'

'What trouble?'

'The hypothetical trouble of this discussion,' Lux said, smoothly.

'And is wakening up dead tired a common thing, would you say?'

'Well, I'm not their medical adviser so I can't run round with a stethoscope and fond inquiries, but I should say that five Seniors out of six in their last term are so tired that each morning is a mild nightmare. It is when one is as tired as that that one's emotional state ceases to be

51

normal. A tiny obstacle becomes an Everest in the path; a careless comment becomes a grievance to be nursed; a small disappointment is all of a sudden a suicidal affair.'

There swam up in Lucy's mind a vision of that circle of faces at tea-time. Brown, laughing, happy faces; careless and for the most part notably confident. Where in that relaxed and healthy crowd had there been the least hint of strain, of bad temper? Nowhere. They had moaned over their hard lot certainly, but it was a humorous and detached complaint.

Tired they might be; in fact tired they certainly were—it would be a miracle if they were not; but tired to the point of abnormality, no. Lucy could not believe it.

'This is my room,' Lux said, and paused. 'Have you something to read? I don't suppose you brought anything if you meant to go back yesterday. Can I lend you something?'

She opened the door, exhibiting a neat bed-sitting-room of which the sole decorations were one engraving, one photograph, and an entire wainscoting of books. From next door came the babble of Swedish chat.

'Poor Fröken,' Lux said unexpectedly, as Lucy cocked an ear. 'She has been so homesick. It must be wonderful to be able to talk family gossip in one's own tongue again.' And then, seeing Lucy's eyes on the photograph: 'My young sister.'

'She is very lovely,' Lucy said; and hoped instantly that there had been no hint of surprise in her tone.

'Yes.' Lux was drawing the curtains. 'I hate moths. Do you? She was born when I was in my teens, and I have practically brought her up. She is in her third year at Medical school.' She came and stood for a moment looking at the photograph with Lucy. 'Well, what can I give you to read? Anything from Runyon to Proust.'

Lucy took *The Young Visiters*. It was a long time since she had read it last, but she found that she was smiling as

the very sight of it. A sort of reflex action; quite in-
voluntary. And when she looked up she found that Lux
was smiling too.

'Well, that is one thing I shall never do,' Lucy said
regretfully.

'What?'

'Write a book that makes all the world smile.'

'Not all the world,' Lux said, her smile broadening. 'I
had a cousin who stopped half-way through. When I
asked her why, she said: "So *unlikely*".'

So Lucy went smiling away towards bed, glad that she
was not going to catch that train tomorrow, and thinking
about the plain Miss Lux who loved a beautiful sister and
liked absurdity. As she turned into the long corridor of the
E-wing she saw Beau Nash standing at the angle of the
stairs at the far end, in the act of lifting a hand-bell to
shoulder height, and in another second the wild yelling of
it filling the wing. She stood where she was, her hands
over her ears, while Beau laughed at her and swung the
evil thing with a will. Lovely, she was, standing there
with that instrument of torture in her hands.

'Is ringing the "bedroom" bell the Head Girl's duty?'
Lucy asked, as Beau at last ceased to swing.

'No, the Seniors take week-about; it just happens to be
my week. Being well down the list alphabetically I don't
have more than one week each term.' She looked at Miss
Pym and lowered her voice in mock confidence. 'I pretend
to be glad about that—everyone thinks it a frightful bore
to have to watch the clock—but I *love* making a row.'

Yes, thought Lucy; no nerves and a body brimming
with health; of course she would love the row. And then,
almost automatically, wondered if it was not the row that
she liked, but the feeling of power in her hands. But no,
she dismissed that thought; Nash was the one that life
had been easy for; the one who had, all her life, had only
to ask, in order to have. She had no need of vicarious

satisfactions; her life was one long satisfaction. She liked the wild clamour of the bell; that was all.

'Anyhow,' Nash said, falling into step with her, 'it isn't the "bedroom bell". It's "Lights Out".'

'I had no idea it was so late. Does that apply to me?'

'Of course not. Olympus does as it likes.'

'Even a boarded-out Olympus?'

'Here is your hovel,' Nash said, switching on the light and standing aside to let Lucy enter the bright little cell, so gay and antiseptic in the unshaded brilliance. After the subtleties of the summer evening and the grace of the Georgian drawing-room, it was like an illustration from one of the glossier American magazines. 'I am glad I happened to see you because I have a confession to make. I won't be bringing your breakfast tomorrow.'

'Oh, that is all right,' Lucy was beginning, 'I ought to get up in any case——'

'No, I don't mean that. Of *course* not. It is just that young Morris asked if she might do it—she is one of the Juniors—and——'

'The abductor of George?'

'Oh, yes, I forgot you were there. Yes, that one. And she seemed to think that her life would not be complete unless she had brought up your breakfast on your last morning, so I said that as long as she didn't ask for your autograph or otherwise make a nuisance of herself, she could. I hope you don't mind. She is a nice child, and it would really give her pleasure.'

Lucy, who didn't mind if her breakfast was brought by a wall-eyed and homicidal negro so long as she could eat the leathery toast in peace and quiet, said she was grateful to young Morris, and anyhow it wasn't going to be her last morning. She was going to stay on and take a lecture on Thursday.

'You *are*! Oh, that's wonderful. I'm so glad. Everyone will be glad. You are so *good* for us.'

54

'A medicine?' Lucy wrinkled her nose in protest.

'No, a tonic.'

'Somebody's Syrup,' Lucy said; but she was pleased.

So pleased that even pushing little hairpins into their appointed places did not bore her with the customary frenzy of boredom. She creamed her face and considered it, unadorned and greasy in the bright hard light, with unaccustomed tolerance. There was no doubt that being a little on the plump side kept the lines away; if you had to have a face like a scone it was at least comforting that it was a smooth scone. And, now she came to think of it, one was given the looks that were appropriate; if she had Garbo's nose she would have to dress up to it, and if she had Miss Lux's cheek-bones she would have to live up to them. Lucy had never been able to live up to anything. Not even The Book.

Remembering in time that there was no bedside light —students were discouraged from working in bed—she switched the light off and crossed to pull aside the curtains of the window looking out on the courtyard. She stood there by the wide-open window, smelling the cool scented night. A great stillness had settled on Leys. The chatter, the bells, the laughter, the wild protests, the drumming of feet, the rush of bath water, the coming and going, had crystallised into this great silent bulk, a deeper darkness in the quiet dark.

'Miss Pym.'

The whisper came from one of the windows opposite.

Could they see her, then? No, of course not. Someone had heard the small noise of her curtains being drawn back.

'Miss Pym, we are so glad you are staying.'

So much for the college grape-vine! Not fifteen minutes since Nash said good-night, but already the news was in the opposite wing.

Before she could answer, a chorus of whispers came

from the unseen windows round the little quadrangle. Yes, Miss Pym. We are glad. Glad. Miss Pym. Yes. Yes. Glad, Miss Pym.

'Good-night, everyone,' Lucy said.

Good-night, they said. Good-night. So glad. Good-night.

She wound her watch and pulled up a chair to put it on —*the* chair, rather: there was only one—so that there should be no burrowing under pillows for it in the morning; and thought how odd it was that only yesterday morning she could not wait to get out of this place.

And perhaps it was because no self-respecting psychologist would have anything to do with a thing so outmoded as Premonition that no small helpful imp from the Unexplainable was there to whisper in her drowsy ear: 'Go away from here. Go away while the going is good. Go away. Away from here.'

6

THE chairs scraped on the parquet floor as the students rose from their kneeling position, and turned to wait while the Staff filed out of morning prayers. Lucy, having become 'temporary staff', had made the gesture of attending this 8.45 ceremony as an off-set to the un-staff-like indulgence of breakfast in bed; and she had spent the last few minutes considering the collective legs of College as spread before her in kneeling rows and marvelling at their individuality. Dress was uniform at this hour of the morning, and heads were bowed in dutiful hands, but a pair of legs were as easy to identify as a face, she found. There they were: stubborn legs, frivolous legs, neat legs, dull legs, doubtful legs—already she needed only a turn of calf and piece of ankle to say: Dakers, or Innes, or Rouse, or Beau, as the case might be. Those elegant ones at the end of the first row were The Nut Tart. Did the nuns not mind that their protégée should listen to Anglican prayers, then? And those rather stick-like ones were Campbell, and those——

'Amen,' said Henrietta, with unction.

'Amen,' murmured the students of Leys, and rose to their feet with the scraping of chairs. And Lucy filed out with the Staff.

'Come in and wait while I arrange this morning's post,' Henrietta said, 'and then I'll go over to the gymnasium with you,' and she led the way into her own sitting-room, where a meek little part-time secretary was waiting for instructions. Lucy sat down on the window seat with the *Telegraph*, and listened with only half an ear to the professional conversation that followed. Mrs So-and-so had written to ask the date of the Demonstration, Mrs Someone-else wanted to know whether there was a hotel near-by where she and her husband could stay when they came to see their daughter perform, the receipt for the butcher must be looked out and presented to his disbelieving eye, the special lecturer for the last Friday of term had cried off, three Prospective Parents wanted prospectuses.

'All quite straightforward, I think,' Henrietta said.

'Yes,' agreed the meek little secretary. 'I'll get on with them at once. There was a letter from Arlinghurst. It doesn't seem to be here.'

'No,' Henrietta said. 'That can be answered later in the week.'

Arlinghurst, Lucy's mind said. Arlinghurst. The school for girls, of course. A sort of female Eton. 'I was at Arlinghurst,' they said, and that settled it. She took her attention from the *Telegraph* leader for a moment and thought that if the 'plum' that Henrietta had been waiting for was Arlinghurst, then indeed it was going to create more than the usual stir among the interested Seniors. She was on the point of asking whether Arlinghurst was in fact the 'plum', but was stopped partly by the presence of the meek little secretary, but more immediately by the expression on Henrietta's face. Henrietta —there was no denying it—Henrietta had a wary, a sort of guilty, look. The look of a person who is Up To Something.

Oh, well, thought Lucy, if she is merely hugging her lovely secret to herself, let her. I shan't spoil it for her. She followed her friend down the long corridor that ran the length of the wing, and out to the covered way that continued the corridor to the gymnasium. The gymnasium lay parallel to the house and to the right-angled wing, so that from the air the buildings made a complete letter E;

the three horizontal strokes being 'old house', the right-angled wing, and the gymnasium; the vertical stroke being the connecting wing and the covered way.

The door to which the covered way led was open, and from inside the gymnasium came the sounds of unco-ordinated activity; voices, laughter, thudding feet. Henrietta paused by the open door and pointed through to the door on the other side, now closed. '*That* is the college crime,' she said. 'Crossing the gymnasium to the field-path instead of using the appointed covered way round the building. That is why we have had to lock it up. One wouldn't think that a few extra steps would mean much to students who took so many in the day, but there was no argument or threat which would stop them using the short-cut through. So we removed the temptation altogether.'

She turned from the open door and led the way to the other end of the building, where a small porch held the stairway to the gallery. As they climbed the stairs Henri-etta paused to point to a piece of mechanism on a low trolley, which filled the well of the staircase. 'That,' she said, 'is the most famous College character of all. That is our vacuum cleaner; known from here to New Zealand as The Abhorrence.'

'Why abhorrent?' Lucy asked.

'It used to be Nature's Abhorrence, but it became shortened to The Abhorrence. You remember the tag one is taught at school: Nature abhors a vacuum.' She looked a moment longer at the monstrous object, caressing it with her eyes. 'It cost us a deplorable sum, The Abhor-rence, but it was money well spent. However well the gymnasium was cleaned in the old days, there was always a residue of dust, which was beaten into the air by the students' feet and sucked up, of course, by the students' respiratory passages; and the result was catarrh. Not universal, of course, but there never was a time, summer or winter, when some student or other was not having a bout of catarrh. It was Dr Knight's predecessor who suggested that it might be invisible dust that was responsible, and she was right. Since we squandered that immense sum on The Abhorrence there has been no more catarrh. And of course,' she added happily, 'it was a saving in the end since it is Giddy the gardener's job to vacuum the gymnasium now, and we don't have to pay cleaners.'

Lucy stopped as they reached the top of the stairs, and looked over the railings into the well again. 'I don't think I like it. It is very well named, it seemed to me. There is something obscene about it.'

'It is unbelievably powerful. And very easy to work. It takes Giddy only about twenty minutes every morning, and when he has finished there is, as he says himself, "nothing left but the fixtures". He is very proud of The Abhorrence. He grooms it as if it were an animal.' Henrietta opened the door at the top of the stairs and they entered the gallery.

A gymnasium as a building does not permit of architecture. It is purely functional. It is an oblong box, lit by windows which are either in the roof or high up the walls. The gymnasium at Leys had windows where the walls met the roof, which is not a beautiful arrangement; but through their far-away panes at no hour of any day could direct sunlight blind a student's eyes, and so cause an accident. The great oblong box of a building was filled with the reflected radiance of a summer morning; golden and soft. Across the floor were scattered the Senior students, limbering up, practising, criticising, and in a few happy instances playing the fool.

'Do they mind an audience?' Lucy asked as they sat down.

'They are very used to one. Hardly a day goes by without a visitor of some kind.'

'What is under the gallery? What is it they watch all the time?'

'Themselves,' said Henrietta succinctly. 'The whole wall below the gallery is one long mirror.'

Lucy admired the impersonal interest on the faces of the students as they watched their reflected performances. To be able to view one's physical entity with such critical detachment was surely no bad thing.

'It is one of the griefs of my life,' the dutch-doll Gage was saying, looking at her up-stretched arms, 'that my arms have that kink at the elbow.'

'If you listened to that Friday-friend and used your will-power, you'd have them straight by now,' Stewart observed, not pausing in her own contortions.

'Probably bent back the other way,' Beau Nash mocked, from a doubled-up position at the rib-stalls.

Lucy deduced that a Friday-friend was the 'interest' lecturer who appeared on Friday evenings; and wondered idly whether that particular one had called his subject 'faith' or 'mind-over-matter'; was it Lourdes or was it Coué?

Hasselt, the South African with the flat Primitive face, was clutching Innes's ankles in the air while Innes stood on her hands. '*Reeeee*-ly on theee *arrrrms*, Mees Innes,' Hasselt was saying, in a would-be Swedish accent that was evidently a quotation from Fröken; and Innes laughed and collapsed. Looking at them, flushed and smiling (this, she thought, is the first time I have seen Mary Innes smile) Lucy felt again how out-of-place these two faces were. Hasselt's belonged above a Madonna-blue robe, with a tiny landscape of hills and castles and roads somewhere at her left ear. And Innes's to a portrait on some ancestral staircase—seventeenth century, perhaps? No, too gay, too adaptable, too arched-of-eyebrow. Sixteenth-century, rather. Withdrawn, uncompromising, unforgiving; the-stake-or-nothing.

Away by herself in a far corner was Rouse, pains-takingly stretching her ham-strings by walking her palms up to her feet. She couldn't really *need* to stretch her ham-strings, not after years of continued stretching, so pre-sumably this was merely a north-country example of 'makking siccar'. There was no fooling about for Miss Rouse; life was real, life was earnest; life was long ham-strings and a good pose in the offing. Lucy wished she liked Miss Rouse better, and looked round for Dakers as a sort of antidote. But there was no tow-head and cheerful pony-face among the collection.

And then, suddenly, the desultory noise and the chatter faded.

No one had come in by the open door at the far end, but there was beyond doubt a Presence in the place. Lucy could feel it coming up through the gallery floor at her feet. She remembered that there was a door at the foot of the stairway; where the Abhorrence stood. Someone had come in down there.

There was no audible word of command, but the students, who a moment before had been scattered over the floor like beads from a broken string, were now, as if by magic, standing in a still, waiting line.

Fröken Gustavsen walked out from under the gallery, and surveyed them.

'Unt wvere ees Mees Dakers?' she asked in a cool small voice.

But even as she said it a flustered Dakers ran in through the open door, and stopped short as she saw the picture that waited her.

'Oh, *catastrophe!*' she wailed, and darted to the gap that someone had accommodatingly left for her. 'Oh, I *am* sorry, Fröken. *Abyssmally* sorry. It was just that——'

'Ees eet proposed to be laate at the Demonstration?' asked Fröken, with almost scientific interest.

'Oh, *no*, of *course* not, Fröken. It was just that——'

'We know. We know. Something was lost, or broke. Eef eet wass possible to come to thees plaace naakid, Mees Dakers would still find somthing to lose or break. Attention!'

They came to attention, and were motionless except for their quick breathing.

'Eef Mees Thomas were to pull een her stow-mach the line would be improved, I theenk.'

Thomas obliged instantly.

'Unt Mees Appleyard shows too much cheen.'

The plump little girl with the red cheeks pulled her chin farther into her neck. 'So!'

They right-turned into file, covered, and marched in single file down the gymnasium; their feet falling so lightly on the hard wood floor that they were almost inaudible.

'Quieter, quieter. Lightly, lightly!'

Was it possible?

But it was possible, apparently. Still more quietly fell those long-trained feet, until it was unbelievable that a collection of solid young females weighing individually anything up to ten stones was marching, marching, round the hall.

Lucy slid an eye round to Henrietta; and almost instantly switched it away again. The fond pride on Henrietta's large pale countenance was startling, almost painful, to see; and for a little Lucy forgot the students below and thought about Henrietta. Henrietta of the sack-like figure and the conscientious soul. Henrietta who had had elderly parents, no sisters, and the instincts of a mother hen. No one had ever lain awake at night over Henrietta; or walked back and fore in the darkness outside her house; or even, perhaps, sent her flowers. (Which reminded her to wonder where Alan was nowadays; there had been several weeks, one spring, when she had thought quite seriously of accepting Alan, in spite of his Adam's apple. It would be nice, she had thought, to be cherished

63

for a change. What had stopped her was the realisation
that the cherishing would have to be mutual. That she
would inevitably have to mend socks, for instance. She
didn't like feet. Even Alan's.) Henrietta had been apparently doomed to a dull if worthy life. But it had not
turned out like that. If the expression on her unguarded
face had been any criterion, Henrietta had built for herself a life that was full, rich, and satisfying. She had said,
in her first reunion gossip with Lucy, that when she took
over Leys a decade ago it had been a small and not very
popular college, and that she and Leys had flourished together; that she was, in fact, a partner now as well as
Principal, and a partner in a flourishing concern. But
until she had surprised that look on Henrietta's face, Lucy
had not realised how much her old friend identified herself with her work. That College was her world, she knew;
Henrietta talked of little else. But absorption in a business
was one thing, and the emotion on Henrietta's face was
quite another.

She was roused from her speculations by the sound of
apparatus being dragged out. The students had stopped
arching themselves into bows at the rib-stalls, puffed out
like figureheads on a ship, and were now bringing out the
booms. Lucy's shins ached with remembered pain; how
often had she barked her bones against that unyielding
piece of wood; certainly one of the compensations
of middle-age was not having to do uncomfortable
things.

The wooden upright was now standing in the middle of
the floor, and the two booms were fitted into its grooved
sides and hoisted as high as hands could reach. The iron
pins with wooden handles shot home through their
appointed holes in the upright to hold the booms up, and
there was the instrument of torture ready. Not that it was
shin-barking time yet; that would come later. Just now
it was only 'travelling'. Two by two, one at each end, the

students proceeded along the boom, hanging by their hands, monkey-wise. First sideways, then backwards, and lastly with a rotary movement, like a travelling top. All this was done with monotonous perfection until it was Rouse's turn to rotate. Rouse had bent her knees for the spring to the boom, and then dropped her hands and looked at her instructor with a kind of panic on her tight, freckled face.

'Oh, Fröken,' she said, 'I'm not going to be able to do it.'

'*Nonsense*, Mees Rouse,' Fröken said, encouraging, but not surprised (this was apparently a repetition of some previous scene), 'you have done eet perfectly since you were a Junior. You do it now of course.'

In a strained silence Rouse sprang to the boom and began her progress along it. For half its length she performed with professional expertness, and then for no apparent reason her hand missed the boom as she turned, and her body swung away, suspended by her other hand. She made an effort to recover herself, pulling up with her sustaining hand, but the rhythm had broken and she dropped to her feet.

'I knew it,' she said. 'I'm going to be like Kenyon, Fröken. Just like Kenyon.'

'*Mees* Rouse; you are not going to be like *anyone*. It is knack, that. And for a moment you haf lost the knack, that is all. You will try again.'

Rouse sprang once more to the boom above her head.

'*No!*' said the Swede with emphasis; and Rouse came back to the ground looking inquiring.

'*Not* saying: Oh, dear, I cannot do eet. But saying: This I do often, with ease, and now al*so*. So!'

Twice more Rouse tried, and failed.

'Ve-ry well, Mees Rouse. That will do. One half of the boom will be put up last thing at night, as it is now, and

65

you will come een the morning early and practise, until the knack has come back.'

'Poor Rouse,' Lucy said, as the booms were being reversed for balance exercises, flat side up instead of rounded.

'Yes, such a pity,' Henrietta said. 'One of our most brilliant students.'

'Brilliant?' said Lucy, surprised. It was not an adjective she would have applied to Rouse.

'In physical work, anyhow. Most brilliant. She finds written work a difficulty, but makes up for it by hard work. A model student, and a great credit to Leys. Such a pity about this little nervous development. Over-anxiety, of course. It happens sometimes. Usually over something quite simple, strangely enough.'

'What did she mean by "being like Kenyon"? That is the girl whose place Teresa Desterro took, isn't it?'

'Yes. How clever of you to remember. That was a case in point. Kenyon suddenly decided that she could not balance. She had always had abnormally good balance, and there was no reason why she should lose it. But she began by being wobbly, took to jumping off in the middle of an exercise, and ended by being unable to get up from sitting position on the boom. She sat there and clung to the boom like a frightened child. Sat there and cried.'

'Some inner insufficiency.'

'Of course. It was not the balance that she was frightened of. But we had to send her home. We are hoping that she will come back to finish her training when she has had a long rest. She was very happy here.'

Was she? thought Lucy. So happy that she broke down. What had reduced the girl who was good at balance to a crying and shivering piece of misery, clutching at the boom?

She watched with a new interest the progress of the balancing that had been poor Kenyon's Waterloo. Two by two the students somersaulted upwards on to the high boom, turned to a sitting position sideways, and then slowly stood up on the narrow ledge. Slowly one leg lifted, the muscles rippling in the light, the arms performed their appointed evolution. The faces were calm, intent. The bodies obedient, sure, and accustomed. When the exercise was finished they sank until they were sitting on their heels, upright and easy, put forward blind hands to seize the boom, descended to sideways sitting once more, and from there to a forward somersault and so to the ground again.

No one fluffed or failed. The perfection was unblemished. Even Fröken found no word to say. Lucy found that she had been holding her breath. She sat back and relaxed and breathed deeply.

'That was lovely. At school the balance was much lower, wasn't it, and so it was not exciting.'

Henrietta looked pleased. 'Sometimes I come in just to see the balance and nothing else. So many people like the more spectacular items. The vaulting and so on. But I find the quiet control of the balance very satisfying.'

The vaulting, when it came, was spectacular enough. The obstacles were, to Lucy's eyes, horrific; and she looked with uncomprehending wonder at the delighted faces of the students. They *liked* this. They liked launching themselves into nothingness, flying through the air to problematical landings, twisting and somersaulting. The restraint that had characterised their attitude up to now had vanished; there was verve in their every movement, a sort of laughter; living was good and this was a physical expression of their joy in living. Amazed, she watched the Rouse who had stumbled and failed over the simple boom exercise, performing hair-raising feats of perfection that must require the maximum of courage, control, and 'knack'. (Henrietta had been right, her physical performance was brilliant. She was also, no doubt, a brilliant

67

games player; her timing was excellent. But still that 'brilliant' stuck in Lucy's throat. 'Brilliant' meant someone like Beau; an all-round fineness; body, mind, and spirit.)

'*Mees* Dakers! Take the left hand off at *wons*. Is eet *mountaineering* you are?'

'I didn't mean to leave it so long, Fröken. Really I didn't.'

'That is understood. It is the not meaning to that ees rrreprehensible. Come again, after Mees Mathews.'

Dakers came again, and this time managed to make her rebellious hand release its grip at the appropriate moment.

'Ha!' she said, delighted with her own success.

'Ha indeed,' agreed Fröken, a smile breaking. 'Co-ordination. All is co-ordination.'

'They like Fröken, don't they,' Lucy said to Henrietta, as the students tidied away the implements of their trade.

'They like all the Staff,' Henrietta said, with a faint return of her head-girl tone. 'It is not advisable to keep a mistress who is unpopular, however good she may be. On the other hand it is desirable that they should be just a little in awe of their preceptors.' She smiled in her senior-clergy-making-a-joke manner; Henrietta did not make jokes easily. 'In their different ways, Fröken, Miss Lux, and Madame Lefevre all inspire a healthy awe.'

'Madame Lefevre? If I were a student, I don't think it would be awe that would knock my knees together, but sheer terror.'

'Oh, Marie is quite human when you know her. She likes being one of the College legends.'

Marie and The Abhorrence, thought Lucy; two College legends. Each with identical qualities; terrible and fascinating.

The students were standing in file, breathing deeply as

they raised their arms and lowered them. Their fifty minutes of concentrated activity had come to an end, and there they were: flushed, triumphant, fulfilled.

Henrietta rose to go, and as she turned to follow Lucy found that Fröken's mother had been sitting behind them in the gallery. She was a plump little woman with her hair in a bun at the back, and reminded Lucy of Mrs Noah, as portrayed by the makers of toy Arks. Lucy bowed and smiled that extra-wide-for-foreigners smile that one uses to bridge the gap of silence, and then, remembering that although this little woman spoke no English she might speak German, she tried a phrase, and the little woman's face lit up.

'To speak with you, Fräulein, is such pleasure that I will even speak German to do it,' she said. 'My daughter tells me that you are very distinguished.'

Lucy said that she had had a success, which was not the same thing as being distinguished unfortunately; and expressed her admiration for the work she had just witnessed. Henrietta who had taken Classics instead of Modern Languages at school, washed her hands of this exchange of civilities, and preceded them down the stairs. As Lucy and Fru Gustavsen came out into the sunlight the students were emerging from the door at the other end, running or dawdling across the covered-way to the house. Last of the group came Rouse, and Lucy could not help suspecting that her emergence was timed to coincide with the passing of Henrietta. There was no need for her to linger a yard or two behind the others like that; she must see out of the tail of her eye that Henrietta was bearing down on her. In similar circumstances Lucy would have bolted, but Rouse was lingering. She liked Miss Rouse even less than usual.

Henrietta overtook the girl and paused to speak to her; and as Lucy and her companion passed them Lucy saw the expression on the tight freckled face turned up to receive the Principal's words of wisdom, and remembered what they had called that at school. 'Being smarmy.' And laying it on with a trowel, too, she thought with vulgar satisfaction.

'And I've always liked freckles, too,' she said regretfully. '*Bitte?*'

But this was not a subject that could be done justice to in German. The Significance of Freckles. She could see it: a thick tome full of portmanteau words and portentousness. No, it would need French to do it justice. Some distilled essence of amiable cynicism. Some pretty little blasting phrase.

'Is this your first visit to England?' she asked; and instead of entering the house with the others they strolled together through the garden towards the front of the house.

Yes, this was Fru Gustavsen's first visit to England, and it amazed her that a people who created gardens like this should also create the buildings in them. 'Not this, of course,' she said, 'this old house is very pleasant. It is of a period that was good, yes? But what one sees from train and taxi; after Sweden it is horrible. Please do not think that I am Russian about things. It is——'

'Russian?'

'Yes. Naïve, and ignorant, and sure that no one can do anything as well as my own country can do it. It is just that I am used to modern houses that are good to look at.'

Lucy said that she might as well get over the subject of our cooking while she was at it.

'Ach, no,' said the little woman surprisingly, 'it is not so, that. My daughter has told me. Here in College it is according to régime'—Lucy thought that 'according to régime' was tact of the most delicate—'and so is not typical. Nor in the hotels is it typical, my daughter says. But she has stayed in private houses in holiday time, and the dishes of the country, she says, are delicious. Not everything she liked. Not everyone likes our raw herring,

70

after all. But the joint roasted in the oven, and the apple tart with cream, and the cold ham very pink and tender, all that is most admirable. Most admirable.'

So, walking through the summer garden Lucy found herself expatiating on herrings fried in oatmeal, and parkins, and Devonshire splits, and hot-pot, and collops, and other regional delicacies. She concealed the existence of the pork pie, which she privately considered a barbarism.

As they turned the corner of the house towards the front door, they passed the windows of a lecture room where the Seniors were already engaged in listening to Miss Lux. The windows were pushed up from the bottom as far as they would go, so that the room was visible in all its details, and Lucy cast an idle glance at the assembled profiles presented to her.

She had looked away before she realised that these were not the faces she had seen only ten minutes ago. She looked back again, startled. Gone was the excitement, the flush of exercise, the satisfaction of achievement. Gone for the moment was even the youth. The faces were tired and spiritless.

Not all of them, of course. Hasselt still had her air of calm well-being. And Beau Nash's face had still its bright indestructible good looks. But the majority looked sunken; indescribably weary. Mary Innes, seated nearest the window, had a marked line from nostrils to chin; a line that had no business there for thirty years yet.

A little saddened and uncomfortable, as one is at the unexpected discovery of an unhappiness in the middle of delight, Lucy turned her head away, and her last glimpse as she walked past was the face of Miss Rouse. And the expression on the face of Miss Rouse surprised her. It reminded her of Walberswick.

Now why Walberswick?

The wary freckled countenance of Miss Rouse had

nothing in common with that formidable grande dame who was Lucy's aunt.

Certainly not.

Then why—but stop! It wasn't her aunt; it was her aunt's cat. The expression on that north-country face in the lecture room was the expression on the face of Philadelphia when she had had cream instead of milk in her saucer. And there was only one word for that expression. The word smug.

Lucy felt, not unreasonably, that someone who had just failed to perform a routine exercise had no right to be looking smug. And the last faint lingering inclination to be sorry for Miss Rouse died in her.

7

'MISS PYM,' said The Nut Tart, materialising at Lucy's elbow, 'let us run away together.'

It was Wednesday morning, and College was sunk in the thick silence of Final Examinations. Lucy was leaning over a five-barred gate behind the gymnasium, staring at a field of buttercups. It was here at the end of the Leys garden that the country began; the real country, free of the last tentacles of Larborough, unraped and unlittered. The field sloped to a stream, beyond which was the cricket field; and beyond that into the far distance stretched the unbroken pattern of hedge and tree and pasture; yellow, and white, and green; asleep in the morning sunshine.

Lucy took her eyes with difficulty from the shimmering yellow of the buttercups that had been mesmerising her, and wondered how many flowered silk frocks the Brazilian possessed. Here was yet another one, shaming the English subtleties with its brilliance.

'Where do you propose that we run to?' she asked.

'Let's go to the village.'

'Is there a village?'

'There is always a village in England; it is that kind of country. But more especially there is Bidlington. You can see the weather thing of the church steeple just over those trees there.'

'It looks a long way,' said Lucy, who was no great walker and was greatly content where she was; it was a long time since she had had a field of buttercups to look at and all time to do it in. 'Is it much of a place?'

'Oh yes. It is a two-pub village,' Desterro said, as one

quoting a calibre. 'Besides, it has everything a village in England should have. Queen Elizabeth slept there, and Charles the Second hid there; and Crusaders are buried in the church—there is one just like the manager of our ranch in Brazil—and all the cottages are obtainable on postcards at the shop; and it appears in books, the village does——'

'Guide books, you mean?'

'No, no. It has an author who specialised in it, you understand. I read one of his books when I came first to Leys. *Rain Over The Sty* it was called. All breasts and incest. And it has the Bidlington Martyrs—that is six men who threw stones at the police station last century some time and got put in jail. Imagine a country that remembers a thing like that! In my country they use knives—when they can't afford revolvers—and we smother the corpses with flowers, and cry a lot, and forget all about it next week.'

'Well——'

'We can have some coffee at The Teapot.'

'A little Hibernian, surely?'

But that was too much for even an intelligent stranger to these shores. 'It is *real* coffee, I may tell you. It both smells and tastes. Oh, come on, Miss Pym. It is a small fifteen minutes away, and it is not yet ten o'clock. And there is nothing to do in this place until we are summoned to eat beans at one o'clock.'

'Are you not taking any of the examinations?' Lucy asked, passing meekly through the gate that was held open for her.

'Anatomy I shall take, I think. Just, as you say, for the hell of it. I have taken all the lectures, so it will be fun to find out how much I know. It is worth knowing anatomy. It is a great labour, of course; it is a subject in which imagination is not appreciated, but it is worth learning.'

'I suppose so. One wouldn't feel a fool in an emergency.'

'Emergency?' said Desterro, whose mind had apparently not been running along these lines. 'Oh, yes, I see. But what I meant is that it is a subject that does not get out of date. Now *your* subject, if you will forgive me, Miss Pym, is continually getting out of date, no? To listen to it is charming, but to work at it would be very foolish. An idea today may be nonsense tomorrow, but a clavicle is a clavicle for all time. You see?'

Lucy saw, and envied such economy of effort.

'So tomorrow, when the Juniors take their Final Anatomy, I take it too. It is a respect-worthy thing; my grandmother would approve of it. But today they are busy about conundrums, and so me, I walk to Bidlington with the charming Miss Pym and we have coffee.'

'Conundrums?'

The Nut Tart fished a folded paper from the minute pocket of her frock and read from it: 'If the ball is over the touch line, but has not reached the ground and a player standing inside hits or catches the ball and brings it into the court again, what decision would you give?'

In a silence more eloquent than speech she folded up the cyclostyled sheet and put it away again.

'How did you get a copy of their paper if they are still busy on the subject of games?'

'Miss Wragg gave me one. She said it might amuse me. It does.'

Down between the yellow field and the may-white hedge the path led them to the stream. They paused by the small bridge to stare at the shadowed water under the willows.

'Over there,' Desterro said, pointing at the level ground across the stream, 'is the games field. In winter it is deep in mud, and they have bars across their shoes to keep them from slipping in it.' Lucy thought that if she were saying: 'They wear rings through their noses to add to their attraction' the tone would be identical. 'Now we walk downstream to the next little bridge and get on to the road there. It is not a road; just a lane.' She moved in silence down the shaded path, a bright dragon-fly of a creature, graceful and alien; and Lucy was surprised to find that she was capable of so unbroken a quiet.

As they came up on to the road at last she said: 'Have you any money, Miss Pym?'

'No,' said Lucy, stopping in dismay.

'Neither have I. But it is all right. Miss Nevill will finance us.'

'Who is Miss Nevill?'

'The lady who runs the tea-house.'

'That is rather unusual, isn't it?'

'Not with me. I am always forgetting my money. But Miss Nevill is charming. Do not feel bad about it, dear Miss Pym, I am in good standing in the village, you will see.'

The village was all the Desterro had claimed for it; and so was Miss Nevill. So, indeed, was The Teapot. It was one of those tea-shops so much despised by the bread-and-cheese-and-beer school, and so gladly welcomed by a generation of tea-drinkers who remember the fly-blown rooms behind village bakers' shops, the primitive buns with currants like dead insects, the cracked and ill-washed cups, and the black evil tea.

It had all the properties stigmatised by the literary frequenters of village inns: the Indian-tree-pattern china, the dark oak tables, the linen curtains in a Jacobean design, the herbaceous bouquets in unglazed brown jugs; yes, even the arts and crafts in the window. But to Lucy, who in the Alan period had had her share of undusted 'snugs', it was quite frankly charming. There was a rich scent of spiced cakes straight from the oven; there was, as well as the long window on the street, a further window that gave on a garden bright with colour; there was peace, and coolness, and welcome.

Miss Nevill, a large lady in a chintz apron, received

Desterro as an old and valued acquaintance, and asked if she were 'playing hookey, as you say on your side of the Atlantic'. The Nut Tart ignored this identification with the back streets of Brooklyn. 'This is Miss Pym who writes books about psychology and is our guest at Leys,' she said, politely introducing Lucy. 'I have told her that here one can drink real coffee, and be in general civilised. We have no money at all, either of us, but we will have a great deal to eat and pay you back later.'

This appeared to Miss Nevill to be quite a normal proposition, and she went away to the kitchen to get the coffee with neither surprise nor demur. The place was empty at this hour of the morning, and Lucy wandered round inspecting the old prints and the new crafts—she was pleased to observe that Miss Nevill drew the line at Brummagem brass door-knockers even if there were raffia mats—and then sat down with Desterro at the table looking on to the village street. Before their coffee arrived, they were joined by a middle-aged couple, husband and wife, who drove up in a car as if they were searching for the place. The car was the kind that a provincial doctor might use; low in petrol consumption and in its third or fourth year of wear. But the woman who came round from the farther seat with a laughing remark to her husband was not a typical doctor's wife. She was grey, and slim, with long legs and narrow feet in good shoes. Lucy watched her with pleasure. It was not often nowadays that one saw good bones; smartness had taken the place of breeding.

'In *my* country,' said Desterro, looking with a considering eye at the woman and with a contemptuous eye on the car, 'that woman would have a chauffeur *and* a *footman.*'

It was not often, moreover, that one saw a middle-aged husband and wife so pleased with each other, Lucy thought, as she watched them come in. They had a holiday air. They came in and looked about them expectantly, questioningly.

'Yes, this is it,' the woman said. 'That is the window on the garden that she talks about, and there is the print of Old London Bridge.'

They moved about looking at things, quietly, unself-consciously, and then took the table at the other window. Lucy was relieved to see that the man was the mate she would have chosen for such a woman; a little saturnine, perhaps, more self-absorbed than the woman; but quite admirable. He reminded her of someone, but she could not think of whom; someone whom she admired. The eyebrows, it was. Dark level brush-marks low over the eyes. His suit was very old, she noticed; well-pressed and kept, but with that much-cleaned air that overtakes a garment in its old age. The woman's suit, a tweed, was frankly shabby, and her stockings were darned—very neatly darned—at the heels. Her hands, too, looked as if they were accustomed to household tasks, and her fine grey hair was washed at home and unwaved. What had she got to look so happy about, this woman who struggled with straitened means? Was it just being on holiday with a husband she loved? Was it that that gave her grey luminous eyes their almost childlike happiness?

Miss Nevill came in with the coffee and a large plate of spiced cakes shining with newness and crisp at the edges. Lucy decided to forget her weight just this once and enjoy herself. This was a decision she made with deplorable frequency.

As she poured the coffee she heard the man say: 'Good morning. We have come all the way from the West Country to taste your griddle cakes. Do you think you could make us some, or are you too busy at this hour of the morning?'

'If you are too busy it doesn't matter,' said the woman

with the hard-worked hands. 'We shall have some of the cakes that smell so good.'

But Miss Nevill would not be a minute in preparing the griddle cakes. She had no batter standing, she said, so the griddle cakes would not be as wonderful as when the batter was allowed to stand; but she was not often asked for them in summer time.

'No, I expect not. But our daughter at Leys has talked so often of them, and this may be our only chance of tasting them.' The woman smiled, half it seemed at the thought of her daughter, half at their own childish desire.

So they were College parents.

Whose? Lucy wondered, watching them over the rim of her coffee cup.

Beau's, perhaps. Oh, no; Beau was rich, of course. Then whose?

She wouldn't mind giving them to Dakers, but there were objections. That tow-head could not be sired by that dark grave man; nor could that adult and intelligent woman have given birth to the through-other piece of nonsense that was Dakers.

And then, quite suddenly, she knew whose eyebrows those were.

Mary Innes's.

They were Mary Innes's parents. And in some odd way they explained Mary Innes. Her gravity; her air of belonging to a century other than this one; her not finding life very amusing. To have standards to live up to, but to have little money to live up to them with, was not a happy combination for a girl burdened with the need to make a success of her training.

Into the silence that had succeeded Miss Nevill's departure, Lucy heard her own voice saying: 'Forgive me, but is your name Innes?'

They turned to her, puzzled for a moment; then the woman smiled. 'Yes,' she said. 'Have we met somewhere?'

'No,' said poor Lucy, growing a little pink as she always did when her impulsiveness had led her into an unexpected situation. 'But I recognised your husband's eyebrows.'

'My *eyebrows*,' said Mr Innes.

But his wife, quicker-witted, laughed. 'Of course,' she said. 'Mary! Are you from Leys, then? Do you know Mary?' Her face lit and her voice sang as she said it. Do you know Mary? Was it because she was going to see her daughter that she was happy today?

Lucy explained who she was, and introduced Desterro, who was pleased to find that this charming couple knew all about her. 'There is very little we don't know about Leys,' Mrs Innes said, 'even if we have never seen the place.'

'Not seen it? Won't you come over and have your coffee with us, by the way?'

'It was too far for us to inspect it before Mary went there. So we decided that we would wait until her training was finished and then come to the Demonstration.' Lucy deduced that if fares had not been a problem, Mary Innes's mother would not have had to wait these years before seeing Leys; she would have come if only so that she could picture her daughter in her setting.

'But you are going there now, surely?'

'No. Oddly enough, we are not. We are on our way to Larborough, where my husband—he's a doctor—has to attend a meeting. We *could* go to Leys, of course, but it is the week of the final examinations, and it would only distract Mary to have her parents descending suddenly on her for no reason. It is a little difficult to pass by when we are so near, but we have waited so long that we can wait another ten days or so. What we couldn't resist was turning off the main West road as far as Bidlington. We didn't expect to run into any College people at this hour of the morning, especially in Examination week, and we did want to see the place that Mary had talked so much about.'

'We knew that we shouldn't have time on Demonstration Day,' Dr Innes said. 'There will be so much to see then. A surprisingly varied training, isn't it?'

Lucy agreed, and described her first impression of the staff-room with its varying worlds.

'Yes. We were a little puzzled when Mary chose that for her career—she had never shown any great interest in games, and I had thoughts that she might take a medical training—but she said she wanted a career with a great many facets; and she seems to have found it!'

Lucy remembered the concentration of purpose in those level brows; she had been right in her face-reading; if Mary Innes had an ambition it would not lightly be given up. Really, eyebrows were the most *helpful* things. If psychology ever went out of fashion she would write a book about face-reading. Under another name, of course. Face-reading was not well seen among the intelligentsia.

'She is very beautiful, your daughter,' said Desterro unexpectedly. She polished off a large mouthful of spice cake, and then, feeling the surprise in their silence, looked up at them. 'Is it not a proper thing in England to compliment parents on their daughter's looks?'

'Oh, yes,' Mrs Innes said hastily, 'it is not that, it is just that we had not thought of Mary as beautiful. She is nice to look at, of course; at least we think so, but then parents are apt to be fatuous about an only daughter. She——'

'When I came first to this place,' Desterro said, reaching out for another cake from the plate (how *did* she keep that figure!), 'it was raining, and all the dirty leaves were hanging down from the trees like dead bats and dripping on everyone, and everyone was rushing round College saying: "Oh *darling*, how *are* you? Did you have nice hols? Darling, you won't believe it, but I left my new hockey stick on *Crewe platform*!" And then I saw a girl who was *not* running about and *not* talking, and who looked a little like my great-grandmother's grandmother who is in the dining-room at the house of my grand-mother's great-nephew, so I said: "It is not after all a barbarism. If it were as it seems to be that girl would not be here. I shall stay." Is there more coffee, Miss Pym, please? She is not only beautiful, your daughter, she is the only beautiful person at Leys.'

'What about Beau Nash?' asked Lucy loyally.

'In England at Christmas time—*very* little milk, Miss Pym, please—the magazines go all gay and give away bright pretty pictures that one can frame and hang above the kitchen mantelpiece to make glad the hearts of the cook and her friends. Very shiny, they are, with——'

'Now that,' said Mrs Innes, 'is sheer libel! Beau is lovely, quite lovely, and you know it. I forgot that you would know Beau, too,' she turned to Lucy, 'that you would know them all, in fact. Beau is the only one we know because she came to us for the holidays once; at Easter time when the West is kinder than the rest of England; and Mary went to them once for some weeks in the summer. We admired Beau so much.' She looked to her husband for confirmation; he had been too withdrawn.

Dr Innes roused himself—he had the wrung-out look of the overworked G.P. when he sank into repose—and the saturnine face took on a boyish and faintly malicious, if tender, amusement. 'It was very odd to see our competent and self-reliant Mary being looked after,' he said.

Mrs Innes evidently felt that this was not the contribution she had been looking for, but decided to make the best of it. 'Perhaps,' she said, as if thinking of it for the first time, 'we have always taken Mary's self-reliance so much for granted that she finds it pleasant to be looked after,' and to Miss Pym: 'It is because they are complementary, I think, that they are such great friends. I am glad about it because we like Beau so much, and because Mary has never made intimate friends easily.'

'It is a very strenuous training, isn't it?' Dr Innes said.

'I sometimes look at my daughter's notebooks and wonder why they bother with stuff that even a doctor forgets as soon as he leaves medical school.'

'The cross-section of the villi,' remembered Lucy.

'Yes; that sort of thing. You seem to have picked up a remarkable amount of physical lore in four days.'

The crumpets came, and even without the ritual standing of the batter they were worth coming even from the West Country for, supposing that had been true. It was a happy party. Indeed, Lucy felt that the whole room was soaked in happiness; that happiness bathed it like a reflexion from the sunlight outside. Even the doctor's tired face looked content and relaxed. As for Mrs Innes, Lucy had rarely seen such happiness on the face of a woman; merely being in this room that her daughter had used so often was, it seemed, a sort of communion with her, and in a few days' time she would see her in the flesh and share her achievement.

If I had gone back to London, Lucy thought, I would have had no share in this. What would I be doing? Eleven o'clock. Going for a walk in the Park, and deciding how to get out of being guest of honour at some literary dinner. Instead I have this. And all because Dr Knight wanted to go to a medical conference tomorrow. No, because once long ago Henrietta stood up for me at school. It was odd to think that this sun-lit moment in an English June began to take shape thirty years ago in a dark crowded school cloakroom filled with little girls putting on their goloshes. What were first causes, anyhow?

'This has been *very* pleasant,' said Mrs Innes, as they stood once more in the village street. 'And it is nice to think that we shall meet again so soon. You will still be at Leys when the Demonstration comes off, won't you?'

'I hope so,' Lucy said, and wondered if she could cadge a bed from Henrietta for so long.

'And you have both promised, solemnly and on your

word of honour, not to tell anyone that you saw us today,' Dr Innes said.

'We have,' they said, waiting to see their new friends get into their car.

'Do you think I can turn the car in one swoop without hitting the Post Office?' Dr Innes said, consideringly.

'I should hate to make any more Bidlington martyrs,' his wife said. 'A tiresome breed. On the other hand, what is this life without some risk?'

So Dr Innes encouraged his engine and swung into this risky evolution. The hub of his off front wheel left a faint smudge on the Post Office's virgin white-wash.

'Gervase Innes, his mark,' said Mrs Innes, and waved her hand to them. 'Till Demonstration Day, and pray for fine weather for it! *Au revoir!*'

They watched the car grow small up the village street, and turned towards the field path and Leys.

'*Nice* people,' Desterro said.

'Charming. Odd to think that we should never have met them if you had not had a craving for good coffee this morning.'

'That is the kind of English, let me tell you in confidence, Miss Pym, that makes every other nation on earth sick with envy. So quiet, so well-bred, so good to look at. They are poor, too, did you notice? Her blouse is quite washed-out. It used to be blue, the blouse; you could see when she leaned forward and her collar lifted a little. It is wrong that they should be so poor, people like that.'

'It must have cost her a lot not to see her daughter when she was so near,' Lucy said reflectively.

'Ah, but she has character, that woman. She was right not to come. None of the Seniors has one little particle of interest to spare this week. Take away even one little particle, and *woops!* the whole thing comes crashing down.' She plucked an ox-eyed daisy from the bank by the bridge and gave the first giggle Lucy had ever heard from her. 'I wonder how my colleagues are getting on with their one-leg-over-the-line puzzles.'

Lucy was wondering how she herself would appear in Mary Innes's Sunday letter home. 'It will be amusing,' Mrs Innes had said, 'to get back home and read all about you in Mary's Sunday letter. Something to do with relativity. Like coming back the previous night.'

'It was strange that Mary Innes should have reminded you of someone in a portrait,' she said to Desterro. 'That is how she seemed to me, too.'

'Ah yes, my great-grandmother's grandmother.' Desterro dropped the daisy on to the surface of the water and watched the stream bear it down under the bridge and away out of sight. 'I did not say it to the nice Inneses, but my great-grandmother's grandmother was a little unpopular with her generation.'

'Oh? Shy, perhaps. What we call nowadays an inferiority complex.'

'I would not know about that. Her husband died too conveniently. It is always sad for a woman when her husband dies too conveniently.'

'You mean that she murdered him!' Lucy said, standing stock-still in the summer landscape, appalled.

'Oh, no. There was no *scandal*.' Desterro sounded reproving. 'It was just that her husband died too conveniently. He drank too much, and was a great gambler, and *not* very attractive. And there was a loose tread at the top of the stairs. A long flight of stairs. And he stepped on it one day when he was drunk. That was all.'

'And did she marry again?' Lucy asked, having absorbed this information.

'Oh, no. She was not in love with anyone else. She had her son to bring up, and the estates were safe for him now that there was no one to gamble them away. She was a very good estate manager. That is where my grandmother got her talent from. When my grandmother came out

from England to marry my grandfather she had never
been farther from her own county than Charles Street,
West One; and in six months she was running the estate.'
Desterro sighed with admiration. 'They are wonderful,
the English.'

8

Miss Pym was invigilating at the Senior Pathology Final, so as to give Miss Lux more time for the correction and marking of previous papers, when Henrietta's meek little secretary tiptoed in and laid the day's letters reverently on the desk in front of her. Miss Pym had been frowning over a copy of the examination paper, and thinking how badly words like *arthritis gonorrhoica* and *suppurative teno-synovitis* went with the clean air of a summer morning after breakfast. *Emphysema* was not so bad; it might be the gardener's name for a flower. A sort of columbine. And *kyphosis* she could picture as something in the dahlia line. *Myelitis* would be a small creeping plant, very blue, with a tendency to turn pink if not watched. And *tabes dorsalis* was obviously an exotic affair of the tiger-lily persuasion, expensive and very faintly obscene.

Chorea. Sclerosis. Pes Varus.

Dear goodness. Did those young things know all that? Differentiate the treatment of something-or-other according to whether it is (a) congenital (b) traumatic (c) hysterical. Well, well. How had she ever erred so far as to feel patronising about these young creatures?

She looked down from her dais with affection on them; all writing away for dear life. The faces were sober, but not on the whole anxious. Only Rouse looked worried, and Lucy decided that her face looked better worried than smug, and withheld her sympathy. Dakers was ploughing steadily over the paper with her tongue protruding and an automatic sigh as she came to the end of each line and

87

began a new one. Beau was confident and detached as if she were writing invitations; doubt was something that had never entered her life; neither her present standing nor her future life was in jeopardy. Stewart's face under the bright red hair was pale, but a faint smile played round her mouth; Stewart's future, too, was assured; she was going to the Cordwainers' School, going home to Scotland bringing her sheaves with her, and Lucy was going to the party she was giving in her room on Saturday night to celebrate. ('We don't ask Staff to individual parties, but since you are not quite Staff you could rank as just a friend.') The Four Disciples, spread across the front row, cast each other communal and encouraging glances now and then; this was their own particular subject and obviously what they did not know about it was not worth mentioning; Manchester was going to get its money's worth. Innes, by the window, lifted her head every now and then to look out at the garden, as if seeking refreshment; that it was not inspiration she sought was apparent from her unhurried progress through the questions; she turned to the garden for some spiritual comfort; it was as if she said: 'Ah yes, you are still there, Beauty; there is a world outside this lecture room.' Innes was beginning to look as if College might be too much with her. That tired line from nostril to mouth was still there.

Lucy picked up the paper-knife from Miss Lux's neat desk, and considered her post. Three bills, which she need not disturb the holy hush by opening. A receipt. An Annual Report. A large, square, deep-blue, and very stiff and expensive envelope with MILLICENT CRAYE embossed in scarlet across the flap (really there was no end to the self-advertising instinct in actresses) which would be five lines of thanks with a broad nib and out-size capitals for her contribution to the Benevolent Fund. That left only Mrs Montmorency. So into Mrs Montmorency she inserted the paper-knife.

Maddam (wrote Mrs Montmorency),

I as done as you sed an sent the urgent by passel post. Registered. Fred put it into Wigmore Street on is way to work reciet enclosed I as packed the blue and the blouses also underclose as per instruxions your pink nitie not having come back from the laundry I as put in the bedge instead hopping this will be all rite.

Maddam, please dont think that I presoom but this is a good thing. It is no life for a woman writin books and not havin no young company please dont think I presoom but I as your welfare at heart you ben one of the nicest ladies I ever worked for Fred says the same. A nice lady like that he says when look at the things thats around not write it isnt please dont think I presoom

yrs respectfully

Mrs Montmorency

P.S. Wire brush in toe of swede shoe

Lucy spent the next fifteen minutes being touched by Mrs Montmorency's concern for her, being furious with the laundry, and wondering why she paid education rates. It wasn't public schools for everyone that was needed, but a great many elementary school classes of not more than a dozen, where the future Mrs Montmorencys could be adequately taken care of in the matter of the Three Rs. Old McLean, their jobbing gardener at home, had left school when he was twelve, but he could write as good a letter as any University acquaintance of hers; and why? Because he came from a small village school with small classes and a good schoolmaster.

And of course because he lived in an age when the Three Rs were more important than Free Milk. They made him literate and left the rest to him. He lived on white-flour scones and stewed tea and died hale and hearty at the age of ninety-two.

She was roused from her musings by Miss Rouse. There was a new expression on Miss Rouse's face, and Lucy didn't like the new expression at all. She had seen Miss Rouse look despairing, smarmy, smug, and worried, but till now she had never seen her look furtive.

Why should she be looking furtive?

She watched her for a moment or two, curiously.

Rouse looked up and caught her gaze and looked quickly away again. Her furtive expression had gone; what had taken its place was one labelled Consciously Carefree. Lucy knew all about that expression. She had not been Form Mistress of the Lower Fourth for nothing. Every eater of illicit sweets wore that expression. So did those who were doing their arithmetic in French lesson.

So did those who were cheating at an examination.

What was it Henrietta had said? 'She finds written work difficult.'

So.

Emphysema and all those flowery sounding things were too much for Miss Rouse, and so she had provided some aids to memory. The question was what kind of aids and where were they? Not on her knee. The desks were open in front, so that a lap was no safe billet for a crib. And one could hardly write enough pathology on one's finger-nails to be of much help; finger-nails were useful only for formulæ. The obvious solution would be the notes up the sleeve, with or without an arrangement of elastic, but these girls had no sleeves below the elbow. Then, what? Where? Or was it that she was just having glimpses of O'Donnell's paper in front of her? Or Thomas's to her right?

Lucy went back to her letters for a moment or two, and waited. All schoolmistresses know this gambit. She looked up casually at the Seniors in general and again went back to her letters. When next she looked up it was straight at Rouse. Rouse's head was low over her paper and in her left hand she held a handkerchief. Now even on a handker-chief it is not possible to write anything that is helpful on so large a subject as pathology, nor is it an easy affair to manipulate; on the other hand handkerchiefs were not common objects at Leys, and certainly no one else was clutching one and dabbing a nose occasionally with it. Lucy decided that whatever sources of information Rouse had lay in her left hand. Her desk was at the back on the window side, so that the wall was to her left; whatever she did with her left hand was not overlooked by anyone.

Well, thought Lucy, what does A do?

Walk down the room and demand the handkerchief and find that it is a square piece of white linen, nine inches by nine inches, with the owner's initials properly marked in one corner, and as candid as a good laundry can make it?

Demand the handkerchief and unearth a scandal that will blast the Senior set like a hurricane at their least stable moment?

See that Rouse gets no chance to use her source of information, and say nothing?

The last was certainly the most sensible. She couldn't have obtained very much aid from anything so far; it would be doing no injustice to anyone to make her a present of that small amount.

Lucy left the desk and strolled down the room to the back, where she stood leaning against the wall, Thomas to her right and Rouse to her left. Thomas stopped writing for a moment and looked up at her with a quick smile. But Rouse did not look up. And Lucy watched the hot blood dye her sandy neck a dull red. And presently she put away the handkerchief—and whatever else that hand contained—in her tunic pocket.

Well, she had foiled the machinations of the evil-intended, but she could feel no satisfaction about it. For the first time it occurred to her that what was very naughty and deplorable in the Fourth Form was quite sickening in a Senior Final. She was glad that it was Rouse and not anyone else. Presently she strolled back to her desk on the dais, and as far as she could see Rouse made no further effort to obtain help with her paper. On the contrary, she was very obviously in deep waters. And Lucy was infuriated to find herself feeling sorry for her. Yes, *sorry*. Sorry for *Rouse*. After all, the girl had worked. Worked like a madman, if all reports were true. It was not as if she had been taking an easy way out to save herself effort. It was just that she found acquiring theoretical knowledge difficult almost to the point of impossibility, and had succumbed to temptation in her desperation.

This point of view made Lucy feel much better about it, and she spent the rest of her invigilating time speculating quite undistressedly about the nature of the crib. She would look again at the examination paper, and consider the enormous range of material it covered, and wonder how Rouse had devised anything at once helpful and invisible. She longed to ask her.

The most likely explanation was that there were two or three particular subjects that Rouse was afraid of, and that help with them was scribbled on a piece of paper.

Innes was the first to shuffle the written sheets together and slip the waiting clip over their upper edge. She read through the pages, making a correction now and then, laid the sheaf down on her desk, sat for a few relaxed moments taking in the beauty of the garden, and then rose quietly and came forward to leave her work on the desk in front of Miss Pym.

'Oh, *catastrophe!*' wailed Dakers; 'is somebody *finished*? And I have a whole question and a half to do yet!'

'Hush, Miss Dakers,' said Lucy, as in duty bound.

Dakers favoured her with a radiant smile, and went back to her steady plodding.

Stewart and Beau Nash followed Innes very shortly; and presently the pile of papers in front of Miss Pym began to grow. With five minutes of the allotted time still to go there were only three students left in the examination room: the little dark Welsh Thomas, who presumably slept too much to be a good 'study'; the imperturbable Dakers still plodding steadily; and a flushed and unhappy Rouse, who was plainly making heavy weather of it. With two minutes still to go there was only Rouse; she was looking confused and desperate; making hasty little excursions back and fore through her papers, deleting, amending, and adding.

The distant yelling of the bell put an end to her indecisions and to her chances; whatever she had done must now abide. She shoved her papers hastily together, aware that the bell meant an instant appearance in the gymnasium and that Fröken would not consider the ordeal of an examination paper any excuse for being late, and brought them up to Lucy at the double. Lucy had expected her to avoid her eye, or otherwise to display symptoms of awkwardness or self-consciousness. But Rouse surprised her by a frank smile and a still franker remark.

'Whoo!' said Rouse, blowing her breath out expressively, 'that was a horror.' And she ran out to join the rest of her set.

Lucy opened the much-scored offering and looked at it with compunction. She had been imagining things. Rouse had not been cheating after all. Or at least not systematically. That furtive look might have been the guilt of inadequacy, now she came to think of it; or perhaps, at the worst, a hope of hints from her neighbour's paper. And that flush that had dyed her neck was due to her awareness of being suspected; Lucy could remember very well even yet times at school when the very knowledge that her innocent act was capable of sinister interpretation was enough to make her face burn with false guilt. Really, she owed Rouse an apology. She would find some way of making it up to her.

She stacked the papers neatly together, put them in alphabetical order from sheer force of habit, checked their number, and carried them upstairs to Miss Lux's room, glad that it would not be her chore to correct them. There was no one in the room, so she left them on the desk and stood for a moment wondering what to do with the hour before lunch. She toyed with the thought of watching the gymnastics, but decided that she must not allow the performance to become familiar, and consequently devoid of wonder, before Demonstration Day. Having induced Henrietta to keep her until then—Henrietta had not required much inducement, it is true—she was not going to mar her own pleasure in the day by too many tastings beforehand. She went downstairs again, lingering by the tall window on the landing—how well eighteenth-century architects had understood how to build houses; nowadays landings were not things to linger on, but breakneck little corners lit, if at all, by a small circular light like a ship's port-hole—and from there, beyond the courtyard and the opposite wing she could see the elms of the field that led to the stream. She would go and look at the buttercups for a little. There was no better way of wasting a summer hour than staring at a field of buttercups. So down she went, and along the wing, and so out to the covered path to the gymnasium, for beyond the gymnasium were the buttercups.

As she went down the covered way her eye caught a spot of colour in the grass that bordered the path. At first she took it for a flower petal and was going to ignore it, when she noticed that it was square, and certainly not a petal. She turned back and picked it up. It was a tiny address-book in faded red leather. It looked as if it had formed part of the fittings of a handbag; an old-fashioned handbag probably since one did not see leather nor workmanship like that nowadays. Idly, with her thoughts on the femininity of that vanished bag with its miniature fittings—there would of course have been a little tube of scent, and a gold pencil, and one of those ivory tablets to scribble engagements on—she opened it, and read, on a page crowded with writing in a tiny script: 'Path. anat. changes as in traumatic. Fibrin in synov. memb. Tissues contr. by fibr. and folds of caps. joined to bone. Anchylosis. Fever.'

It meant nothing to Lucy as information, but its meaning was obvious. She turned the pages, finding nearly all of them crowded with the same succinct information. Even the X page—devoted by the keepers of address-books to measurements for new curtains or that good story that would do for the W.R.I. speech next Tuesday—even the X page had cryptic remarks about rays. What bowled Lucy over was the comprehensiveness of it; the premeditation. This was no product of a last-minute panic; it was a cold-blooded insurance against failure. By the neatness and method shown in the compiling, it looked as though the entries had been made as each subject was studied. Had the notebook been of a normal size, in fact, it would have been nothing more than a legitimate précis of a subject. But no one making a précis would have chosen a book not much larger than a good-sized postage stamp when an equally portable but normal-sized notebook could be had for a few pence. The use of a book so tiny that a mapping pen had been necessary in order to make the entries legible could have only one explanation.

Lucy knew very well what had happened. Rouse had pulled out her handkerchief as she ran. She had never before carried the little book in a pocket, and her mind was divided urgently between the bad paper she had done and the fear of being late for gymnastics, so there was no care in the pulling out of the handkerchief. And so the little book dropped on to the grass at the edge of the path.

She walked on beyond the gymnasium and through the five-barred gate into the field, but she had no eye for the buttercups. She walked on slowly down the field to the coolness under the willows and the quiet green water. She hung over the rail of the bridge watching the weeds trail and the occasional fish dart, and thought about Rouse. There was no name on the fly-leaf, nor as far as she could see any means of identification in the book itself. Most schools taught script as well as current form in writing nowadays; and script was much less easily recognisable than current writing. A handwriting expert would no doubt be easily able to trace the author, but to what end? There was no evidence that the book had been used for any illegitimate purpose; no evidence even that it had been compiled with any sinister intent—although the presumption was strong. If she handed it over to Henrietta as lost property what would happen? No one would claim it, and Henrietta would be faced with the fact that one of her Seniors had prepared a précis that could be conveniently palmed at an examination.

If nothing was ever said about the book, then Rouse's punishment would be a perpetual and lifelong doubt as to what had become of it. Lucy felt that such a punishment fitted the crime admirably. She thumbed the tiny India-paper pages once more, wondered again what Edwardian elegancy had given it birth, and, leaning over, dropped it into the water.

As she walked back to the house she wondered how Rouse had managed the other Final Examinations. Pathology could be no less easy to memorise than Kinesiology or any of the other obscurities studied by the budding P.T.I. How had Rouse, the difficult 'study', managed with these? Was the little red leather book only one of five or six? Did one invest in a mapping pen for one subject only? One *could*, she supposed, buy very tiny address books if one searched long enough; though not perhaps so fine or so tiny as the little red one. It may have been the possession of the little red one which first put the thought of insurance against failure into Rouse's mind.

She remembered that the results of the previous examinations would be exhibited on the letter-board by the students' entrance, so instead of walking round to the front of the house as she had meant to she turned in at the quadrangle door. There were several Junior lists pinned to the green baize, and three Senior lists. Lucy read them with interest.

FINAL PHYSIOLOGY

Honours

Mary Innes	- - -	93

First Class

Wilhelmina Hasselt	-	87
Pamela Nash -	- -	86
Sheena Stewart	- -	82
Pauline Lucas	-	79
Janet Gage	- -	79
Barbara Rouse	-	77

Second Class

Dorothy Littlejohn	-	74
Beatrice Appleyard	-	71
Joan Dakers -	- -	69
Eileen O'Donnell	- -	68
Margaret Campbell	-	67
Ruth Waymark	-	66
Lilian Mathews	- -	65

and the rest, below that mark, mere Passes.

Well, Rouse had scraped into a First by two marks, it seemed.

Lucy turned to the next list.

FINAL MEDICALS

First Class

Pauline Lucas	- -	89
Pamela Nash	- - -	89
Mary Innes	- -	89
Dorothy Littlejohn	-	89
Ruth Waymark	- -	85
Wilhelmina Hasselt	-	82
Sheena Stewart	- -	80
Lilian Mathews	- -	79
Barbara Rouse	- -	79

Second Class

Jenny Burton	- -	73
Janet Gage	- - -	72
Eileen O'Donnell	- -	71
Joan Dakers	- - -	69

and the rest mere Passes.

And again Rouse managed to scrape a First.

FINAL KINESIOLOGY

Honours

Mary Innes	- - -	96

First Class

Pauline Lucas	- -	89
Pamela Nash	- -	88
Sheena Stewart	- -	87
Wilhelmina Hasselt	-	85
Ruth Waymark	- -	80
Janet Gage	- - -	79
Joan Dakers	- -	78
Barbara Rouse	- -	78

Another First! Three Firsts out of three tries. The girl who found written work so difficult? There was surely a strong case for the existence of more little notebooks?

Oh, well; this being Friday, tomorrow would see the end of examinations, and it was not likely that Rouse would, after this morning's experience, bring any extraneous help to the test tomorrow morning. The little book prepared for tomorrow, if it existed, would be still-born.

While she mused over the lists (it was nice to see that Dakers had managed at least one First) Miss Lux arrived with the results of yesterday's Final.

'Thank you for bringing up the Path. papers,' she said. 'And thank you for invigilating. It helped me to get these done.'

She thumbed the drawing-pin into the board and stood back to look at the list.

FINAL HYGIENE

Honours

    Mary Innes - - - 91

First Class

    Pamela Nash - - - 88
    Wilhelmina Hasselt - 87
    Sheena Stewart - - 86
    Pauline Lucas - - 81
    Barbara Rouse - - 81

'Barbara Rouse, eighty-one,' Lucy said, before she thought.

'Yes, surprising, isn't it?' Miss Lux said placidly. 'But she works like a black. She is so brilliant in her physical work that I think it maddens her to be far down any list.'

'Innes seems to make a habit of heading the lists.'

'Oh, Innes is wasted here.'

'Why? The more intelligence one brings to a profession the better surely?'

'Yes, but with an intelligence like Innes's one could head much more thrilling lists than these. It's a waste.'

'I somehow don't think that Rouse will get eighty-one

for today's paper,' Lucy said, as they moved away from the board.

'Why? Was she in difficulties?'

'Bogged down,' said Lucy; and hoped that she did not sound too pleased. '*What* a life it is,' she added, as the five-minute bell rang, and the dripping Seniors came running in from the gymnasium, ripping off their tunics as they tore into the bathrooms for a shower before the gong went. 'When you think of the leisurely way we acquired knowledge. At university, I mean. If we sat a final examination, the rest of the day would almost certainly be our own to recover in. But these young creatures do it as part of their time-table.'

From the bathrooms came cursing and chaos. 'Oh, Donnie, you *swine*, that was *my* shower!' 'Mark, you brute, get off my foot!' 'Oh, no, you don't, my girl; these are *my* tights!' 'God, look at my blisters!' 'Kick over my shoe, Greengage, the floor's sopping.' '*Must* you shoot the cold water round like that, you chump!'

'They like it, you know,' Lux said. 'In their heart they like the rush and the overwork. It makes them feel important. Very few of them will ever have any legitimate reason for feeling important, and so it is comforting for them to have the image of it at least.'

'Cynic,' said Lucy.

'No, psychologist.' She inclined her head towards the row as they moved away. 'It sounds like a free fight, doesn't it? Everyone sounds desperate and furious. But it is all play-acting. In five minutes they will be sitting like good children in the dining-room with not a hair out of place.'

And so they were. When the staff filed in to the top table five minutes later, there were the scramblers of the bathroom, standing dutifully behind their chairs, calm, and combed, and neat, their interest already absorbed by the thought of food. Truly, they *were* children. Whatever heart-breaks they suffered would be forgotten in to-morrow's toy. It was absurd to think of them as harassed adults, trembling on the precipice edge of break-down. They were volatile children; their griefs were loud, and vocal, and transient. For five days now, ever since The Nut Tart had been so knowing under the cedar tree last Saturday afternoon, she had looked for some hint of abnormality, of aberration, of lack of control, and what had she found? One very normal and highly controlled piece of dishonesty; unremarkable except for its neatness.

'Isn't it nice,' Henrietta said, helping out something that looked like cheese-and-vegetable pie, 'I've got a post in Wales for little Miss Thomas. Near Aberystwyth. I am so delighted.'

'A very soporific atmosphere, Wales,' Madame Lefevre said, consideringly; blasting Henrietta's whole conception with five gentle words.

'Yes,' said Miss Lux, 'who is going to keep her awake?'

'It's not who is going to *keep* her awake, it's who is going to wake her in the first place,' Wragg said, with a greedy eye on the pie. Wragg was still near enough her College days to be possessed of a large hunger and no gastronomic judgement.

'Wales is her native atmosphere,' Henrietta said, repressive, 'and I have no doubt she will know how to deal with it. In any case she is not likely to have any great success *outside* Wales; the Welsh are extraordinarily provincial, using the word in its literal sense. I have noticed before how they gravitate back to their own province. It is as well for them to go there in the first place if the chance offers. And luckily, in this case, it has offered very conveniently. The junior gymnast of three. That will suit Miss Thomas very nicely. She has no great initiative, I'm afraid.'

'Is Thomas's the only new post?' Wragg asked, falling on the pie.

'No, there was one that I wanted to discuss with you.'

Aha, thought Lucy, here comes Arlinghurst at last.

'Ling Abbey want someone to be wholly responsible for the younger children, and to take dancing as well all through the school. That is to say, the dancing would have to be of a high standard. I wanted to give the post to Miss Dakers—she is very good with small children—but I wanted to know what you thought of her dancing, Marie.'

'She is a cow,' said Madame.

'She *is* very good with little ones, though,' Wragg said.

'A *heavy* cow,' said Madame.

'It isn't her personal performance that is important,' Henrietta said. 'It is her power to inspire performance in others. Does she understand the subject sufficiently, that is the point?'

'Oh, she knows the difference between three-four time and four-four, certainly.'

'I saw Dakers teaching the babies at West Larborough their dances for their do last Christmas,' Wragg said, 'and she was wonderful. I was there to crit. her, and I was so fascinated I forgot to make any notes at all. I think she would be just right for that post.'

'Well, Marie?'

'I can't imagine why anyone bothers,' Madame said. The dancing at Ling Abbey is quite frightful anyhow.'

This Pilatian washing of hands, in spite of its negative quality, seemed positive enough to all concerned. It was apparent that Dakers was going to Ling Abbey. And since Ling Abbey was a good place to be going to—if one had to be going to a school—Lucy was glad for her. She glanced down the room to where, even above this babel, Dakers' high voice could be heard italicising her opinion of the Pathology paper. 'I said that a joint went *gummy*, my dear, and I'm certain that's not the *technical* word.'

'Shall I warn them both, Miss Hodge?' Wragg asked, later.

(Warn?)

'No, just Miss Thomas today, I think. I shall tell Miss Dakers tomorrow. It is better to spread the excitement out.'

As the Staff rose from their table and filed out, Wragg turned to the politely standing and temporarily silent students and said: 'Miss Hodge will see Miss Thomas in her office when luncheon is over.'

This was apparently a ritual pronouncement, for the buzz broke out almost before the Staff had reached the door. 'A post, Tommy!' 'Congrats, Tommy.' 'Hoorah, old Thomas.' 'Up the Welsh!' 'Hope it's a thousand a year, Tom.' 'Iss nott thatt the lucky thing, now!' 'Cheers, Tommy!'

And still no one had mentioned Arlinghurst.

9

WHEN Lucy first heard Arlinghurst mentioned it was not by any of the Staff but by the students themselves. She had spent Saturday afternoon with Fröken and her mother, helping to finish the Swedish folk costumes which the Juniors would wear for some of the country dances at the Demonstration. It was a lovely day and they had taken the piles of bright primitive colour to the farthest corner of the garden, where they could sit and look over the English countryside. Both cricket and tennis matches were 'away' this week, so the garden was deserted, and no toiling figures marred the virgin green of the field beyond the stream. They had sewed in great beatitude, and Fru Gustavsen seemed to have reported well of Lucy to her daughter, for Fröken's reticence had largely vanished, and Lucy was delighted to find that a young woman who had always reminded her of sunlight on snow was the possessor of a rich warm chuckle and a sense of humour to match. (It is true that Lucy's sewing considerably shook Fru Gustavsen's faith in her, but much must be forgiven the English.) Fru Gustavsen had gone back to the subject of food, and had held forth at great length on the virtues of something called 'frikadellar'; which, it appeared, was a kind of mince. Lucy (whose cooking consisted of chopping up a few tomatoes in a pan at the last moment, adding whatever was to be cooked, and pouring some cream over the lot) thought it a very lengthy and complicated affair, and decided to have nothing to do with it.

'Are you doing anything tonight?' Fröken had asked. 'My mother and I are going into Larborough to the theatre. She has not yet seen an English company. We would be delighted if you would care to come with us.'

Lucy explained that tonight she was going to a party in Stewart's room to celebrate her Post. 'I understand that Staff don't usually go, but I am not real Staff.'

Fröken slid an eye round at her and said: 'You ought to be. You are very good for them.'

That medicinal phrase again. As if she were a prescription.

'How?'

'Oh, in ways too subtle for my English—and *much* too subtle for the German language. It is, a little, that you wear heels; a little, that you have written a book; a little, that they don't have to be just a tiny bit afraid of you; a little that—oh, a thousand littles. You have come at a good time for them; a time when they need a distraction that is not—distracting. Oh, dear, I wish my English was better.'

'You mean, I am a dose of alkali on an acid stomach.'

Fröken gave her unexpected chuckle. 'Yes, just that. I am sorry you will not be coming to the theatre, but it is a great mark of favour to be invited to a students' party, and you will enjoy it, I think. Everyone will be happy tonight, now that the examinations are over. Once they come back from the match they are free for the week-end. So they will be gay this Saturday. Off the chain,' she added, in English.

And off the chain they certainly were. As Lucy came in by the quadrangle door, leaving Fröken and her mother to go round to the front of the house where they lived, a blast of sound rose up round her. The rush of bath water on two floors, the calling of innumerable voices, the drumfire of feet on bare oak stairs, singing, whistling, crooning. Both teams had apparently come back—victorious to judge by the atmosphere—and the place was alive. The place was also excited, and one word was woven like a leitmotiv through the babble. Arlinghurst. Arlinghurst. As she walked past the ground-floor bathrooms on her way to the stairs, she heard the first of it. '*Have* you *heard*, my dear! *Arlinghurst!*'

'What?'

'*Arling-hurst!*'

A tap was turned off.

'I can't hear with the blasted water. Where, did you say?'

'Arlinghurst!'

'I don't believe it.'

'But yes,' said another voice, 'it's true.'

'It can't be; they don't send First Posters to Arlinghurst.'

'No, really it's true. Miss Hodge's sec. told Jolly in confidence and Jolly told her sister in the village and *she* told Miss Nevill at The Teapot, and Miss Nevill talked about it to The Nut Tart when she was there to tea this afternoon with that cousin of hers.'

'Is that gigolo here again?'

'I say, *Arlinghurst!* Who would believe it! Whom do you think they'll give it to?'

'Oh, that's easy.'

'Yes, Innes of course.'

'Lucky Innes.'

'Oh, well, she deserves it.'

'Just imagine. *Arlinghurst!*'

And on the first floor it was the same; the rushing of bath water, the splashing, the babble, and Arlinghurst.

'But who told you?'

'The Nut Tart.'

'Oh, my dear, she's dippy, everyone knows.'

'Well, it's a cert for Innes, anyhow, so it's nothing to do with me. I'll probably wind up in the L.C.C.'

'She may be dippy, but she's not M.D., and she'd got it pat. She didn't even know what Arlinghurst *was*, so she wasn't making it up. She said: "Is it a school?"'

'*Is it a school!* My hat!'

'I say, won't The Hodge be just dizzy with pride, my dears!'

'D'you suppose she'll be dizzy enough to give us tart for supper instead of that milk pudding?'

'I expect Jolly made the puddings yesterday and they're all standing waiting in rows on the hatch.'

'Oh, well, they can wait as far as I'm concerned. I'm for Larborough.'

'Me, too. I say, is Innes there?'

'No, she's finished. She's dressing.'

'I say, let's throw Innes a party, all of us, instead of letting her give a little private one. After all, it's——'

'Yes. Let's do that, shall we? After all, it isn't every day that someone gets a post like that, and Innes deserves it, and everyone will be glad about it, and——'

'Yes, let's have a do in the common-room.'

'After all, it's a sort of communal honour. A decoration for Leys.'

'Arlinghurst! Who'd have believed it?'

'Arlinghurst!'

'Arlinghurst! My hat!'

Lucy wondered if the meek little secretary's indiscretion had been prompted by the knowledge that the news was about to be made public. Even the cautious and secretive Henrietta could not sit on such a piece of information much longer; if for no other reason than that Arlinghurst would be expecting an answer. Lucy supposed that Henrietta had been waiting until the 'bad' week was over before providing her sensation; she could not help feeling that it was a very neat piece of timing.

As she walked along the corridor to her cell at the end, she met Innes, buttoning herself into a fresh cotton frock.

'Well,' said Lucy, 'it seems to have been a successful afternoon.'

'The row, you mean?' Innes said. 'Yes, we won. But

the row is not a war chant. It's a paean of praise that they will never have to live this week again.'

Lucy noticed how unconsciously she had used the word 'they'. She wondered for a moment at the girl's calm. Had she, possibly, not yet heard about the Arlinghurst vacancy? And then, as Innes moved from the dimness of the corridor into the light from Dakers' wide-open door, Lucy saw the radiance on her face. And her own heart turned over in sympathy. *That* was how it felt, was it? Like seeing Heaven opened.

'*You* look happy, anyhow,' she said, falling back on bald platitude since there were no words to describe what was shining in Innes's eyes.

'To use a phrase of O'Donnell's, I wouldn't call the king my cousin,' Innes said, as they moved apart. 'You are coming to Stewart's party, aren't you? That's good. We'll meet again there.'

Lucy powdered her nose, and decided to go over to the 'old house' and see how the Staff were reacting to the news of Arlinghurst. Perhaps there would still be some tea; she had forgotten all about tea and so apparently had the Gustavsens. She rearranged the bottle of champagne which was waiting for Stewart's party in the ice she had begged from Miss Joliffe, regretted yet once more that the Larborough wine merchant had not been able to supply a better year, but trusted (rightly) that Rheims and all its products were simply 'champagne' to a student.

To go over to the 'old house' one had to pass both the Seniors' bedrooms and the first floor bathrooms again, and it seemed to Lucy that the orchestration of sound had reached a new pitch of intensity, as more and more students heard the news and passed it on and commented on it above the roar of water, and banging of doors, and the thudding of feet. It was strange to come from that blare of sound and excitement into the quiet, the cream paint and mahogany, the tall windows and space, the waiting peace of the 'house'. She crossed the wide landing and opened the door of the drawing-room. Here too there was quiet, and she had shut the door behind her and come forward into the room before becoming aware of the exact quality of that quiet. Before realising, in fact, that the quiet was electric, and that she had walked into the middle of a Staff row. A row, moreover, if one was to judge from the faces, of most unholy proportions. Henrietta was standing, flushed and defensive and stubborn, with her back to the fireplace, and the others were staring at her, accusing and angry.

Lucy would have beaten a retreat, but someone had automatically poured out a cup of tea and thrust it at her, and she could hardly put it down again and walk out. Though she would have liked to for more reasons than one. The tea was almost black and quite cold.

No one took any notice of Lucy. Either they accepted her as one of themselves, or they were too absorbed in their quarrel to realise her fully. Their eyes had acknowledged her presence with the same absent acquiescence that greets a ticket-collector in a railway carriage; a legitimate intruder, but not a partaker in discussion.

'It's monstrous,' Madame was saying. 'Monstrous!' For the first time within Lucy's experience she had discarded her Récamier pose and was sitting with both slender feet planted firmly on the floor.

Miss Lux was standing behind her, her bleak face even bleaker than usual, and two very unusual spots of bright red high on her cheek-bones. Fröken was sitting back in one of the chintz-covered chairs looking contemptuous and sullen. And Wragg, hovering by the window, looked as much confused and embarrassed as angry; as if, having so lately come up from the mortal world, she found this battling of Olympians disconcerting.

'I fail to see anything monstrous about it,' Henrietta said with an attempt at her head-girl manner; but even to

Lucy's ears it had a synthetic quality. Henrietta was obviously in a spot.

'It is more than monstrous,' Madame said, 'it is very nearly criminal.'

'Marie, don't be absurd.'

'Criminal from more than one point of view. You propose to palm off an inferior product on someone who expects the best; and you propose at the same time to lower the credit of Leys so that it will take twenty years to recover, if it ever recovers. And for what, I ask you? For what? Just to satisfy some whim of your own!'

'I fail to see where the whim comes in,' Henrietta snapped, dropping some of her Great Dane dignity at this thrust. 'No one here can deny that she is a brilliant student, that she has worked hard and deserved her reward. Even her theoretical work has been consistently good this term.'

'Not consistently,' said Miss Lux in a voice like water dropping on to a metal pan. 'According to the paper I corrected last night, she could not even get a Second in Pathology.'

It was here that Lucy stopped wondering what to do with her tea, and pricked up her ears.

'Oh, dear, that is a pity,' Henrietta said, genuinely distracted from the main point by this news. 'She was doing so well. So much better than I had dared to hope.'

'The girl is a moron, and you know it,' Madame said.

'But this is nonsense. She is one of the most brilliant students Leys has ever——'

'For God's sake, Henrietta, stop saying that. You know as well as any of us what they mean by brilliant.' She flourished a sheet of blue note-paper in her thin brown hand, and holding it at arm's length (she was 'getting on' was Madame, and she hated to wear glasses) read aloud. '"We wondered if, among your leaving students, you had one brilliant enough to fill this place. Someone who would be 'Arlinghurst' from the beginning, and so more part of the school and its traditions than a migrant can ever be, and at the same time continue the Leys connection that has been so fortunate for us." The Leys connection that has been so fortunate! And you propose to end it by sending them Rouse!'

'I don't know why you are all so stubbornly against her. It can be nothing but prejudice. She has been a model student, and no one has ever said a word against her until now. Until I am prepared to give her the rewards of her work. And then you are all suddenly furious. I am entirely at a loss. Fröken! Surely you will bear me out. You can never have had a better pupil than Miss Rouse.'

'Mees Rouse is a very good gymnast. She is also, I understand from Mees Wragg, a very fine games player. But when she goes out from thees plaace it will not matter any longer that she can do a handstand better than anyone else and that she ees a good half-back. What will matter then is character. And what Mees Rouse has of character is neither very much nor very admirable.'

'Fröken!' Henrietta sounded shocked. 'I thought you liked her.'

'Did you?' The two cold, disinterested little words said: I am expected to like all my students; if you had known whom I liked or disliked I should be unworthy.

'Well, you *asked* Sigrid, and you've certainly been told,' Madame said, delighted. 'I could not have put it better myself.'

'Perhaps——' began Miss Wragg. 'I mean, it *is* for gymnastics they want her. They are separate departments at Arlinghurst: the gym., and the games, and the dancing; one person for each. So perhaps Rouse wouldn't be too bad.'

Lucy wondered whether this tentative offering was inspired by Rouse's performance for Miss Wragg's department at half-back, or by a desire to smooth things over and draw the two edges of the yawning gap even a little nearer.

'Doreen, my pet,' said Madame, in the tolerant tones that one uses to a half-wit, 'what they are looking for is not someone who "wouldn't be too bad"; what they are looking for is someone so outstanding that she can step straight from College to be one of the three gymnasts at the best girls' school in England. Does that sound to you like Miss Rouse, do you think?'

'No. No, I suppose not. It does sound like Innes, I must admit.'

'Quite so. It does sound like Innes. And it is beyond the wit of man why it doesn't sound like Innes to Miss Hodge.' She fixed Henrietta with her enormous black eyes, and Henrietta winced.

'I've told you! There is a vacancy at the Wycherley Orthopædic Hospital that would be ideal for Miss Innes. She is excellent at medical work.'

'God give me patience! The Wycherley Orthopædic Hospital!'

'Doesn't the unity of the opposition persuade you that you are wrong, Miss Hodge?' It was Miss Lux, incisive even in her anger. 'Being a minority of one is not a very strong position.'

But that was the wrong thing to say. If Henrietta had ever been open to persuasion, she was by now far past that stage. She reacted to Miss Lux's logic with a spurt of fury.

'My position as a minority may not be very strong, Miss Lux, but my position as Principal of this college is unquestioned, and what you think or do not think of my decisions is immaterial. I took you into my confidence, as I always have, about the disposal of this vacancy. That you do not agree with me is, of course, regrettable, but of no consequence. It is for me to make decisions here, and in this case I have made it. You are free to disapprove, of course; but not to interfere, I am glad to say.'

She picked up her cup with a hand that shook, and put it away on the tea-tray, as was her habit; and then made for the door. Lumbering and hurt, like a wounded elephant, thought Lucy.

'Just a minute, Henrietta!' Madame said, her eyes having lighted on Lucy and a spark of amused malice appearing therein. 'Let us ask the outsider and the trained psychologist.'

'But I am *not* a trained psychologist,' said poor Lucy.

'Just let us hear what Miss Pym thinks.'

'I don't know what Miss Pym has to do with the vacancies——'

'No, not about the appointment. Just what she thinks of these two students. Come along, Miss Pym. Give us your frank opinion. After a mere week among us you cannot be accused of bias.'

'You mean Rouse and Innes?' asked Lucy, playing for time. Henrietta had paused with her hand on the door. 'I don't know them, of course; but it certainly surprises me that Miss Hodge should think of giving that appointment to Rouse. I don't think she is at all—in fact I think she would be *quite* the wrong person.'

Henrietta, to whom this was apparently the last straw, cast her an *et tu Brute* look and blundered out of the room, with a muttered remark about it being 'surprising what a pretty face can do to influence people.' Which Lucy took to refer to Innes, not to herself.

In the drawing-room was a very crowded silence.

'I thought I knew all about Henrietta,' Madame said at last, reflective and puzzled.

'I thought one could trust her to do justice,' Miss Lux said, bitter.

Fröken got to her feet without a word, and still looking contemptuous and sullen, walked out of the room. They watched her go with gloomy approbation; her silence was comment enough.

'It is a pity that this should have happened, when everything was going so well,' Wragg said, producing another of her unhelpful offerings. She was like someone running round with black-currant lozenges to the victims of an earthquake. 'Everyone has been so pleased with their posts, and——'

'Do you think she will come to her senses when she has had time to think it over?' Lux asked Madame.

'She has been thinking it over for nearly a week. Or rather she has had it settled in her mind for nearly a week; so that by now it has become established fact and she will not be able to see it any other way.'

'And yet she couldn't have been sure about it—I mean, sure of our reaction—or she would not have kept it to herself until now. Perhaps when she thinks it over——'

'When she thinks it over she will remember that Catherine Lux questioned the Royal Prerogative——'

'But there is a Board in the background. There is no question of Divine Right. There must be someone who can be appealed to against her decision. An injustice like this can't be allowed to happen just because——'

'Of course there is a Board. You met them when you got the job here. You see one of them when she comes to supper on the Friday nights when the lecture happens to be on Yoga, or Theosophy, or Voodoo, or what not. A greedy slug in amber beads and black satin, with the brains of a louse. She thinks Henrietta is wonderful. So do the rest of the Board. And so, let me say it here and now, do I. That is what makes it all so shocking. That Henrietta, the shrewd Henrietta who built this place up from something not much better than a dame's school, should be so blind, so suddenly devoid of the most elementary judgement—it's fantastic. Fantastic!'

'But there must be *something* we can do——'

'My good if tactless Catherine,' Madame said rising gracefully to her feet, 'all we can do is go to our rooms and pray.' She reached for the scarf that even in the hottest weather draped her thin body as she moved from one room to another. 'There are also the lesser resorts of aspirin and a hot bath. They may not move the Almighty, but they are beneficial to the blood pressure.' She floated out of the room; as nearly without substance as a human being can be.

'If Madame can't do anything to influence Miss Hodge, I don't see that anyone else can,' Wragg said.

'I certainly can't,' Lux said. 'I just rub her the wrong way. Even if I didn't, even if I had the charm of Cleopatra and she hung on my every word, how can one reduce a mental astigmatism like that? She is quite honest about it, you see. She is one of the most honest persons I have ever met. She really *sees* the thing like that; she really sees Rouse as everything that is admirable and deserving, and thinks we are prejudiced and oppositious. How can one alter a thing like that?' She stared a moment, blankly, at the bright window, and then picked up her book. 'I must go and change, if I can find a free bathroom.'

Her going left Lucy alone with Miss Wragg, who obviously wanted to go too, but did not know how to make her departure sufficiently graceful.

'It is a mess, isn't it?' she proffered.

'Yes, it seems a pity,' Lucy said, thinking how inadequately it summed up the situation; she was still stunned by the new aspect presented to her. She became aware that Wragg was still in her outdoor clothes. 'When did you hear about it?'

'I heard the students talking about it downstairs— when we came in from the match, I mean—and I bolted up here to see if it was true, and I walked straight into it. Into the row, I mean. It *is* a pity; everything was going so well.'

'You know that the students take it for granted that Innes will get the post,' Lucy said.

'Yes,' Wragg sounded sober. 'I heard them in the bath-rooms. It was a natural thing to think. All of us would take it for granted that Innes would be the one. She is not very good for me—in games, I mean—but she is a good coach. She understands what she is doing. And of course in other things she is brilliant. She really should have been a doctor or something brainy like that. Oh, well, I suppose I must go and get out of these things.' She hesitated a moment. 'Don't think we do this often, will you, Miss Pym? This is the first time I have seen the Staff het up about any-thing. We are all such good friends as a rule. That's what makes this such a pity. I wish someone could change Miss Hodge's point of view. But if I know her no one can do that.'

10

No one can do that, they said; but it was just possible that she, Lucy, might. When the door closed behind Wragg she found herself faced with her own dilemma. She had reason to know that Miss Lux's first view of Henrietta's reaction was much truer than her second. That mental astigmatism that Lux talked about was not great enough to exclude a doubt of her own judgement; Lucy had not forgotten the odd guilty look on Henrietta's face last Monday morning when her secretary had tried to bring up the subject of the Arlinghurst letter. It had been an up-to-something look. Not a Father Christmas up-to-something, either. Quite definitely it was something she was a little ashamed of. Astigmatic enough she might be to find Rouse worthy, but not cock-eyed enough to be unaware that Innes had a prior claim.

And that being so, then it was Lucy's duty to put certain facts before her. It was a great pity about the little red book now dissolving into pulp among the weeds—she had been altogether too impulsive about its disposal—but, book or no book, she must brave Henrietta and produce some cogent reasons for her belief that Rouse was not a suitable person to be appointed to Arlinghurst.

It surprised her a little to find that an interview with Henrietta on this footing brought back a school-girl qualm that had no place in the bosom of any adult; least of all one who was a Celebrity. But she was greatly fortified by that remark of Henrietta's about 'pretty faces'. That was a remark that Henrietta really should not have made.

She got up and put the cup of black, cold tea on the

tray; noticing regretfully that they had had almond-fingers for tea; she would have very much liked an almond-finger ten minutes ago, but now she could not have eaten even an éclair. It would not be true to say that she had discovered feet of clay in Henrietta, since she had never made any sort of image in Henrietta's likeness. But she *had* looked up to Henrietta as a person of superior worth to her own, and the habit of mind acquired at school had stayed with her. She was therefore shocked to find her capable of what was at worst cheating, and at the very least a *bêtise*. She wondered what there had been in Rouse to unseat so solid a judgement as Henrietta's. That remark about 'pretty faces'. That unconsidered, blurted remark. Was there something in that plain, north-country face that had touched a woman so used to good looks in her students? Was there something in the plain, unloved, hardworking, ambitious Rouse that Henrietta identified with herself? Was it like seeing some old struggle of her own? So that she adopted, and championed, and watched over her unconsciously. Her disappointment over Rouse's comparative failure in Pathology had been so keen that it had distracted her even from the urgent quarrel with her Staff.

Or was it just that Rouse had made good use of those admiring—not to say adoring—looks that she had sampled on the covered way the other morning?

No, not that. Henrietta had her faults, but silliness was not one of them. She had, moreover, like everyone else in the scholastic world, served a long apprenticeship to adoration, both real and synthetic. Her interest in Rouse might be heightened by Rouse's obvious discipleship, but the origin of that interest was elsewhere. It was most likely that the Henrietta who had been plain, and un-loved, and ambitious, had viewed the plain, and unloved, and ambitious young Rouse with a kindliness that was half recognition.

Lucy wondered whether to go to Henrietta at once, or to wait until she simmered down. The snag was that as Henrietta simmered down, so would her own determination to beard Henrietta on the subject. All things considered, and with the memory of previous fiascos, she thought that she had better go now while her feet would still carry her in the proper direction.

There was no immediate answer to her tap at the office door, and for a moment she hoped that Henrietta had retired to her own room upstairs and so reprieved her from her plain duty for a few hours longer. But no; there was her voice bidding her come in, and in went Lucy, feeling horribly like a culprit and furious with herself for being such a rabbit. Henrietta was still flushed and wounded-looking, and if she had not been Henrietta, Lucy would have said that there were tears in her eyes; but that was manifestly impossible. She was very busy about some papers on her desk, but Lucy felt that until she had knocked Henrietta's only activity had been mental.

'Henrietta,' she began, 'I'm afraid you thought it presumptuous of me to express an opinion about Miss Rouse.' (Oh dear, that sounded very pompous!)

'A little uncalled-for,' Henrietta said coldly.

Of all the Henrietta phrases! 'Uncalled-for'! 'But it *was* called for,' she pointed out. 'That is just what it was. I should never have dreamed of offering my opinion unasked. The point is, that opinion——'

'I don't think we need discuss it, Lucy. It is a small matter, anyhow, and not one to——'

'But it *isn't* a small matter. That is why I've come to see you.'

'We pride ourselves in this country, don't we, that everyone has a right to his opinion, and a right to express it. Well, you expressed it——'

'When I was asked to.'

'When you were asked to. And all I say is that it was a

little tactless of you to take sides in a matter of which you can know very little, if anything at all.'

'But that is just it. I *do* know something about it. You think I am just prejudiced against Miss Rouse because she is not very attractive——'

'Not very attractive to *you*, perhaps,' amended Henrietta quickly.

'Shall we say not very obviously attractive,' Lucy said, annoyed and beginning to feel better. 'You think I have judged her merely on her social graces, but that is not so.'

'On what else could you judge her? You know nothing of her work.'

'I invigilated at one of her examinations.'

Lucy observed with satisfaction that this brought Henrietta up short.

There was silence while one could count five.

'And what quality of a student could you possibly test by invigilating at an examination?'

'Her honesty.'

'Lucy!' But the tone was not shocked. It was a warning. It meant, if it meant anything: Do-you-know-what-the-punishment-for-slander-is?

'Yes, I said her honesty.'

'Are you trying to tell me that you found Miss Rouse—obtaining help during an examination?'

'She did her best. I haven't spent the best years of my life in Fourth-Form circles without knowing the routine. It was at the beginning that I noticed what she was about, and since I didn't want to make a scandal of it I thought the best way was to prevent her from using it.'

'Using it? Using what?'

'The little book.'

'You mean that you saw a student using a small book at an examination, and *said nothing about it*?'

'No, of course not. It was only afterwards that I knew about the book. All that I knew at the time was that there was something she was trying to refer to. She had a handkerchief in her left hand—although she hadn't a cold, and seemed to have no legitimate use for the thing—and she had that bag-of-sweets-under-the-desk look that you know as well as I do. There wasn't anything under her desk, so I deduced that whatever she had was in her hand with the handkerchief. As I had no proof——'

'Ah! You had no proof.'

'No. I had no proof, and I didn't want to upset the whole room by demanding any, so I invigilated from the back of the room, where I was directly behind her, and could see to it that she got no help from anything or anybody.'

'But if you did not ask her about the affair, how did you know about a book?'

'I found the book lying by the path to the gymnasium. It was——'

'You mean the book was not in her desk? Not *in the room at all*?'

'No. If it had been in her desk you would have known about it five minutes later. And if I had found such a book in the examination room I would have brought it to you at once.'

'Such a book? What kind of book?'

'A tiny address-book filled with Pathology notes.'

'An address-book?'

'Yes. A, arthritis—and so on.'

'You mean that the book was merely a book of reference compiled by a student in the course of her study?'

'Not "merely".'

'And *why* not "merely"?'

'Because the whole thing was not much bigger than an out-size postage stamp.'

Lucy waited for this to sink in.

'And what connection is there between this book you found and Miss Rouse?'

'Only that no one else in the room had a bag-of-sweets-under-the-desk expression; in fact, no one else seemed to be particularly worried about the paper. And that Rouse was the last to leave the room.'

'What has that to do with it?'

'If the book had been dropped before Rouse came out of the examination room it would almost certainly have been picked up by one of the other students. It was a sort of dahlia red, and was lying very obviously on the grass at the edge of the path.'

'Not *on the path*?'

'No,' said Lucy, reluctantly. 'About half an inch off it.'

'So that it could have been passed many times by a crowd of chattering students excited over an examination, and anxious not to be late for their next class?'

'Yes, I suppose it could.'

'And was there a name on the book?'

'No.'

'No name? No means of identification?'

'Nothing except the script. It was in script, not current form.'

'I see.' One could see Henrietta bracing herself. 'Then you had better bring me the book and we will take the proper steps to have the owner identified.'

'I haven't got it,' said poor Lucy. 'I drowned it.'

'You what?'

'I mean, I dropped it into the stream by the games field.'

'That was surely a very extraordinary thing to do?' *Was* there a spark of relief in Henrietta's eye?

'Not really. I suppose it was impetuous. But what was I to do with it? It was a précis of Pathology, and the Pathology Final was over and the book had not been used. Whatever had been planned had not been carried out. Why, then, worry you by bringing the book to you? It seemed to me that the best punishment for whoever had compiled the thing was never to know what had become of it. To live the rest of their days with a question at the back of their mind.'

'"Whoever had compiled it." That describes the situation, doesn't it? There is not one iota of evidence to connect the book with Miss Rouse.'

'If there had been evidence, as I said before, I would have brought it to you. There is only presumption. But the presumption is very strong. A great many people are ruled out altogether.'

'Why?'

'Those who don't consider themselves likely to be at a loss don't waste time insuring against it. That is to say, those who are good on the theoretical side are innocent. But you yourself told me that Rouse finds written work extraordinarily difficult.'

'So do a great many others.'

'Yes. But there is another factor. A great many no doubt find difficulty with theory, but don't particularly care as long as they struggle through. But Rouse is brilliant at practical work, and it galls her to be also-ran in examinations. She is ambitious, and a hard-worker. She wants the fruits of her labours, and she is very doubtful of getting them. Hence the little book.'

'That, my dear Lucy, is psychological theorising.'

'Maybe. But psychological theorising is what Madame asked me to do, in the drawing-room. You thought I had based my opinion on a mere prejudice. I thought you ought to know that I had some better foundation for my theorising.' She watched Henrietta's flushed face, and wondered if she might venture into the minefield again, now that she had proved that she was not merely wantonly trespassing. 'As one friend to another, Henrietta, I don't understand why you even consider sending Rouse to Arlinghurst when you have someone as suitable as Innes.' And she waited for the explosion.

But there was no explosion. Henrietta sat in heavy

silence, making a dotted pattern with her pen on the fine clean blotting-paper; a measure of her troubled state, since neither doodling nor wasting paper was a habit of Henrietta's.

'I don't think you know much about Innes,' she said at length, in a reasonably friendly tone. 'Because she has a brilliant mind and good looks you credit her with all the other virtues. Virtues that she quite definitely does not possess. She has no sense of humour, and she does not make friends easily—two serious disabilities in anyone who plans to live the communal life of a residential school. Her very brilliance is a drawback in that it makes it difficult for her to suffer fools gladly. She has a tendency —quite unconscious, I am sure—to look down her nose at the rest of the world.' (Lucy remembered suddenly how, this very afternoon, Innes had automatically used the word 'they' in referring to the students. Old Henrietta was shrewd enough.) 'In fact, ever since she came here she has left me with the impression that she despises Leys, and is using it only as a means to an end.'

'Oh, surely not,' Lucy protested mechanically, while her inner self was wondering whether that were indeed so, and whether that accounted for a great deal that had puzzled her about Mary Innes. If being at Leys had indeed been a secret purgatory, a trial endured as a means to an end, that might explain that too-adult reticence, that air of concentration in a person who had no natural need of concentration, that inability to smile.

She remembered, irrelevantly, Desterro's light-hearted account of how she changed her mind and decided to stay at Leys when she saw Innes. It was because Innes was not 'of' Leys that Desterro had noticed her on that dreary autumn afternoon, picking her out from the milling crowd as someone from an alien, more adult world.

'But she is very popular with her colleagues,' Lucy said aloud.

'Yes, her own set like her well enough. They find her aloofness—intriguing, I think. She is not so popular with children, unfortunately; they find her intimidating. If you looked at her crit. book—the book that the Staff use for reports when they go to outside classes with students—you would find that the word 'antagonistic' appears again and again in describing her attitude.'

'Perhaps it is just those eyebrows,' Lucy said. She saw that Henrietta, uncomprehending, thought this a mere frivolousness, and added: 'Or perhaps like so many people she has an inner doubt about herself, in spite of all appearances to the contrary. That is the usual explanation of antagonism as an attitude.'

'I find psychologists' explanations a little too glib,' Henrietta said. 'If one has not the natural graces to attract friendship, one can at least make an *effort* to be friendly. Miss Rouse does.'

(I bet! thought Lucy.)

'It is a great tragedy to lack the natural graces; one is not only denied the ready friendship of one's colleagues, but one has to overcome the unreasoning prejudice of those in office. Miss Rouse has fought hard to overcome her natural disabilities: her slowness of mind and her lack of good looks; she goes more than half-way to meet people and puts herself to great pains to be adaptable and pleasant and—and—and acceptable to people. And with her pupils she succeeds. They like her and look forward to seeing her; her reports from her classes are excellent. But with the Staff in their private capacity she has failed. They see only her personal—unattractiveness, and her efforts to be friendly and adaptable have merely annoyed them.' She looked up from her pen-patterns and caught Lucy's expression. 'Oh, yes, you thought my preference for Rouse as a candidate was the result of blind prejudice, didn't you? Believe me, I have not brought up Leys to its present position without understanding something of how the human mind works. Rouse has worked hard during her years here and has made a success of them, she is popular with her pupils and sufficiently adaptable to make herself acceptable to her colleagues; she has the friendliness and the adaptability that Innes so conspicuously lacks; and there is no reason why she should not go to Arlinghurst with my warm recommendation.'

'Except that she is dishonest.'

Henrietta flung the pen down on its tray with a clatter.

'That is a sample of what the unattractive girl has to struggle against,' she said, all righteousness and wrath. 'You think that one out of a score of girls has tried to cheat at an examination, and you pick on Rouse. Why? Because you don't like her face—or her expression, if one must be accurate.'

So it had been no use. Lucy drew her feet under her and prepared to go.

'There is nothing at all to connect the little book you found with any particular student. You just remembered that you hadn't liked the looks of Miss Rouse; and so she was the culprit. The culprit—if there is one; I should be sorry to think that any senior student of mine would stoop to such a subterfuge—the culprit is probably the prettiest and most innocent member of the set. You should know enough of human nature, as distinct from psychology, to know that.'

Lucy was not sure whether it was this last thrust or the accusation of fastening crime on to plain faces, but she was very angry by the time she reached the door.

'There is just one point, Henrietta,' she said, pausing with the door-knob in her hand.

'Yes?'

'Rouse managed to get a First in all her Finals so far.'

'Yes.'

'That is odd, isn't it.'

'Not at all odd. She has worked very hard.'

'It's odd, all the same; because on the occasion when someone was prevented from using the little red book she could not even get a Second.'

And she closed the door quietly behind her.

'Let her stew over that,' she thought.

As she made her way over to the wing her anger gave way to depression. Henrietta was, as Lux said, honest, and that honesty made arguing with her hopeless. Up to a point she was shrewd and clear-minded, and beyond that she suffered from Miss Lux's 'astigmatism'; and for mental astigmatism nothing could be done. Henrietta was not consciously cheating, and therefore could not be reasoned, frightened, nor cajoled into a different course. Lucy thought with something like dismay of the party she was to attend presently. How was she going to face a gathering of Seniors, all speculating about Arlinghurst and rejoicing openly over Innes's good luck?

How was she going to face Innes herself, with the radiance in her eyes? The Innes who 'wouldn't call the king her cousin'.

II

SUPPER at Leys was the formal meal of the day, with the Seniors in their dancing silks and the rest in supper frocks, but on Saturdays when so many had 'Larborough leave' it was a much more casual affair. Students sat where they pleased, and, within the bounds of convention, wore what they pleased. Tonight the atmosphere was even more informal than usual since so many had departed to celebrate the end of Examination Week elsewhere, and still more were planning celebration on the spot after supper. Henrietta did not appear—it was understood that she was having a tray in her room—and Madame Lefevre was absent on concerns of her own. Fröken and her mother were at the theatre in Larborough, so Lucy shared the top table with Miss Lux and Miss Wragg, and found it very pleasant. By tacit consent the burning question of Arlinghurst was not referred to.

'One would think,' said Miss Lux, turning over with a fastidious fork the vegetable mysteries on her plate, 'that on a night of celebration Miss Joliffe would have provided something more alluring than a scranbag.'

'It's *because* it's a celebration night that she doesn't bother,' said Wragg, eating heartily. 'She knows quite well that there is enough good food waiting upstairs to sink a battleship.'

'Not for us, unfortunately. Miss Pym must put something in her pocket for us when she is coming away.'

'I bought some cream puffs in Larborough on the way home from the match,' Wragg confessed. 'We can have our coffee in my room and have a gorge.'

Miss Lux looked as if she would have preferred cheese straws, but in spite of her chill incisiveness she was a kind person, so she said: 'I take that very kindly of you, so I do.'

'I thought you would be going to the theatre, or I would have suggested it before.'

'An out-moded convention,' said Miss Lux.

'Don't you like the theatre?' asked the surprised Lucy, to whom the theatre was still a part of childhood's magic.

Miss Lux stopped looking with a questioning revulsion at a piece of carrot, and said: 'Have you ever considered what you would think of the theatre if you were taken to it for the first time, now, without the referred affection of childhood pantomimes and what not? Would you really find a few dressed-up figures posturing in a lighted box *entertaining*? And the absurd convention of intervals— once devoted to the promenade of toilets and now perpetuated for the benefit of the bar. What other entertainment would permit of such arbitrary interruption? Does one stop in the middle of a symphony to go and have a drink?'

'But a play is made that way.' Lucy protested.

'Yes. As I said; an out-moded convention.'

This dashed Lucy a little, not because of her lingering affection for the theatre, but because she had been so wrong about Miss Lux. She would have said that Miss Lux would be a passionate attender of try-out performances in the drearier suburbs of plays devoted to a Cause and Effects.

'Well, I nearly went tonight myself,' Wragg said, 'just to see Edward Adrian again. I had a terrific rave on him when I was a student. I expect he's a bit *passé* now. Have you ever seen him?'

'Not on the stage. He used to spend his holidays with us when he was a boy.' Miss Lux ran her fork once more through the heap on her plate and decided that there was nothing further worth her attention.

'*Used to spend the holidays!* At your *house*?'

'Yes, he went to school with my brother.'

'Good heavens! how absolutely incredible!'

'What is incredible about it?'

'I mean, one just doesn't think of Edward Adrian as being an ordinary person that people *know*. Just a schoolboy like anyone else.'

'A very horrid little boy.'

'Oh, *no!*'

'A quite revolting little boy. Always watching himself in mirrors. And possessed of a remarkable talent for getting the best of everything that was going.' She sounded calm, and clinical, and detached.

'Oh, Catherine, you shatter me.'

'No one I have ever met had the same genius for leaving someone else holding the baby as Teddy Adrian.'

'He has other kinds of genius though, surely,' Lucy ventured.

'He has talent, yes.'

'Do you still see him?' asked Wragg, still a little dazzled to be getting first-hand news of Olympus.

'Only by accident. When my brother died we gave up the house that our parents had had, and there were no more family gatherings.'

'And you've never seen him on the stage?'

'Never.'

'And you didn't even go a sixpenny bus-ride into Larborough to see him play tonight.'

'I did not. I told you, the theatre bores me inexpressibly.'

'But it's Shakespeare!'

'Very well, it's Shakespeare. I would rather sit at home and read him in the company of Doreen Wragg and her cream puffs. You won't forget to put something in your pocket for us when you leave your feast, will you, Miss Pym? Anything gratefully received by the starving proletariat. Macaroons, Mars bars, blood oranges, left-over sandwiches, squashed sausage rolls——'

'I'll put a hat round,' promised Lucy. 'I'll pass the hat and quaver: "Don't forget the Staff".'

But as she lifted the champagne bottle out of its melting ice in her wash-bowl she did not feel so gay about it. This party was going to be an ordeal, there was no denying it. She tied a big bow of ribbon to the neck of the bottle, to make it look festive and to take away any suggestion of 'bringing her own liquor'; the result was rather like a duchess in a paper cap, but she didn't think that the simile would occur to the students. She had hesitated over her own toilet, being divided between a rough-and-tumble outfit suitable to a cushions-on-the-floor gathering, and the desire to do her hosts honour. She had paid them the compliment of putting on her 'lecture' frock, and doing an extra-careful make-up. If Henrietta had taken away from this party by her vagaries, she, Lucy, would bring all she could to it.

Judging by the noise in other rooms, and the running back and fore with kettles, Stewart's was not the only party in Leys that evening. The corridors smelt strongly of coffee, and waves of laughter and talk rose and died away as doors were opened and shut. Even the Juniors seemed to be entertaining; if they had no Posts to celebrate they had the glory of having their first Final behind them. Lucy remembered that she had not found out from The Nut Tart how she had fared in that Anatomy Final. ('Today's idea may be nonsense tomorrow, but a clavicle is a clavicle for all time.') When she passed the students' notice-board again she must look for Desterro's name.

She had to knock twice at the door of Number Ten before the sound penetrated, but when a flushed Stewart opened the door and drew her in a sudden shyness fell on the group, so that they got to their feet in polite silence like well-brought-up children.

'We are so glad to have you,' Stewart was beginning, when Dakers sighted the bottle and all formality was at an end.

'*Drink!*' she shrieked. 'As I live and breathe, *drink!* Oh, Miss Pym you are a *poppet!*'

'I hope that I am not breaking any rules,' Lucy said, remembering that there had been an expression in Miss Joliffe's eye that she had still not accounted for, 'but it seemed to me an occasion for champagne.'

'It's a triple occasion,' Stewart said. 'Dakers and Thomas are celebrating too. It couldn't be *more* of an occasion. It was lovely of you to think of the champagne.'

'It will be sacrilege to drink it out of tooth-glasses,' Hasselt said.

'Well, anyhow, we drink it now, as aperitif. A course by itself. Pass up your glasses everyone. Miss Pym, the chair is for you.'

A basket chair had been imported and lined with a motley collection of cushions; except for the hard chair at the desk it was the only legitimate seat in the room, the rest of the party having brought their cushions with them and being now disposed about the floor or piled in relaxed heaps like kittens on the bed. Someone had tied a yellow silk handkerchief over the light so that a golden benevolence took the place of the usual hard brightness. The twilight beyond the wide-open window made a pale blue back-cloth that would soon be a dark one. It was like any student party of her own college days, but as a picture it had more brilliance than her own parties had had. Was it just that the colours of the cushions were gayer? That the guests were better physical types, without lank hair, spectacles, and studious pallor?

No, of course it wasn't that. She knew what it was. There was no cigarette smoke.

'O'Donnell isn't here yet,' Thomas said, collecting tooth-glasses from the guests and laying them on the cloth that covered the desk.

'I expect she's helping Rouse to put up the boom,' a Disciple said.

'She can't be,' a second Disciple said, 'it's Saturday.'

'Even a P.T.I. stops work on a Sunday,' said a third.

'Even Rouse,' commented the fourth.

'Is Miss Rouse still practising rotatory travelling?' Lucy asked.

'Oh, yes,' they said. 'She will be, up to the day of the Dem.'

'And when does she find time?'

'She goes when she is dressed in the morning. Before first class.'

'Six o'clock,' said Lucy. 'Horrible.'

'It's no worse than any other time,' they said. 'At least one is fresh, and there is no hurry, and you can have the gym to yourself. Besides, it's the only possible time. The boom has to be put away before first class.'

'She doesn't have to go,' Stewart said, 'the knack has come back. But she is terrified she will lose it again before the Dem.'

'I can understand that, my dear,' Dakers said. 'Think what an *immortal* fool one would feel hanging like a sick monkey from the boom, with all the *élite* looking on, and Fröken simply *stabbing* one with that eye of hers. My dear, *death* would be a happy release. If Donnie isn't doing her usual chore for Rouse, *where* is she? She's the only one not here.'

'Poor Don,' Thomas said, 'she hasn't got a post yet.' Thomas with her junior-of-three in Wales was feeling like a millionaire.

'Don't worry over Dòn,' Hasselt said, 'the Irish always fall on their feet.'

But Miss Pym was looking round for Innes, and not finding her. Nor was Beau there.

Stewart, seeing her wandering eye, interpreted the question in it and said: 'Beau and Innes wanted me to tell you how sorry they were to miss the party, and to hope that you would be their guest at another one before the end of term.'

'Beau will be giving one for Innes,' Hasselt said. 'To celebrate Arlinghurst.'

'As a matter of fact, we're *all* giving a party for Innes,' a Disciple said.

'A sort of general jamboree,' said a second Disciple.

'It's an honour for College, after all,' said a third.

'You'll come to that, won't you, Miss Pym,' said a fourth, making it a statement rather than a question.

'Nothing would please me more,' Lucy said. And then, glad to skate away from such thin ice: 'What has happened to Beau and Innes?'

'Beau's people turned up unexpectedly and took them off to the theatre in Larborough,' Stewart said.

'That's what it is to own a Rolls,' Thomas said, quite without envy. 'You just dash around England as the fit takes you. When *my* people want to move they have to yoke up the old grey mare—a brown cob, actually—and trot twenty miles before they reach any place at all.'

'Farmers?' Lucy asked, seeing the lonely narrow Welsh road winding through desolation.

'No, my father is a clergyman. But we have to keep a horse to work the place, and we can't have a horse and a car too.'

'Oh, well,' said a Disciple arranging herself more comfortably on the bed, 'who wants to go to the theatre, anyhow?'

'Of all the boring ways of spending an evening,' said a second.

'Sitting with one's knees in someone's back,' said a third.

'With one's eyes glued to opera glasses,' said a fourth.

'Why opera glasses?' asked Lucy, surprised to find Miss Lux's attitude repeated in a gathering where sophistication had not yet destroyed a juvenile thirst for entertainment.

'What would you see without them?'

'Little dolls walking about in a box.'

'Like something on Brighton pier.'

'Except that on Brighton pier you can see the expression on the faces.'

They were rather like something from Brighton pier themselves, Lucy thought. A turn. A sort of extended Tweedledum and Tweedledee. They were apparently not moved to speech unless one of their number made a remark; when the others felt called upon to produce corroborative evidence.

'Me, I'm only too glad to put my feet up and do nothing for a change,' Hasselt said. 'I'm breaking in a new pair of ballet shoes for the Dem. and my blisters are spectacular.'

'Miss Hasselt,' said Stewart, obviously quoting, 'it is a student's business to preserve her body in a state of fitness at all times.'

'That may be,' said Hasselt, 'but I'm not standing in a bus for five miles on a Saturday night to go anywhere, least of all to a theatre.'

'Anyhow, it's only Shakespeare, my dears,' Dakers said. '"It is the cause, my soul!"' she burlesqued, clutching at her breast.

'Edward Adrian, though,' volunteered Lucy, feeling that her beloved theatre must have one champion.

'Who is Edward Adrian?' Dakers asked, in genuine inquiry.

'He's that weary-looking creature who looks like a moulting eagle,' Stewart said, too busy about her hostess's duties to be aware of the reaction on Lucy: that was a horribly vivid summing-up of Edward Adrian, as seen by the unsentimental eyes of modern youth. 'We used to be taken to see him when I was at school in Edinburgh.'

'And didn't you enjoy it?' Lucy asked, remembering that Stewart's name headed the lists on the notice-board along with Innes's and Beau's, and that mental activity would not be for her the chore that it probably was for some of the others.

'Oh, it was better than sitting in a class-room,' Stewart allowed. 'But it was all terribly—old-fashioned. Nice to look at, but a bit dreary. I'm a tooth-glass short.'

'Mine, I suppose,' O'Donnell said, coming in on the words and handing over her glass. 'I'm afraid I'm late. I was looking for some shoes that my feet would go into. Forgive these, won't you, Miss Pym,' she indicated the bedroom slippers she was wearing. 'My feet have died on me.'

'Do *you* know who Edward Adrian is?' Lucy asked her.

'Certainly I do,' O'Donnell said. 'I've had a rave on him ever since I went to see him at the age of twelve in Belfast.'

'You seem to be the only person in this room either to know or to admire him.'

'Ah, the heathen,' said O'Donnell, casting a scornful eye on the gathering—and it seemed to Lucy that O'Donnell was suspiciously bright about the eyes, as if she had been crying. 'It's in Larborough I would be this minute, sitting at his feet, if it wasn't practically the end of term and I lacked the price of a seat.'

And if, thought Lucy pitying, you hadn't felt that backing out of this party would be put down to your being the only one present not yet to have a post. She liked the girl who had dried her eyes and thought of the bedroom slipper excuse and come gaily to the party that was none of hers.

'Well,' said Stewart, busy with the wire of the cork, 'now that O'Donnell is here we can open the bottle.'

'Good heavens, champagne!' O'Donnell said.

The wine came foaming into the thick blunt tooth-glasses, and they turned to Lucy expectantly.

'To Stewart in Scotland, to Thomas in Wales, to Dakers at Ling Abbey,' she said.

They drank that.

'And to all our friends between Cape Town and Manchester,' Stewart said.

And they drank that too.

'Now, Miss Pym what will you eat?'

And Lucy settled down happily to enjoy herself. Rouse was not going to be a guest; and she was by some special intervention of Providence in the shape of rich parents in a Rolls-Royce going to be spared the ordeal of sitting opposite an Innes bursting with happiness that had no vestige of foundation.

12

BUT by noon on Sunday she was much less happy, and
was wishing that she had had the foresight to invent a
luncheon engagement in Larborough and so remove herself out of the area of the explosion that was coming. She
had always hated explosions, literal and metaphorical;
people who blew into paper bags and then burst them
had always been regarded by Lucy with a mixture of
abhorrence and awe. And the paper bag that was going to
be burst after lunch was a particularly nasty affair; an
explosion whose reverberations would be endless and un-
predictable. At the back of her mind was the faint hope
that Henrietta might have changed her mind; that the
silent witness of those tell-tale lists on the notice-board
might have proved more eloquent than her own poor
words. But no amount of encouragement could make this
hope anything but embryonic. She remembered only too
clearly that a shaking of Henrietta's faith in Rouse would
not mean a corresponding access of belief in Innes as a
candidate. The best that could be hoped for was that she
might write to the Head at Arlinghurst and say that there
was no Leaving Student good enough for so exalted a
post; and that would do nothing to save Innes from the
grief that was coming to her. No, she really should have
got herself out of Leys for Sunday lunch and come back
when it was all over. Even in Larborough, it was to be
supposed, there were people that one might conceivably
be going to see. Beyond those over-rich villas of the outskirts with their smooth sanded avenues and their pseudo
everything, somewhere between them and the soot of the

city there must be a belt of people like herself. Doctors, there must be, for instance. She could have invented a doctor friend—except that doctors were listed in registers. If she had thought in time she could have invited herself to lunch with Dr Knight; after all, Knight owed her something. Or she could have taken sandwiches and just walked out into the landscape and not come home till bed-time.

Now she sat in the window-seat in the drawing-room, waiting for the Staff to assemble there before going down to the dining-room; watching the students come back from church and wondering if she had sufficient courage and resolution to seek out Miss Joliffe even yet and ask for sandwiches; or even just walk out of college with no word said—after all, one didn't starve in the English country even on a Sunday. As Desterro said, there were always villages.

Desterro was the first to come back from church; leisured and fashionable as always. Lucy leant out and said: 'Congratulations on your knowledge of the clavicle.' For she had looked at the board on the way to bed last night.

'Yes, I surprised myself,' said The Nut Tart. 'My grandmother will be so pleased. A "first" sounds so well, don't you think? I boasted about it to my cousin, but he said that was most unseemly. In England one waits to be asked about one's successes.'

'Yes,' agreed Lucy, sadly, 'and the worst of it is so few people ask. The number of lights under bushels in Great Britain is tragic.'

'Not Great Britain,' amended Desterro. 'He says—my cousin—that it is all right north of the river Tweed. That is the river between England and Scotland, you know. You can boast in Dunbar, but not in Berwick, Rick says.'

'I should like to meet Rick,' Lucy said.

'He thinks you are quite adorable, by the way.'

'*Me?*'

'I have been telling him about you. We spent all the intervals talking about you.'

'Oh, you went to the theatre, did you?'

'He went. I was taken.'

'Did you not enjoy it, then?' asked Lucy, mentally applauding the young man who made The Nut Tart do anything at all that she did not want to.

'Oh, it was as they say "not too bad". A little of the grand manner is nice for a change. Ballet would have been better. He is a dancer *manqué*, that one.'

'Edward Adrian?'

'Yes.' Her mind seemed to have strayed away. 'The English wear all one kind of hat,' she said reflectively. 'Up at the back and down in front.'

With which irrelevance she trailed away round the house, leaving Lucy wondering whether the remark was occasioned by last night's audience or Dakers' advent up the avenue. Dakers' Sunday hat was certainly a mere superior copy of the hat she had worn at school, and under its short brim her pleasant, waggish, pony's face looked more youthful than ever. She took off the hat with a gesture when she saw Miss Pym, and loudly expressed her delight in finding Lucy alive and well after the rigours of the night before. This was the first morning in *all* her college career, it seemed, when she had positively *failed* to eat a fifth slice of bread and marmalade.

'Gluttony is one of the seven deadly sins,' she observed, 'so I had need of shriving this morning. I went to the Baptist place because it is nearest.'

'And do you feel shriven?'

'I *don't* know that I *do*, now you come to mention it. It was all very *conversational*.'

Lucy took it that a shamed soul demanded ritual.

'Very friendly, though, I understand.'

'Oh, *frightfully*. The clergyman began his sermon by

leaning on one elbow and remarking: "Well, my friends, it's a very fine day." And everyone shook hands with everyone coming out. And they had some fine warlike hymns,' she added, having thought over the Baptist good points. She looked thoughtful for a moment longer and then said: 'There are some Portsmouth Brothers on the Larborough road——'

'Plymouth.'

'Plymouth what?'

'Plymouth Brethren, I suppose you mean.'

'Oh, yes; I knew it had something to do with the Navy. And I'm Pompey by inclination. Well, I think I shall sample *them* next Sunday. You don't suppose they're *private*, or anything like that?'

Miss Pym thought not, and Dakers swung her hat in a wide gesture of burlesque farewell and went on round the house.

By ones and twos, and in little groups, the students returned from their compulsory hour out of College. Waving or calling a greeting or merely smiling, as their temperaments were. Even Rouse called a happy 'Good morning, Miss Pym!' as she passed. Almost last came Beau and Innes; walking slowly, serene and relaxed. They came to rest beneath the window looking up at her.

'Heathen!' said Beau, smiling at her.

They were sorry they missed the party, they said, but there would be others.

'I shall be giving one myself when the Dem. is over,' Beau said. 'You'll come to that, won't you?'

'I shall be delighted. How was the theatre?'

'It might have been worse. We sat behind Colin Barry.'

'Who is he?'

'The All-England hockey "half".'

'And I suppose that helped *Othello* a lot.'

'It helped the intervals, I assure you.'

'Didn't you want to see *Othello*?'

141

'Not us! We were dying to go to Irma Ireland's new film—*Flaming Barriers*. It sounds very sultry, but actually, I believe, it's just a good clean forest fire. But my parents' idea of a night out is the theatre and a box of chocolates for the intervals. We couldn't disappoint the old dears.'

'Did *they* like it?'

'Oh, they *loved* it. They spent the whole of supper talking about it.'

'You're a fine pair to call anyone "heathen",' Lucy observed.

'Come to tea with the Seniors this afternoon,' Beau said.

Lucy said hastily that she was going out to tea.

Beau eyed her guilty face with something like amusement, but Innes said soberly: 'We should have asked you before. You are not going away before the Dem., are you?'

'Not if I can help it.'

'Then will you come to tea with the Seniors next Sunday?'

'Thank you. If I am here I should be delighted.'

'My lesson in manners,' said Beau.

They stood there on the gravel looking up at her, smiling. That was how she always remembered them afterwards. Standing there in the sunlight, easy and graceful; secure in their belief in the world's rightness and in their trust in each other. Untouched by doubt or blemish. Taking it for granted that the warm gravel under their feet was lasting earth, and not the precipice edge of disaster.

It was the five-minute bell that roused them. As they moved away, Miss Lux came into the room behind, looking grimmer than Lucy had ever seen her.

'I can't imagine why I'm here,' she said. 'If I had thought in time I wouldn't be taking part in this God-forsaken farce at all.'

142

Lucy said that that was exactly what she herself had been thinking.

'I suppose there has been no word of Miss Hodge having a change of heart?'

'Not as far as I know. I'm afraid it isn't likely.'

'What a pity we didn't *all* go out to lunch. If Miss Hodge had to call Rouse's name from a completely deserted table, College would at least be aware that we had no part in this travesty.'

'If you didn't have to mark yourself "out" on the slate before eleven, I would go now, but I haven't the nerve.'

'Oh well, perhaps we can do something with our expressions to convey that we consider the whole thing just a bad smell.'

It's the being there to countenance it she minds, thought Lucy; while I just want to run away from unpleasantness like a child. Not for the first time, she wished she was a more admirable character.

Madame Lefèvre came floating in wearing a nigger-brown silk affair that was shot with metallic blue in the high-lights; which made her look more than ever like some exotic kind of dragonfly. It was partly those enormous headlamps of eyes, of course; like some close-up of an insect in half-remembered Nature 'shorts'; the eyes and the thin brown body, so angular yet so graceful. Madame, having got over her immediate rage, had, it seemed, recovered her detached contempt for the human species, and was regarding the situation with malicious if slightly enjoyable distaste.

'Never having attended a wake,' she said, 'I look forward with interest to the performance today.'

'You are a ghoul,' Lux said; but without feeling, as if she were too depressed to care greatly. 'Haven't you done anything to alter her mind?'

'Oh, yes, I have wrestled with the Powers of Darkness.

Wrestled very mightily. Also very cogently, may I say. With example and precept. Who was it who was condemned to push an enormous stone up a hill for ever? Extraordinary how appropriate these mythological fancies still are. I wonder if a ballet of Punishments would be any good? Sweeping out stables, and so forth. To Bach, perhaps. Though Bach is not very inspirational, choreographically speaking. And a great many people rise up and call one damned, of course, if one uses him.'

'Oh, stop it,' Lux said. 'We are going to connive at an abomination and you speculate about choreography!'

'My good, if too earnest, Catherine, you must learn to take life as it comes, and to withdraw yourself from what you cannot alter. As the Chinese so rightly advise: When rape is inevitable, relax and enjoy it. We connive at an abomination, as you so exquisitely put it. True. But as intelligent human beings we concern ourselves with the by-products of the action. It will be interesting to see how, for instance, the little Innes reacts to the stimulus. Will the shock be a mortal one, will it galvanise her into action, or will it send her into crazy throes of galvanic activity that has no meaning?'

'Damn your metaphors. You are talking nonsense and you know it. It is someone else's rape we are invited to countenance; and as far as I know there is nothing in the history of philosophy, Chinese or otherwise, to recommend that.'

'Rape?' said Fröken, coming in followed by her mother. 'Who is going to be raped?'

'Innes,' Lux said dryly.

'Oh.' The twinkle died out of Fröken's eye, leaving it cold and pale. 'Yes,' she said, reflectively. 'Yes.'

Fru Gustavsen's round 'Mrs Noah' face looked troubled. She looked from one to another, as if hoping for some gleam of assurance, some suggestion that the problem

144

was capable of being resolved. She came over to Lucy in the window-seat, ducked her head in a sharp Good-morning, and said in German:

'You know about this thing the Principal does? My daughter is very angry. Very angry my daughter is. Not since she was a little girl have I seen her so angry. It is very bad what they do? You think so too?'

'Yes, I'm afraid I do.'

'Miss Hodge is a very good woman. I admire her very much. But when a good woman makes a mistake it is apt to be much worse than a bad woman's mistake. More colossal. It is a pity.'

It was a great pity, Lucy agreed.

The door opened and Henrietta came in, with a nervous Wragg in tow. Henrietta appeared serene, if a little more stately than usual (or than circumstances demanded), but Wragg cast a placatory smile round the gathering as if pleading with them to be all girls together and look on the bright side. Their close-hedged antagonism dismayed her, and she sent an appealing glance at Madame, whose dogs-body she normally was. But Madame's wide sardonic gaze was fixed on Henrietta.

Henrietta wished them all good-morning (she had breakfasted in her own room) and she had timed her en-trance very neatly, for before her greeting was finished, the murmur of the distant gong made the moment one for action, not conversation.

'It is time for us to go down, I think,' Henrietta said, and led the way out.

Madame rolled her eye at Lux in admiration of this piece of generalship, and fell in behind.

'A wake, indeed!' Lux said to Lucy as they went downstairs. 'It feels more like Fotheringay.'

The demure silence waiting them in the dining-room seemed to Lucy's heightened imagination to be charged with expectation, and certainly during the meal College seemed to be more excited than she had ever seen it. The babble of conversation deepened to a roar, so that Henrietta, coming-to between her busy gobbling of the meat course and her expectation of the pudding, sent a message by Wragg to Beau, asking that College should contain themselves.

For a little they were circumspect, but soon they forgot and the talk and laughter rose again.

'They are excited to have Examinations Week over,' Henrietta said indulgently, and let them be.

This was her only contribution to conversation—she never did converse while eating—but Wragg served up brave little platitudes at regular intervals, looking from one to the other of the shut faces round the table hopefully, like a terrier which has brought a bone to lay at one's feet. One could almost see her tail wag. Wragg was to be the innocent means of execution, the passive knife in the guillotine, and she felt her position and was tacitly apologising for it. Oh, for Pete's sake, she seemed to be saying, I'm only the Junior Gymnast in this set-up, it's not my fault that I have to tag along in her rear; what do you expect me to do?—tell her to announce the damned thing herself?

Lucy was sorry for her, even while her pious pieces of the obvious made her want to scream. Be quiet, she wanted to say, do be quiet, there is nothing for a situation like this but silence.

At last Henrietta folded up her napkin, looked round the table to make sure that all her Staff had finished eating, and rose. As the Staff rose with her, College came to its feet with an alacrity and a unanimity that was rare. It was apparent that they had been waiting for this moment. Against her will, Lucy turned to look at them; at the rows of bright expectant faces, half-smiling in their eagerness; it did nothing to comfort her that they looked as if at the slightest provocation they would break into a cheer.

146

As Henrietta turned to the door and the Staff filed after her, Wragg faced the delighted throng and said the words that had been given her to say.

'Miss Hodge will see Miss Rouse in her office when luncheon is over.'

13

Lucy could no longer see the faces, but she felt the silence go suddenly blank. Become void and dead. It was the difference between a summer silence full of bird-notes and leaves and wind in the grasses, and the frozen stillness of some Arctic waste. And then, into the dead void just as she reached the door, came the first faint sibilant whisper as they repeated the name.

'Rouse!' they were saying. 'Rouse!'

And Lucy, stepping into the warm sunlight, shivered. The sound reminded her of frozen particles being swept over a snow surface by a bitter wind. She even remembered where she had seen and heard those particles: that Easter she had spent on Speyside when they had missed the Grantown bus and they were a long way from home and they had to walk it every foot of the way, under a leaden sky into a bitter wind over a frozen world. She felt a long way from home now, crossing the sunny courtyard to the quadrangle door, and the sky seemed to her as leaden as any Highland one in a March storm. She wished for a moment that she were at home, in her own quiet little sitting-room, settling down for a Sunday afternoon of unbroken peace, untouched by human problems and unhurt by human griefs. She toyed with the idea of inventing an excuse to go when tomorrow morning's post would give her a chance; but she had looked forward like a child to the Demonstration on Friday, and she had now a quite personal interest in what had promised to be for her merely something new in spectacles. She knew all the Seniors personally and a great many of the Juniors; she had talked 'Dem.' with them, shared their half-fearful anticipation of it, even helped to make their costumes. It was the summit, the triumphant flower, the resounding full-stop of their College careers, and she could not bear to go without seeing it; without being part of it.

She had dropped the rest of the Staff, who were bound for the front of the house, but Wragg, coming behind her to pin a notice on the students' board, mopped her forehead in frank relief and said: 'Thank heaven that is over. I think it was the worst thing I have ever had to do. I couldn't eat my lunch with thinking of it.' And Lucy remembered that there had indeed been the phenomenon of a large piece of tart unfinished on Miss Wragg's plate.

That was life, that was. Innes had Heaven's door shut in her face, and Wragg couldn't finish her pudding!

No one had yet come out of the dining-room—College appetites being so much larger than Staff ones, their meals lasted at least ten or fifteen minutes longer—so the corridors were still deserted as Lucy went up to her room. She resolved to get away from Leys before the crowd of students overran the countryside. She would go away deep into the green and white and yellow countryside, and smell the may and lie in the grass and feel the world turning on its axis, and remember that it was a very large world, and that College griefs were wild and bitter, but soon over, and that in the Scale of Things they were undeniably Very Small Beer.

She changed her shoes to something more appropriate to field paths, crossed to the 'old house' and ran down the front stairs and out by the front door so as to avoid the students who would now be percolating out of the dining-room. The 'old house' was very silent and she deduced that there had been no lingering in the drawing-room after lunch today. She skirted the house and made for the field behind the gymnasium, with vague thoughts of Bidlington and The Teapot stirring in her mind. The hedge of may was a creamy foam on her right, and on her left the buttercups were a golden sea. The elms, half-floating in the warm light, were anchored each to its purple shadow, and daisies patterned the short grass under her feet. It was a lovely world, a fine round gracious world, and no day for—Oh, poor Innes! *poor* Innes!—no day for the world to turn over and crush one.

It was when she was debating with herself whether to cross the little bridge, to turn downstream to Bidlington, or up-stream to the unknown, that she saw Beau. Beau was standing in the middle of the bridge watching the water, but with her green linen dress and bright hair she was so much a part of the sunlight-and-shadow under the willows that Lucy had been unaware that anyone was there. As she came into the shade herself and could see more clearly, Lucy saw that Beau was watching her come, but she gave her no greeting. This was so unlike Beau that Lucy was daunted.

'Hullo,' she said, and leaned beside her on the wooden rail. 'Isn't it beautiful this afternoon?' *Must* you sound so idiotic? she asked herself.

There was no answer to this, but presently Beau said: 'Did you know about this appointment?'

'Yes,' said Lucy. 'I—I heard the Staff talking about it.'

'When?'

'Yesterday.'

'Then you knew this morning when you were talking to us.'

'Yes. Why?'

'It would have been kind if someone had warned her.'

'Warned whom?'

'Innes. It isn't very nice to have your teeth kicked in in public.'

She realised that Beau was sick with rage. Never before

had she seen her even out of temper, and now she was so angry that she could hardly talk.

'But how could I have done that?' she asked reasonably, dismayed to be taken personally to task for something that she considered none of her business. 'It would have been disloyal to mention it before Miss Hodge had announced her decision. For all I knew she might have altered that decision; when I left her it was still possible that she might see things from——' She stopped, realising where she was headed. But Beau too had realised. She turned her head sharply to look at Miss Pym.

'Oh. You argued with her about it. You didn't approve of her choice, then?'

'Of course not.' She looked at the angry young face so near her own and decided to be frank. 'You might as well know, Beau, that no one approves. The Staff feel about it very much as you do. Miss Hodge is an old friend of mine, and I owe her a great deal, and admire her, but where this appointment is concerned she is "on her own". I have been desolated ever since I first heard of it, I would do anything to reverse it, to waken up tomorrow and find that it is just a bad dream; but as to warning anyone——' She lifted her hand in a gesture of helplessness.

Beau had gone back to glaring at the water. 'A clever woman like you could have thought of something,' she muttered.

The 'clever woman' somehow made Beau of a sudden very young and appealing; it was not like the confident and sophisticated Beau to look for help or to think of her very ordinary Pym self as clever. She was after all a child; a child raging and hurt at the wrong that had been done her friend. Lucy had never liked her so well.

'Even a hint,' Beau went on, muttering at the water. 'Even a suggestion that there might be someone else in the running. *Anything* to warn her. To make the shock less shattering. To put her on her guard, so that she wasn't wide open. It had to be punishment, but it needn't have been a massacre. You could have sacrificed a little scruple in so good a cause, couldn't you?'

Lucy felt, belatedly, that perhaps she might have.

'Where is she?' she asked. 'Where is Innes?'

'I don't know. She ran straight out of College before I could catch her up. I know she came this way, but I don't know where she went from here.'

'She will take it very badly?'

'Did you expect her to be brave and noble about the hideous mess?' Beau said savagely, and then, instantly: 'Oh, I'm sorry. I do beg your pardon. I know you're sorry about it too. I'm just not fit to be spoken to just now.'

'Yes, I am sorry,' Lucy said. 'I admired Innes the first time I saw her, and I think she would have been an enormous success at Arlinghurst.'

'Would have been,' muttered Beau.

'How did Miss Rouse take the news? Was she surprised, do you think?'

'I didn't wait to see,' Beau said shortly. And presently: 'I think I shall go up-stream. There is a little thorn wood up there that she is very fond of; she may be there.'

'Are you worried about her?' Lucy asked; feeling that if it were merely comforting that Beau planned, Innes would surely prefer solitude at the moment.

'I don't think she is busy committing suicide, if that is what you mean. But of course I am worried about her. A shock like that would be bad for anyone—especially coming now, at the end of term when one is tired. But Innes—Innes has always cared too much about things.' She paused to look at the water again. 'When we were Juniors and Madame used to blister us with her sarcasm —Madame can be simply unspeakable, you know—the rest of us just came up in weals, but Innes was actually flayed; just raw flesh. She never cried, as some of the others did when they'd had too much for one go. She just —just burned up inside. It's bad for you to burn up inside. And once when——' She stopped, and seemed to decide that she had said enough. Either she had been on the verge of an indiscretion or she came to the conclusion that discussing her friend with a comparative stranger, however sympathetic, was not after all the thing to do. 'She has no oil on her feathers, Innes,' she finished.

She stepped off the bridge and began to walk away up the path by the willows. 'If I was rude,' she said, pausing just before she disappeared, 'do forgive me. I didn't mean to be.'

Lucy went on looking at the smooth silent water, wishing passionately that she could recover the little red book which she had consigned so smugly to the brook two days ago, and thinking of the girl who had no 'duck's back'—no protective mechanism against the world's weather. The girl who could neither whimper nor laugh; who 'burned up inside' instead. She rather hoped that Beau would not find her until the worst was over; she had not run to Beau for sympathy, she had run as far and as fast from human company as she could, and it seemed only fair to let her have the solitude she sought.

It would do Beau no harm at any rate, Lucy thought, to find that the world had its snags and its disappointments; life had been much too easy for Beau. It was a pity that she had to learn at Innes's expense.

She crossed the bridge into the games field, turned her face to open country and took the hedge gaps as they came; hoping that she might not overtake Innes, and determined to turn a blind eye in her direction if she did. But there was no Innes. No one at all moved in the Sunday landscape. Everyone was still digesting roast beef. She was alone with the hedges of may, the pasture, and the blue sky. Presently she came to the edge of a slope, from which she could look across a shallow valley to successive distances, and there she sat with her back against an oak, while the insects hummed in the grass, and the fat white clouds sailed up and passed, and the slow shadow of the tree circled round her feet. Lucy's capacity for doing nothing was almost endless, and had been the despair of both her preceptors and her friends.

It was not until the sun was at hedge level that she roused herself to further decision. The result of her self-communing was a realisation that she could *not* face College supper tonight; she would walk until she found an inn, and in the half-dark she would come back to College already hushed by the 'bedroom' bell. She made a wide circle round, and in half an hour saw in the distance a steeple she recognised, whereupon she jettisoned her thoughts of an inn and wondered if The Teapot was open on Sundays. Even if it wasn't perhaps she could persuade Miss Nevill to stay her pangs with something out of a can. It was after seven before she reached the outskirts of Bidlington, and she looked at the Martyrs' Memorial—the only ugly erection in the place—with something of a fellow interest, but the open door of The Teapot restored her. *Dear* Miss Nevill. Dear large clever business-like accommodating Miss Nevill.

She walked into the pleasant room, already shadowed by the opposite cottages, and found it almost empty. A family party occupied the front window, and in the far corner were a young couple who presumably owned the expensive coupé which was backed in at the end of the garden. She thought it clever of Miss Nevill to manage that the room should still look spotless and smell of flowers after the deluge of a Sunday's traffic in June.

She was looking round for a table when a voice said: 'Miss Pym!'

Lucy's first instinct was to bolt: she was in no mood for student chat at the moment; and then she noticed that it was The Nut Tart. The Nut Tart was the female half of the couple in the corner. The male half was undoubtedly 'my cousin'; the Rick who thought her adorable and who was referred to in College parlance as 'that gigolo'.

Desterro rose and came over to meet her—she had charming manners on formal occasions—and drew her over to their table. 'But this is lovely!' she said. 'We were talking of you, and Rick was saying how much he would like to meet you, and here you are. It is magic. This is my cousin, Richard Gillespie. He was christened Riccardo, but he thinks it sounds too like a cinema star.'

'Or a band leader,' Gillespie said, shaking hands with her and putting her into a chair. His unaccented manner was very English, and did something to counteract his undoubted resemblance to the more Latin types of screen hero. Lucy saw where the 'gigolo' came from; the black smooth hair that grew so thick, the eyelashes, the flare of the nostrils, the thin line of dark moustache were all according to the recipe; but nothing else was, it seemed to Lucy. Looks were what he had inherited from some Latin ancestor; but manner, breeding, and character seemed to be ordinary public school. He was considerably older than Desterro—nearly thirty, Lucy reckoned—and looked a pleasant and responsible person.

They had just ordered, it seemed, and Richard went away to the back premises to command another portion of Bidlington rarebit. 'It is a cheese affair,' Desterro said, 'but not those Welsh things you get in London teashops. It is a very rich cheese sauce on very soft buttery toast, and it is flavoured with odd things like nutmeg—I think it is nutmeg—and things like that, and it tastes divine.'

Lucy, who was in no state to care what food tasted like, said that it sounded delicious. 'Your cousin is English, then?'

'Oh, yes. We are not what you call first cousins,' she explained as Richard came back. 'The sister of my father's father married his mother's father.'

'In simpler words,' Richard said, 'our grandparents were brother and sister.'

'It may be simpler, but it is not explicit,' Desterro said, with all the scorn of a Latin for the Saxon indifference to relationships.

'Do you live in Larborough?' Lucy asked Richard.

'No, I work in London, at our head office. But just now I am doing liaison work in Larborough.'

In spite of herself Lucy's eye swivelled round to Desterro, busy with a copy of the menu.

'One of our associated firms is here, and I am working with them for a week or two,' Rick said smoothly; and laughed at her with his eyes. And then, to put her mind completely at rest: 'I came with a chit to Miss Hodge, vouching for my relationship, my respectability, my solvency, my presentability, my orthodoxy——'

'Oh, be quiet, Rick,' Desterro said, 'it is not my fault that my father is Brazilian and my mother French. What is saffron dough-cake?'

'Teresa is the loveliest person to take out to a meal,' Rick said. 'She eats like a starved lion. My other women friends spend the whole evening reckoning the calories and imagining what is happening to their waists.'

'Your other women friends,' his cousin pointed out a trifle astringently, 'have not spent twelve months at Leys Physical Training College, being sweated down to vanishing point and fed on vegetable macedoine.'

Lucy, remembering the piles of bread wolfed by the students at every meal, thought this an overstatement.

'When I go back to Brazil I shall live like a lady and eat like a civilised person, and it will be time then to consider my calories.'

Lucy asked when she was going back.

'I am sailing on the last day of August. That will give me a little of the English summer to enjoy between the last day of College and my going away. I like the English summer. So green, and gentle, and kind. I like everything about the English except their clothes, their winter, and their teeth. Where is Arlinghurst?'

Lucy, who had forgotten Desterro's abrupt hopping from one subject to another, was too surprised by the name to answer immediately and Rick answered for her. 'It's the best girls' school in England,' he finished, having described the place. 'Why?'

'It is the College excitement at the moment. One of our students is going there straight from Leys. One would think she had at least been made a Dame, to listen to them.'

'A legitimate reason for excitement, it seems to me,' Rick observed. 'Not many people get professional plums straight out of college.'

'Yes? It really is an honour then, you think?'

'A very great one, I imagine. Isn't it, Miss Pym?'

'Very.'

'Oh, well. I am glad of it. It is sad to think of her wasting the years in a girls' school, but if it is an honour for her, then I am glad.'

'For whom?' Lucy asked.

'For Innes, of course.'

'Were you not at lunch today?' asked Lucy, puzzled.

'No. Rick came with the car and we went over to the Saracen's Head at Beauminster. Why? What has that to do with this school affair?'

'It isn't Innes who is going at Arlinghurst.'

'Not Innes! But they all said she was. Everyone said so.'

'Yes, that is what everyone expected, but it didn't turn out like that.'

'No? Who is going, then?'

'Rouse.'

Desterro stared.

'Oh, no. No, that I refuse to believe. It is quite simply not possible.'

'It is true, I am afraid.'

'You mean that—that someone—that they have preferred that *canaille*, that *espèce d'une*——!'

'Teresa!' warned Rick, amused to see her moved for once.

Desterro sat silent for a space, communing with herself.

'If I were not a lady,' she said at length in clear tones, 'I would *spit*!'

The family party looked over, surprised and faintly alarmed. They decided that it was time they were going, and began to collect their things and reckon up what they had had.

'Now look what you have done,' Rick said. 'Alarmed the lieges.'

At this moment the rarebits arrived from the kitchen, with Miss Nevill's large chintz presence behind them; but The Nut Tart, far from being distracted by the savoury food, remembered that it was from Miss Nevill that she had first had news of the Arlinghurst vacancy, and the subject took a fresh lease of life. It was Rick who rescued Lucy from the loathed subject by pointing out that the rarebit was rapidly cooling; Lucy had a strong feeling that he himself cared nothing for the rarebit, but that he had somehow become aware of her tiredness and her distaste for the affair; and she felt warm and grateful to him and on the point of tears.

'After all,' Rick pointed out as The Nut Tart at last turned her attention to her food, 'I don't know Miss Innes, but if she is as wonderful as you say she is bound to get a very good post, even if it isn't exactly Arlinghurst.'

This was the argument with which Lucy had sought to comfort herself all the long afternoon. It was reasonable, logical, and balanced; and as a sort of moral belladonna-plaster it was so much red flannel. Lucy understood why The Nut Tart rejected it with scorn.

'How would *you* like to have *that* preferred to you?' she demanded through a large mouthful of rarebit. 'That' was Rouse. 'How would you like to believe that they were going to pay you honour, a fine public honour, and then have them slap your face in front of everyone?'

'Having your teeth kicked in,' Beau had called it. Their reactions were remarkably similar. The only difference was that Desterro saw the insult, and Beau the injury.

'And we had such a lovely happy morning in this very room the other day with Innes's father and mother,' Desterro went on, her fine eyes wandering to the table where they had sat. This, too, Lucy had been remembering. 'Such nice people, Rick; I wish you could see them. We were all nice people together: me, and Miss Pym, and the Inneses *père et mère*, and we had an interval of civilisation and some good coffee. It was charming. And now——'

Between them, Lucy and Rick steered her away from the subject; and it was not until they were getting into the car to go back to Leys that she remembered and began to mourn again. But the distance between Bidlington and Leys as covered by Rick's car was so short that she had no time to work herself up before they were at the door. Lucy said good-night and was going to withdraw tactfully, but The Nut Tart came with her. 'Good-night, Rick,' she said, casually. 'You are coming on Friday, aren't you?'

'Nothing will stop me,' Rick assured her. 'Three o'clock, is it?'

'No, half-past two. It is written on your invitation card. The invitation I sent you. For a business person you are not very accurate.'

'Oh, well, my business things I naturally keep in files.'

'And where do you keep my invitation?'

'On a gold chain between my vest and my heart,' Rick said, and went the winner out of that exchange.

'Your cousin is charming,' Lucy said, as they went up the steps together.

'You think so? I am very glad. I think so too. He has all the English virtues, and a little spice of something that is not English virtue at all. I am glad that he is coming to see me dance on Friday. What makes you smile?'

Lucy, who had been smiling at this typically Desterro view of her cousin's presence on Friday, hastened to change the subject.

'Shouldn't you be going in by the other door?'

'Oh, yes, but I don't suppose anyone will mind. In a fortnight I shall be free to come up these steps if I like—I shall not like, incidentally—so I might as well use them now. I do not take well to tradesmen's entrances.'

Lucy had meant to pay her respects to the Staff before going to her room in the wing, but the hall was so quiet, the air of the house so withdrawn, that she was discouraged and took the line of least resistance. She would see them all in the morning.

The Nut Tart paid at least a token obedience to College rules, and it was apparent from the hush in the wing corridor that the 'bedroom' bell must have gone some minutes ago; so they said good-night at the top of the stairs, and Lucy went away to her room at the far end. As she undressed she found that her ear was waiting for a sound from next door. But there was no sound at all; nor was there any visible light from the window, as she noticed when she drew her own curtains. Had Innes not come back?

She sat for a while wondering whether she should do something about it. If Innes had not come back, Beau would be in need of comfort. And if Innes had come back and was silent, was there perhaps some impersonal piece of kindness, some small service, that she could do to express her sympathy without intrusion?

She switched off her light and drew back the curtains, and sat by the open window looking at the brightly lit squares all round the little quadrangle—it was considered an eccentricity to draw a curtain in this community—watching the separate activities of the now silent and individual students. One was brushing her hair, one sewing something, one putting a bandage on her foot (a Foolish Virgin that one: she was hopping about looking for a pair of scissors instead of having begun with the implement already laid out, like a good masseuse), one wriggling into a pyjama jacket, one swatting a moth.

Two lights went out as she watched. Tomorrow the waking bell would go at half-past five again, and now that examinations were over they need no longer stay awake till the last moment over their notebooks.

She heard footsteps come along her own corridor, and got up, thinking they were coming to her. Innes's door opened quietly, and shut. No light was switched on, but she heard the soft movements of someone getting ready for bed. Then bedroom slippers in the corridor, and a knock. No answer.

'It's me: Beau,' a voice said; and the door was opened. The murmur of voices as the door closed. The smell of coffee and the faint chink of china.

It was sensible of Beau to meet the situation with food. Whatever demons Innes had wrestled with during the long hours between one o'clock and ten she must now be empty of emotion and ready to eat what was put in front of her. The murmur of voices went on until the 'lights out' bell sounded; then the door opened and closed again, and the silence next-door merged into the greater silence that enveloped Leys.

Lucy fell into bed, too tired almost to pull up the covers;

angry with Henrietta, sad for Innes, and a little envious of her in that she had a friend like Beau.

She decided to stay awake a little and think of some way in which she could express to poor Innes how great was her own sympathy and how deep her own indignation; and fell instantly asleep.

14

MONDAY was an anticlimax. Lucy came back into a community that had talked itself out on the subject of Arlinghurst. Both Staff and students had had a whole day's leisure in which to spread themselves over the sensation, and by night-time there was nothing more to be said; indeed every possible view had already been repeated *ad nauseam*; so that with the resumption of routine on Monday the affair had already slipped into the background. Since she still had her breakfast brought to her by the devoted Miss Morris, she was not there to see Innes's first public appearance; and by the time she came face to face with the students as a body, at lunch, habit had smoothed over the rough places and College looked much as usual.

Innes's face was composed, but Lucy thought that its normal withdrawn expression had become a shut-down look; whatever emotions she still wrestled with, they were under hatches and battened down. Rouse looked more than ever like Aunt Celia's cat, Philadelphia, and Lucy longed to shut her out of doors and let her mew. The only curiosity she had had about the affair was to know how Rouse took that unexpected announcement; she had even gone the length of asking Miss Lux on the way down to lunch.

'What did Rouse look like when she heard the news?'

'Ectoplasm,' said Miss Lux.

'Why ectoplasm?' Lucy had asked, puzzled.

'It is the most revolting thing I can think of.'

So her curiosity remained unsatisfied. Madame twitted

her about her desertion of them yesterday, but no one wanted to harp on the probable reason for it. Already the shadow of the Demonstration, only four days away, loomed large over them all; Arlinghurst was a yesterday's sensation and already a little stale. College was once more into its stride.

Indeed only two small incidents livened the monotony of routine between Monday and Friday.

The first was Miss Hodge's offer to Innes of the post at the Wycherley Orthopaedic Hospital, and Innes's refusal of it. The post was then offered to and gratefully accepted by a much-relieved O'Donnell. ('*Darling*, how *nice*!' Dakers had said. 'Now I can sell you my clinic overalls which I shall *never* use again, my dear.' And sell them she did; and was so delighted to have good hard cash in her purse so near the end of term that she instantly began to hawk the rest of her belongings round the wing, and was only dissuaded when Stewart asked caustically if the safety-pins were standard equipment.)

The second incident was the arrival of Edward Adrian, thespian.

This unlooked-for occurrence took place on Wednesday. Wednesday was swimming afternoon, and all the Juniors and such Seniors as had no afternoon patients were down at the pool. Lucy, who by prayer, counting, and determination, could just get across the bath, took no part in this exercise in spite of warm invitations to come in and be cool. She spent half an hour watching the gambols, and then walked back to the house for tea. She was crossing the hall to the stairs when one of the Disciples—she thought it was Luke, but she was still not quite certain about them—dashed out of the clinic door and said:

'Oh, Miss Pym, would you be an angel and sit on Albert's feet for a moment?'

'Sit on Albert's feet?' repeated Lucy, not quite sure that she had heard aright.

'Yes, or hold them. But it's easier to sit on them. The hole in the strap has given way, and there isn't another that isn't in use.' She ushered the dazed Lucy into the quiet of the clinic, where students swathed in unfamiliar white linen superintended their patients' contortions, and indicated a plinth where a boy of eleven or so was lying face down. 'You see,' she said, holding up a leather strap, 'the thing has torn away from the hole, and the hole in front is too tight and the one behind too loose. If you would just hang on to his feet for a moment; if you wouldn't rather sit on them.'

Lucy said hastily that she would prefer to hang on.

'All right. This is Miss Pym, Albert. She is going to be the strap for the nonce.'

'Hullo, Miss Pym,' said Albert, rolling an eye round at her.

Luke—if it was she—seized the boy under the shoulders and yanked him forward till only his legs remained on the plinth. 'Now clamp a hand over each ankle and hang on, Miss Pym,' she commanded, and Lucy obeyed, thinking how well this breezy bluntness was going to suit Manchester and how extremely heavy a small boy of eleven was when you were trying to keep his ankles down. Her eyes strayed from what Luke was doing to the others, so strange and remote in this new guise. Was there no end to the facets of this odd life? Even the ones she knew well, like Stewart, were different, seen like this. Their movements were slower, and there was a special bright artificially-interested voice that they used to patients. There were no smiles and no chatter; just a bright hospital quiet. 'Just a *little* further. *That's* right.' 'That is looking much better today, isn't it!' 'Now, we'll try that once more and then that will be all for today.'

Through a gap in Hasselt's overall as she moved, Lucy caught a glimpse of silk, and realised that she was already changed for dancing, there being no interval between finishing her patient and appearing in the gym. Either she had already had tea, or would snatch a cup *en route*.

While she was thinking of the oddity of this life of dancing-silks under hospital clothes, a car passed the window and stopped at the front door. A very fashionable and expensive car of inordinate length and great glossiness, chauffeur-driven. It was so seldom nowadays that one saw anyone but an invalid driven by a chauffeur that she watched with interest to see who might emerge from it.

Beau's mother, perhaps? That was the kind of car that went with a butler, undoubtedly.

But what came out of the car was a youngish man—she could see only his back—in the kind of suit one sees anywhere between St James's Street and the Duke of York's Steps any time between October and the end of June. What with the chauffeur and the suit Lucy ran through in her mind the available Royalties, but could not find an appropriate one; Royalty drove itself nowadays, anyhow.

'Thank you very much, Miss Pym. You've been an enormous help. Say thank you, Albert.'

'Thank you, Miss Pym,' Albert said dutifully; and then, catching her eye, winked at her. Lucy winked back, gravely.

At this moment O'Donnell erupted into the room clutching the large sifter of talcum powder that she had been having refilled by Fröken in the farther room, and hissed in an excited whisper: 'What do you think! *Edward Adrian!* In the car. *Edward Adrian!*'

'Who cares?' Stewart said, relieving her of the sifter. 'You were a damned long time getting the talc.'

Lucy closed the clinic door behind her and emerged into the hall. O'Donnell had spoken truth. It was Edward Adrian who was standing in the hall. And Miss Lux had also spoken truth. For Edward Adrian was examining himself in the mirror.

As Lucy climbed the stairs she met Miss Lux coming down, and as she turned to the second flight could see their meeting.

'Hullo, Teddy,' Miss Lux said, without enthusiasm.

'Catherine!' Adrian said, with the most delighted enthusiasm, going forward to meet her as if about to embrace her. But her cool solitary hand, outstretched in conventional greeting, stopped him.

'What are you doing here? Don't tell me you have developed a "niece" at Leys.'

'Don't be a beast, Cath. I came to see you, of course. Why didn't you tell me you were here? Why didn't you come to see me, so that we could have had a meal together, and a talk about old——'

'Miss Pym,' Miss Lux's clear accents came floating up the staircase, 'don't run away. I want you to meet a friend of mine.'

'But Catherine——' she heard him say in quick low protest.

'It's the *famous* Miss Pym,' Miss Lux said, in a you'll-like-that-you-silly-creature tone, 'and a great admirer of yours,' she added as a final snare.

Does he realise how cruel she is being? she wondered as she waited for them to come up to her, or is his self-satisfaction too great to be pierced by her rating of him?

As they went together into the deserted drawing-room, she remembered suddenly Stewart's description of him as a 'weary-looking creature who looked like a moulting eagle' and thought how apt it was. He had good looks of a sort, but although he could not be much older than forty —forty-three or four, perhaps—they already had a preserved air. Without his paints and his pencils and his toupees, he looked tired and worn, and his dark hair was receding. Lucy felt suddenly sorry for him. With the youth and strength and beauty of Desterro's Rick fresh in her mind, she found the spoiled and famous actor somehow pitiful.

He was being charming to her—he knew all about her book; he read all the best-sellers—but with one eye on Miss Lux while she examined what was left of tea, inspected the contents of the tea-pot, and apparently deciding that a little more hot water would meet the case, lit the burner under the tea-kettle again. There was something in that consciousness of Catherine Lux's presence that puzzled Lucy. It wasn't in the part, as she had imagined the part for him. The successful star calling on the humble lecturer at a girls' college should surely show more detachment; more willingness to peacock in front of the stranger, after the manner of actors. He was 'doing his act' for her, of course; all his charm was turned full on, and it was a very considerable charm; but it was mere reflex action. All his interest was centred round the cool scraggy woman who rated him at some washy tea. It couldn't be very often, Lucy thought with amusement, that Edward Adrian arrived on any doorstep without trumpets; for nearly twenty years—ever since that first heart-breaking Romeo had brought tears to the eyes of critics sick of the very name of Montague—his comings and goings had been matters of moment. He had moved in a constant small eddy of importance; people ran to do his bidding and waited for his pleasure; they gave him things and asked nothing in return; they gave up things for him and expected no thanks. He was Edward Adrian, household word, two feet high on the bills, national possession.

But he had come out this afternoon to Leys to see Catherine Lux, and his eyes followed her round like an eager dog's. The Catherine whose estimate of him was a little hot water added to the tea-pot.

It was all very strange.

168

'I hope you are doing well in Larborough, Teddy?'
Lux asked with more politeness than interest.

'Oh, yes; fair. Too many schools, but one must put up
with that when one plays Shakespeare.'

'Don't you like playing to young people?' Lucy asked,
remembering that the young people she had met lately
had not greatly liked having to listen to him.

'Well—they don't make the best audience in the world,
you know. One would prefer adults. And they get cut
rates, of course; which doesn't help the takings. But we
look on it as an investment,' he added with generous
tolerance. 'They are the future theatre-goers, and must
be trained up in the way they should go.'

Lucy thought that the training, if judged by results,
had been singularly unsuccessful. The way the young
went was in a bee-line to something called *Flaming
Barriers*. It wasn't even true to say that they 'didn't go' to
the theatre; it was much more positive than that: they
fled from it.

However, this was a polite tea-party and no time for
home truths. Lucy asked if he was coming to the
Demonstration—at which Miss Lux looked annoyed. He
had never heard of a Demonstration and was all eagerness.
It was years since he had seen anyone do any more P.T.
than putting their toes under the wardrobe and waving
their torso about. Dancing? Goodness, was there dancing?
But of course he would come. And what was more, they
should come back with him to the theatre and have supper
with him afterwards.

'I know Catherine hates the theatre, but you could
stand it for once, couldn't you, Catherine? It's *Richard III*
on Friday night, so you wouldn't have to put up with me
in a romantic effort. It isn't a good play, but the production is wonderful, even if it is I who say it that shouldn't.'

'A criminal libel on a fine man, a blatant piece of political
propaganda, and an extremely silly play,' Lux opined.

169

Adrian smiled broadly, like a schoolboy. 'All right, but sit through it and you shall see how good a supper the Midland at Larborough can provide when egged on by a miserable actor. They even have a Johannisberger.'

A faint colour showed in Lux's cheek at that.

'You see I remember what you like. Johannisberger, as you once remarked, tastes of flowers, and will take the stink of the theatre out of your nostrils.'

'I never said it stank. It creaks.'

'Of course it does. It has been on its last legs for quite two hundred years.'

'Do you know what it reminds me of? The Coronation Coach. A lumbering anachronism; an absurd convention that we go on making use of because of inherited affection. A gilded relic——'

The kettle boiled, and Miss Lux poured the hot water into the pot.

'Give Miss Pym something to eat, Teddy.'

An almost nursery tone, Lucy thought, taking one of the curled-up sandwiches from the plate he offered her. Was that what attracted him? Was it a sort of nostalgia for a world where he was taken for granted? He would not like such a world for long, that was certain, but it was quite possible that he wearied sometimes of the goldfish life he led, and would find a refreshment in the company of someone to whom he was just Teddy Adrian who used to come in the holidays.

She turned to say something to him, and surprised the look in his eyes as he watched Catherine spurning the various eatables. The amusement, the affection, that lit them might be a brother's, but there was something else. A—hopelessness, was it? Something like that. Something, anyhow, that had nothing to do with brotherliness; and that was very odd in a Great Star looking at the plain and ironic Mistress of Theory at Leys.

She looked across at the unconscious Catherine, and for

the first time saw her as Edward Adrian saw her. As a woman with the makings of a *belle laide*. In this scholastic world one accepted her 'good' clothes, her simple hair-dressing, her lack of make-up, as the right and appropriate thing, and took her fine bones and lithe carriage for granted. She was just the plain and clever Miss Lux. But in the theatre world how different she would be! That wide supple mouth, those high cheek-bones with the hollow under them, the short straight nose, the good line of the lean jaw—they cried aloud for make-up. From the conventional point of view Lux had the kind of face that, as errand boys say, would 'stop a clock'; but from any other view-point it was a face that would stop them eating at the Iris if she walked in at lunch-time properly dressed and made-up.

A combination of *belle laide* and someone who knew him 'when' was no inconsiderable attraction. For the rest of tea-time Lucy's mind was busy with revision.

As soon as she decently could she retired, leaving them to the *tête-à-tête* that he had so obviously sought; the *tête-à-tête* that Miss Lux had done her best to deny him. He pleaded once more for a theatre party on Friday night —his car would be there and the Dem. would be over by six o'clock and College supper would be nothing but an anticlimax, and *Richard III* might be a lot of nonsense, but it *was* lovely to look at, he promised them, and the food at the Midland was really wonderful since they had lured the chef away from Bono in Dover Street, and it was a very long time since he had seen Catherine and he had not talked half enough to the clever Miss Pym who had written that wonderful book, and he was dead sick anyhow of the company of actors who talked nothing but theatre and golf, and just to please him they might come—and altogether what with his practised actor's charm and his genuine desire that they should say yes, it was agreed that on Friday night they should go back to Larborough with him, witness his production of *Richard III*, and be rewarded with a good supper and a lift home.

As she crossed to the wing, however, Lucy found herself a little depressed. Yet once more she had been wrong about Miss Lux. Miss Lux was not an unwanted plain woman who found compensation in life by devoting herself to a beautiful younger sister. She was a potentially attractive creature who so little needed compensation that she couldn't be bothered with one of the most successful and handsome men in the world today.

She had been all wrong about Miss Lux. As a psychologist she began to suspect she was a very good teacher of French.

15

THE only person who was moved by Edward Adrian's incursion into the College world was Madame Lefevre. Madame, as the representative of the theatre world in College, evidently felt that her own share in this visit should have been a larger one. She also gave Miss Lux to understand that she had, in the first place, no right to know Edward Adrian, but that, in the second place, having known him she had no right to keep him to herself. She was comforted by the knowledge that on Friday she would see him in person, and be able to talk to him in his own language, so to speak. He must have felt greatly at sea, she gave them to understand, among the aborigines of Leys Physical Training College.

Lucy, listening to her barbed silkinesses at lunch on Thursday, hoped that she would not ingratiate herself sufficiently with Adrian to be included in the supper party; she was looking forward to Friday night, and she most certainly would not look forward any more if Madame was going to be watching her all evening with those eyes of hers. Perhaps Miss Lux would put a spoke in her wheel in time. It was not Miss Lux's habit to put up with something that was not to her mind.

Still thinking of Madame and Miss Lux and tomorrow night, she turned her eyes absently on the students, and saw Innes's face. And her heart stopped.

It was three days, she supposed, since she had seen Innes for more than a moment in passing; but could three days have done this to a young girl's face? She stared, trying to decide where the change actually lay. Innes was thinner, and very pale, certainly, but it was not that. It was not even the shadows under her eyes and the small hollow at the temple. Not even the expression; she was eating her lunch with her eyes on the plate in apparent calm. And yet the face shocked Lucy. She wondered if the others saw; she wondered that no one had mentioned it. The thing was as subtle and as obvious as the expression on the face of the Mona Lisa; as indefinable and as impossible to ignore.

So that is what it is to 'burn up inside', she thought. 'It is bad to burn up inside', Beau had said. Verily it must be bad if it ravaged a face like that. How could a face be at the same time calm and—and look like that? How, if it came to that, could one have birds tearing at one's vitals and still keep that calm face?

Her glance went to Beau, at the head of the nearer table, and she caught Beau's anxious look at Innes.

'I hope you gave Mr Adrian an invitation card?' Miss Hodge said to Lux.

'No,' said Lux, bored with the subject of Adrian.

'And I hope you have told Miss Joliffe that there will be one more for tea.'

'He doesn't eat at tea-time, so I didn't bother.'

Oh, stop talking little sillinesses, Lucy wanted to say, and look at Innes. What is happening to her? Look at the girl who was so radiant only last Saturday afternoon. *Look* at her. What does she remind you of? Sitting there so cam and beautiful and all wrong inside. What does she remind you of? One of those brilliant things that grow in the woods, isn't it? One of those apparently perfect things that collapse into dust at a touch because they are hollow inside.

'Innes is not looking well,' she said in careful understatement to Lux as they went upstairs.

'She is looking very ill,' Lux said bluntly. 'And would you wonder?'

'Isn't there something one can do about it?' Lucy asked.

'One could find her the kind of post she deserves,' Lux said dryly. 'As there is no post available at all, that doesn't seem likely to materialise.'

'You mean that she will just have to begin to answer advertisements?'

'Yes. It is only a fortnight to the end of term, and there are not likely to be any more posts in Miss Hodge's gift now. Most places for September are filled by this time. The final irony, isn't it? That the most brilliant student we have had for years is reduced to application-in-own-handwriting - with - five - copies - of - testimonials - not - returnable.'

It was damnable, Lucy thought; quite damnable.

'She *was* offered a post, so that lets Miss Hodge out.'

'But it was a medical one, and she doesn't want that,' Lucy said.

'Oh, yes, yes; you don't have to convert me; I'm enlisted already.'

Lucy thought of tomorrow, when the parents would come and radiant daughters would show them round, full of the years they had spent here and the new achievement that was theirs. How Innes must have looked forward to that; looked forward to seeing the two people who loved her so well and who had by care and deprivation managed to give her the training she wanted; looked forward to putting Arlinghurst in their laps.

It was bad enough to be a leaving student without a post, but that was a matter susceptible to remedy. What could never be remedied was the injustice of it. It was Lucy's private opinion that injustice was harder to bear than almost any other inflicted ill. She could remember yet the surprised hurt, the helpless rage, the despair that used to consume her when she was young and the victim of an injustice. It was the helpless rage that was worst; it consumed one like a slow fire. There was no outlet, because there was nothing one could do about it. A very destructive emotion indeed. Lucy supposed that she had been like Innes, and lacked a sense of humour. But did the young ever have the detachment necessary for a proper focusing of their own griefs? Of course not. It was not people of forty who went upstairs and hanged themselves because someone had said a wrong word to them at the wrong moment; it was adolescents of fourteen.

Lucy thought she knew the passion of rage and disappointment and hate that was eating Innes up. It was enormously to her credit that she had taken the shock with outward dignity. A different type would have babbled to all and sundry, and collected sympathy like a street singer catching coins in a hat. But not Innes. A sense of humour she might lack—oil on her feathers, as Beau said—but the suffering that lack entailed was her own affair; not to be exhibited to anyone—least of all to people she unconsciously referred to as 'them'.

Lucy had failed to think of a nice non-committal way of expressing her sympathy; flowers and sweets and all the conventional marks of active friendship were not to be considered, and she had found no substitute; and she was disgusted with herself now to realise that Innes's trouble, even though it was next-door to her all night, had begun to fade into the background for her. She had remembered it each night as Innes came to her room after the 'bedroom' bell, and while the small noises next-door reminded her of the girl's existence. She had wondered and fretted about her for a little before falling to sleep. But during the crowded many-faceted days she had come near forgetting her.

Rouse had made no move to give a Post party on Saturday night; but whether this was due to tact, an awareness of College feeling on the subject, or the natural thrift with which, it seemed, she was credited, no one knew. The universal party that had been so triumphantly planned for Innes was no more heard of; a universal party for Rouse was something that was apparently not contemplated.

Altogether, even allowing for the fact that Lucy had not been present at the height of the excitement when presumably tongues would have wagged with greater freedom, College had been strangely reticent about the Arlinghurst appointment. Even little Miss Morris, who chattered with a fine lack of inhibition every morning as she planked the tray down, made no reference to it. In this affair Lucy was for College purposes 'Staff'; an outsider; perhaps a sharer in blame. She did not like the idea at all.

But what she liked least of all, and now could not get out of her mind, was Innes's barren tomorrow. The tomorrow that she had slaved those years for, the tomorrow that was to have been such a triumph. Lucy longed to provide her with a post at once, instantly, here and now; so that when tomorrow that tired happy woman with the luminous eyes came at last to see her daughter she would not find her empty-handed.

But of course one could not hawk a P.T.I. from door to door like a writing-pad; nor offer her to one's friends like a misfit frock. Goodwill was not enough. And goodwill was practically all she had.

Well, she would use the goodwill and see where it got her. She followed Miss Hodge into her office as the others went upstairs, and said: 'Henrietta, can't we *invent* a post for Miss Innes? It seems all wrong that she should be jobless.'

'Miss Innes will not be long jobless. And I can't imagine what consolation an imaginary post would be to her meanwhile.'

'I didn't say imagine, I said invent; manufacture. There must be dozens of places all up and down the country that are still vacant. Couldn't we bring the job and Innes together somehow without her going through the slow suspense of applying? That waiting, Henrietta. Do you remember what it used to be like? The beautifully written applications and the testimonials that never came back.'

'I have already offered Miss Innes a post and she has refused it. I don't know what more I can do. I have no more vacancies to offer.'

'No, but you could get in touch with some of those advertised vacancies on her behalf, couldn't you?'

'I? But that would be most irregular. And quite unnecessary. She naturally gives my name as a reference when she applies; and if she were not commendable——'

'But you could—oh, you could ask for particulars of the post since you have a particularly brilliant student——'

'You are being absurd, Lucy.'

'I know, but I want Innes to be very much sought-after by five o'clock this afternoon.'

Miss Hodge, who did not read Kipling—or indeed, acknowledge his existence—stared.

'For a woman who has written such a noteworthy book —Professor Beatock praised it yesterday at the University College tea—you have an extraordinarily impulsive and frivolous mind.'

This defeated Lucy, who was well aware of her mental limitations. Punctured, she stood looking at Henrietta's broad back in the window.

'I am greatly afraid,' Henrietta said, 'that the weather is going to break. The forecast this morning was anything but reassuring, and after so long a spell of perfect summer we are due for a change. It would be a tragedy if it decided to change tomorrow of all days.'

A tragedy, would it! My God, you big lumbering silly woman, it is you who has the frivolous mind. I may have a C3 intelligence and childish impulses, but I know tragedy when I see it and it has nothing to do with a lot

178

of people running to save their party frocks or the cucumber sandwiches getting wet. No, by God, it hasnt'.

'Yes, it would be a pity, Henrietta,' she said meekly, and went away upstairs.

She stood for a little at the landing window watching the thick black clouds massing on the horizon, and hoping evilly that tomorrow they would swamp Leys in one grand Niagara so that the whole place steamed with damp people drying like a laundry. But she noticed almost immediately the heinousness of this, and hastily revised her wish. Tomorrow was their great day, bless them; the day they had sweated for, borne bruises and sarcasm for, been pummelled, broken, and straightened for, hoped, wept, and lived for. It was plain justice that the sun should shine on them.

Besides, it was pretty certain that Mrs Innes had only one pair of 'best' shoes.

16

EACH successive day of her stay at Leys saw Lucy a little
more wide awake in the mornings. When the monstrous
clamour of the 5.30 bell had first hurled her into wakefulness, she had turned on her other side as soon as the noise
stopped and had fallen asleep again. But habit was beginning to have its way. Not only did she not fall asleep
again after the early waking, but for the last day or two
she had been sufficiently conscious to know in some
drowsy depths of her that the waking bell was about to
ring. On Demonstration morning she made history by
wakening before the reveille.

What woke her was a faint fluttering under the point of
her sternum: a feeling that she had not had since she was
a child. It was associated with prize-giving days at school.
Lucy had always had a prize of sorts. Never anything
spectacular, alas—2nd French, 3rd Drawing, 3rd Singing
—but she was definitely in the money. Occasionally, too,
there was a 'piece' to be played—the Rachmaninoff
Prelude, for one; not the DA, DA, DA one but the DA-
de-de-de; with terrific concentration on the de-de-de—
and consequently a new frock. Hence the tremor under
the breastbone. And today, all those years afterwards, she
had recaptured the sensation. For years any flutterings in
that region had been mere indigestion—if indigestion can
ever be mere. Now, because she was part of all the young
emotion round her, she shared the thrill and the anticipation.

She sat up and looked at the weather. It was blank and
grey, with a cool mist that might later lift on a blazing

day. She got up and went to the window. The silence was absolute. Nothing stirred in the still greyness but the College cat, picking its way in an annoyed fashion over the dew-wet stones, and shaking each foot in turn as protest against the discomfort. The grass was heavy with dew, and Lucy, who had always had a perverted affection for wet grass, regarded it with satisfaction.

The silence was ripped in two by the bell. The cat, as if suddenly reminded of urgent business, sprang into wild flight. Giddy crunched past on his way to the gymnasium; and presently the faint whine of his vacuum-cleaner could be heard, like some far-distant siren. Groans and yawns and inquiries as to the weather came from the little rooms all round the courtyard, but no one came to a window to look; getting up was an agony to be postponed to the last moment.

Lucy decided to dress and go out into the dew-grey morning, so cool and damp and beneficent. She would go and see how the buttercups looked without the sun on them. Wet gamboge, probably. She washed sketchily, dressed in the warmest things she had with her, and slinging a coat over her shoulders went out into the silent corridor and down the deserted stairs. She paused by the quadrangle door to read the notices on the students' board; cryptic, esoteric, and plain. 'Students are reminded that parents and visitors may be shown over the bedroom wings and the clinic, but not the front of the house.' 'Juniors are reminded that it is their duty to wait on the guests at tea and so help the domestic staff.' And, by itself, in capitals, the simple statement:

DIPLOMAS WILL BE PRESENTED ON
TUESDAY MORNING AT 9 O'CLOCK

As she moved on towards the covered way, Lucy visualised the diploma as an imposing roll of parchment tied up with ribbon, and then remembered that even in the matter of diplomas this place was a law unto itself. Their diploma was a badge to stick in their coat; a little enamel-and-silver affair that, pinned to the left breast of their working garment, would tell all and sundry where they had spent their student years and to what end.

Lucy came out into the covered way and dawdled along it to the gymnasium. Giddy had long since finished his cleaning operations—she had seen him from her window before she left her room contemplating his roses at the far side of the lawn—and it was apparent that Rouse had already performed her morning routine—the faint damp marks of her gym. shoes were visible on the concrete path —so the gymnasium was deserted. Lucy paused as she was about to turn along the path by its side wall, and stepped in at the wide-open door. Just as a race-course is more dramatic before the crowds blur it or an arena before its traffic writes scribbles over it, so the great waiting hall had a fascination for her. The emptiness, the quiet, the green sub-aqueous light, gave it a dignity and a mysteriousness that did not belong to its daytime personality. The single boom that Rouse used swam in the shadows, and the liquid light of the mirrors under the gallery wavered at the far end in vague repetition.

Lucy longed to shout a command so as to hear her voice in this empty space; or to climb a ribstall and see if she could do it without having heart-failure; but she contented herself with gazing. At her age gazing was enough; and it was a thing that she was good at.

Something winked on the floor half-way between her and the boom; something tiny and bright. A nail-head or something, she thought; and then remembered that there were no nail-heads in a gymnasium floor. She moved forward, idly curious, and picked the thing up. It was a small filigree rosette, flat, and made of silvery metal; and as she put it absently into her jersey pocket and turned

182

away to continue her walk, she smiled. If the quiver under her sternum this morning had reminded her of school days, that small metal circle brought back even more clearly the parties of her childhood. Almost before her conscious mind had recognised it for what it was she was back in the atmosphere of crackers and jellies and white silk frocks, and was wearing on her feet a pair of bronze leather pumps with elastic that criss-crossed over the ankle and a tiny silver filigree rosette on each toe. Going down the path to the field gate, she took it out again and smiled over it, remembering. She had quite forgotten those bronze pumps; there were black ones, too, but all the best people wore bronze ones. She wondered who in College possessed a pair. College wore ballet shoes for dancing, with or without blocked toes; and their gymnasium shoes were welted leather with an elastic instep. She had never seen anyone wear those pumps with the little ornament at the toe.

Perhaps Rouse used them for running down to the gymnasium in the mornings. It was certainly this morning the ornament had been dropped, since The Abhorrence under Giddy's direction was guaranteed to abstract from the gymnasium everything that was not nailed down.

She hung over the gate for a little, but it was chilly there and disappointing; the trees were invisible in the mist, the buttercups a mere rust on the grey meadow, and the may hedges looked like dirty snow. She did not want to go back to the house before breakfast, so she walked along to the tennis courts where the Juniors were mending nets— this was odd-job day for everyone, they said, this being the one day in the year when they conserved their energies against a greater demand to come—and with them she stayed, talking and lending a hand, until they went up to College for breakfast. When they marvelled at her early rising little Miss Morris had suggested that she was tired of cold toast in her room, but when she said frankly that she could not sleep for excitement they were gratified by so proper an emotion in an alien breast, and promised that the reality would beggar expectation. She had not seen anything yet, it seemed.

She changed her wet shoes, suffered the friendly gibes of the assembled Staff at her access of energy, and went down with them to breakfast.

It was when she turned to see how Innes was looking this morning that she became aware of a gap in the pattern of bright heads. She did not know the pattern well enough to know who was missing, but there was certainly an empty place at one of the tables. She wondered if Henrietta knew. Henrietta had cast the usual critical eye over the assembly as she sat down, but as the assembly was also at that moment in the act of sitting down the pattern was blurred and any gap not immediately visible.

Hastily, in case Henrietta did not in fact know about that gap, she withdrew her gaze without further investigation. It was none of her wish to call down retribution on the head of any student, however delinquent. Perhaps, of course, someone had just 'gone sick'; which would account for the lack of remark where their absence was concerned.

Miss Hodge, having wolfed her fish-cake, laid down her fork and swept the students with her small elephant eye. 'Miss Wragg,' she said, 'ask Miss Nash to speak to me.'

Nash got up from her place at the head of the nearest table and presented herself.

'Is it Miss Rouse who is missing from Miss Stewart's table?'

'Yes, Miss Hodge.'

'Why has she not come to breakfast?'

'I don't know, Miss Hodge.'

'Send one of the Juniors to her room to ask why she is not here.'

Yes, Miss Hodge.'

A stolid amiable Junior called Tuttle, who was always having to take the can back, was sent on the mission, and came back to say that Rouse was not in her room; which report Beau bore to the head table.

'Where was Miss Rouse when you saw her last?'

'I can't remember actually seeing her at all, Miss Hodge. We were all over the place this morning doing different things. It wasn't like sitting in class or being in the gym.'

'Does anyone,' said Henrietta addressing the students as a whole, 'know where Miss Rouse is?'

But no one did, apparently.

'Has anyone seen her this morning?'

But no one, now they came to think of it, had seen her.

Henrietta, who had put away two slices of toast while Tuttle was upstairs, said: 'Very well, Miss Nash,' and Beau went back to her breakfast. Henrietta rolled up her napkin and caught Fröken's eye, but Fröken was already rising from table, her face anxious.

'You and I will go to the gymnasium, Fröken,' Henrietta said, and they went out together, the rest of the Staff trailing after them, but not following them out to the gymnasium. It was only on the way upstairs to make her bed that it occurred to Lucy to think: 'I could have told them that she wasn't in the gymnasium. How silly of me not to think of it.' She tidied her room—a task that the students were expected to perform for themselves and which she thought it only fair that she likewise should do for herself—wondering all the time where Rouse could have disappeared to. And why. Could she suddenly have failed again this morning to do that simple boom exercise and been overtaken by a *crise des nerfs*? That was the only explanation that would fit the odd fact of any College student missing a meal; especially breakfast.

She crossed into the old house' and went down the front stairs and out into the garden. From the office came

Henrietta's voice talking rapidly to someone on the telephone, so she did not interrupt her. There was still more than half an hour before Prayers; she would spend it reading her mail in the garden, where the mist was rapidly lifting and a shimmer had come into the atmosphere that had been so dead a grey. She went to her favourite seat at the far edge of the garden overlooking the countryside, and it was not until nine o'clock that she came back. There was no doubt about the weather now: it was going to be a lovely day; Henrietta's 'tragedy' was not going to happen.

As she came round the corner of the house an ambulance drove away from the front door down the avenue. She looked at it, puzzled; but decided that in a place like this an ambulance was not the thing of dread that it was to the ordinary civilian. Something to do with the clinic, probably.

In the drawing-room, instead of the full Staff muster demanded by two minutes to nine o'clock, there was only Miss Lux.

'Has Rouse turned up?' Lucy asked.

'Yes.'

'Where was she?'

'In the gymnasium, with a fractured skull.'

Even in that moment of shock Lucy thought how typical of Lux that succinct sentence was. 'But *how*? What happened?'

'The pin that holds up the boom wasn't properly in. When she jumped up to it it came down on her head.'

'Good heavens!' Lucy could feel that inert log crash down on her own skull; she had always hated the boom.

'Fröken has just gone away with her in the ambulance to West Larborough.'

'That was smart work.'

'Yes. West Larborough is not far, and luckily at this hour of the morning the ambulance hadn't gone out, and once it was on the way here there was no traffic to hold it up.'

'What dreadful luck for everyone. On Demonstration Day.'

'Yes. We tried to keep it from the students, but that was hopeless, of course. So all we can do is to minimise it.'

'How bad is it, do you think?'

'No one knows. Miss Hodge has wired to her people.'

'Weren't they coming to the Dem.?'

'Apparently not. She has no parents; just an aunt and uncle who brought her up. Come to think of it,' she added after a moment's silence, 'that is what she looked like: a stray.' She did not seem to notice that she had used the past tense.

'I suppose it was Rouse's own fault?' Lucy asked.

'Or the student who helped her put up the thing last night.'

'Who was that?'

'O'Donnell, it seems. Miss Hodge has sent for her to ask her about it.'

At that moment Henrietta herself came in, and all the vague resentments that Lucy had been nursing against her friend in the last few days melted at sight of Henrietta's face. She looked ten years older, and in some odd fashion at least a stone less heavy.

'They have a telephone, it seems,' she said, continuing the subject that was the only one in her mind, 'so I shall be able to talk to them perhaps before the telegram reaches them. They are getting the trunk call for me now. They should be here before night. I want to be available for the telephone call, so will you take prayers, Miss Lux. Fröken will not be back in time.' Fröken was, as Senior Gymnast, second in rank to Miss Hodge. 'Miss Wragg may not be at prayers; she is getting the gymnasium put to rights. But Madame will be there, and Lucy will back you up.'

'But of course,' said Lucy. 'I wish there was something more that I could do.'

There was a tap at the door, and O'Donnell appeared.

'Miss Hodge? You wanted to see me?'

'Oh, in my office, Miss O'Donnell.'

'You weren't there, so I——'

'Not that it matters, now that you are here. Tell me: when you put up the boom with Miss Rouse last night— It *was* you who helped her?'

'Yes, Miss Hodge.'

'When you put up the boom with her, which end did you take?'

There was a tense moment of silence. It was obvious that O'Donnell did not know which end of the boom had given way and that what she said in the next few seconds would either damn her or save her. But when she spoke it was with a sort of despairing resolution that stamped what she said with truth.

'The wall end, Miss Hodge.'

'You put the pin into the upright that is fixed to the wall?'

'Yes.'

'And Miss Rouse took care of the upright in the middle of the floor.'

'Yes, Miss Hodge.'

'You have no doubt as to which end you attended to?'

'No, none at all.'

'Why are you so certain?'

'Because I always did do the end by the wall.'

'Why was that?'

'Rouse is taller than I am and could shove the boom higher than I could. So I always took the end by the wall so that I could put a foot in the ribstalls when I was putting the pin in.'

'I see. Very well. Thank you, Miss O'Donnell, for being so frank.'

O'Donnell turned to go, and then turned back.

'Which end came down, Miss Hodge?'

'The middle end,' Miss Hodge said, looking with something like affection on the girl, though she had been on the point of letting her go without putting her out of suspense.

A great wave of colour rushed into O'Donnell's normally pale face. 'Oh, thank you!' she said, in a whisper, and almost ran out of the room.

'Poor wretch,' said Lux. 'That was a horrible moment for her.'

'It is most unlike Miss Rouse to be careless about apparatus,' Henrietta said thoughtfully.

'You are not suggesting that O'Donnell is not telling the truth?'

'No, no. What she said was obviously true. It was the natural thing for her to take the wall end where she would have the help of the ribstalls. But I still cannot see how it happened. Apart from Miss Rouse's natural carefulness, a pin would have to be very badly put in indeed for it to be so far *not* in that it let the boom come down. And the hoisting rope so slack that it let the boom fall nearly three feet!'

'I suppose Giddy couldn't have done something to it accidentally?'

'I don't know what he could have done to it. You can't alter a pin put in at that height without stretching up deliberately to it. It is not as if it were something he might possibly touch with his apparatus. And much as he prides himself on the strength of The Abhorrence there is no suction that will pull a pin out from under a boom.'

'No.' Lux thought a little. 'Vibration is the only kind of force that would alter a pin's position. Some kind of tremor. And there was nothing like that.'

'Not inside the gymnasium, certainly. Miss Rouse

189

locked it as usual last night and gave the key to Giddy, and he unlocked it just after first bell this morning.'

'Then there is no alternative to the theory that for once Rouse was too casual. She was the last to leave the place and the first to come back to it—you wouldn't get anyone there at that hour of the morning who wasn't under the direst compulsion—so the blame is Rouse's. And let us be thankful for it. It is bad enough as it is, but it would be far worse if someone else had been careless and had to bear the knowledge that she was responsible for——'

The bell rang for Prayers, and downstairs the telephone shrilled in its own hysterical manner.

'Have you marked the place in the prayer book?' Lux asked.

'Where the blue ribbon is,' Miss Hodge said, and hurried out to the telephone.

'Has Fröken not come back?' asked Madame, appearing in the doorway. 'Ah, well, let us proceed. Life must go on, if I may coin a phrase. And let us hope that this morning's ration of uplift is not too apposite. Holy Writ has a horrible habit of being apposite.'

Not for the first time, Lucy wished Madame Lefevre on a lonely island off Australia.

It was a silent and subdued gathering that awaited them, and prayers proceeded in an atmosphere of despondency that was foreign and unprecedented. But with the hymn they recovered a little. It was Blake's and had a fine martial swing, and they sang it with a will. So did Lucy.

'Nor shall the sword sleep in my hand,' she sang, making the most of it. And stopped suddenly, hit in the wind.

Hit in the wind by a jolt that left her speechless.

She had just remembered something. She had just remembered why she had been so sure that Rouse would not be found in the gymnasium. Rouse's damp footprints had been visible on the concrete path, and so she had taken it for granted that Rouse had already been and gone. But Rouse had not been. Rouse had come later, and had sprung to the insecure boom and had lain there until after breakfast when she was searched for.

Then—whose footprints were they?

17

'STUDENTS,' said Miss Hodge, rising in her place after lunch and motioning the rest of the Staff to remain seated, 'You are all aware of the unfortunate accident which occurred this morning—entirely through the carelessness of the student concerned. The first thing a gymnast learns is to examine apparatus before she uses it. That a student as responsible and altogether admirable as Miss Rouse should have failed in so simple and fundamental a duty is a warning to you all. That is one point. This is the other. This afternoon we are entertaining guests. There is no secret about what happened this morning—we could not keep it secret even if we wanted to —but I do ask you not to make it a subject of conversation. Our guests are coming here to enjoy themselves; and to know that this morning an accident took place sufficiently serious to send one of our students to hospital would undoubtedly take the edge off their pleasure; if indeed it did not fill them with a quite unnecessary apprehension when watching gymnastics. So if any of you have a desire to dramatise today's happening, please curb it. It is your business to see that your guests go away happy, without reservations or regrets. I leave the matter to your own good sense.'

It had been a morning of adjustment; physical, mental, and spiritual. Fröken had come back from the West Larborough hospital to put a worried lot of Seniors through a routine that would allow for the fact that they were one short. Under her robust calm they took the alterations, and necessity for them, with a fair degree of equanimity; although she reported that at least a third of them shied like nervous colts each time they handled the right-hand front boom, or passed the place where it had fallen. It was going to be a miracle, Fröken said with resignation, if they got through this afternoon's performance without someone or other making a fool of themselves. As soon as Fröken had released them Madame Lefevre took them over for a much lengthier session. Thanks to her physical prowess, Rouse had been part of almost every item on the ballet programme; which meant that almost every item had to undergo either patching or reconstruction. This thankless and wearisome business had lasted until nearly lunch-time, and the echoes of it were still audible. Most of the lunch-table conversation appeared to consist of remarks like: 'Is it you I give my right hand to when Stewart passes in front of me?' and Dakers lightened the universal anxiety by being overtaken by one of those sudden silences common to all gatherings, which left her announcing loudly that my *dears*, the last hour had *proved* that one could be in two places at the same time.

The most fundamental adjustment, however, occurred when both Fröken and Madame had finished their respective revisions. It was then that Miss Hodge had sent for Innes and offered her Rouse's place at Arlinghurst. Hospital had confirmed Fröken's diagnosis of a fracture, and there was no chance that Rouse would be fit for work until many months had passed. How Innes had taken this no one knew; all that anyone knew was that she had accepted. The appointment, having all the qualities of anticlimax and being overshadowed by an authentic sensation, was taken as a matter of course; and as far as Lucy could see neither Staff nor students gave it a thought. Madame's sardonic: 'The Deity disposes,' was the solitary comment.

But Lucy was less happy about it. A vague uneasy stirring plagued her like some mental indigestion. The patness of the thing worried her. The accident had happened not only opportunely, but at the last available moment. Tomorrow there would have been no need for Rouse to go to the gymnasium and practise; there would have been no boom set up and no pin to be insecurely placed. And there were those damp foot-marks in the early morning. If they were not Rouse's own, whose were they? As Lux had very truly observed, no one could be dragged anywhere near the gymnasium at that hour by anything less compelling than wild horses.

It was possible that they were Rouse's prints and that she had done something else before going into the gymnasium for her few minutes on the boom. Lucy could not swear that the footprints actually went into the building; she could remember no actual print on either of the two steps. She had merely seen the damp marks on the covered way and concluded, without thinking about it at all, that Rouse was ahead of her. The prints may have continued round the building, for all she knew. They may have had nothing to do with the gymnasium at all. Nothing to do with the students, even. It was possible that those heelless impressions, so vague and blurred, were made by a maid-servant's early-morning shoes.

All that was possible. But allied to the steps that were not likely to be Rouse's was the oddity of a small metal ornament lying on a floor that had been swept twenty minutes before by a powerful vacuum-cleaner. An ornament lying directly between the door and the waiting boom. And whatever was conjecture, one thing was certain: the ornament was not lost by Rouse. Not only had she almost certainly not been in the gymnasium this morning before Lucy entered it, but she did not possess a pair of pumps. Lucy knew, because one of her helpful chores today had been to pack poor Rouse's things. Miss Joliffe, whose task it would nominally have been, was overwhelmed by preparations for the afternoon's entertainment, and had passed the duty on to Wragg. Wragg had no student to enlist as substitute, since they were all busy with Madame, and it was not a duty that could be entrusted to a Junior. So Lucy had willingly taken over the job, glad to find a way to be of use. And her first action in Number Fourteen had been to take Rouse's shoes out of the cupboard and look at them.

The only pair that were not there were her gymnastic shoes, which presumably had been what she wore this morning. But to be sure she summoned O'Donnell when she heard the Seniors come back from the gymnasium and said: 'You know Miss Rouse very well, don't you? Would you cast your eye over these shoes and tell me whether they are all she had, before I begin packing them.'

O'Donnell considered, and said yes, these were all. 'Except her gym. shoes,' she added. 'She was wearing those.'

That seemed to settle it.

'Nothing away being cleaned?'

'No, we clean our own—except for our hockey boots in winter.'

Well, that seemed to be that. What Rouse had worn this morning were regulation College gym. shoes. It was not off any shoes of Rouse's that the little filigree rosette had come.

Then from where? Lucy asked herself as she packed Rouse's belongings with a care she never accorded her own. From where?

She was still asking herself that as she changed her dress for the party. She put the rosette into one of the small drawers of the dressing-table-desk affair, and dully looked over her scanty collection of clothes for something that would be suitable to a garden-party afternoon. From her second window, the one looking out on the garden, she could see the Juniors busy with small tables and basket-chairs and tea-umbrellas. Their ant-like running about was producing a gay border of colour round three sides of the lawn. The sun streamed down on them, and the picture in its definition and variety of detail was like a Brueghel gone suddenly gay.

But Lucy, looking down at the picture and remembering how she had looked forward to this occasion, felt sick at heart; and could not bring herself yet to acknowledge why she should be heartsick. Only one thing was clear to her. Tonight she must go to Henrietta with the little rosette. When all the excitement was over and Henrietta had time to be quiet and consider, then the problem—if there was a problem—must be handed over to her. She, Lucy, had been wrong last time when she had tried to save Henrietta suffering by dropping the little red book into the water; this time she must do her duty. The rosette was no concern of hers.

No. It was no concern of hers. Certainly not.

She decided that the blue linen with the narrow red belt was sufficiently Hanover Square to satisfy the most critical of parents from the provinces, brushed the suède shoes with the brush so dutifully included by Mrs Montmorency, and went down to help wherever she could be useful.

By two o'clock the first guests were arriving; going into the office to pay their respects to Miss Hodge, and then being claimed by excited offspring. Fathers prodded doubtfully at odd gadgets in the clinic, mothers prodded the beds in the wing, and horticultural uncles prodded Giddy's roses in the garden. She tried to find distraction in 'pairing' the parents she met with the appropriate student. She noticed that she was searching unconsciously for Mr and Mrs Innes and anticipating their meeting with something that was half dread. Why dread? she asked herself. There was nothing in the world to dread, was there? Certainly not. Everything was lovely. Innes had after all got Arlinghurst; the day was after all a triumph for her.

She came on them unexpectedly, round the corner of the sweet-pea hedge; Innes walking between them with her arms through theirs and a light on her face. It was not the radiance that had shone in her eyes a week ago, but it was a good enough substitute. She looked worn but at peace; as if some inner battle was over, the issue settled for good or bad.

'You knew them,' she said to Miss Pym, indicating her parents, 'and you never told me.'

It was like meeting old friends, Lucy thought. It was unbelievable that her only traffic with these people had been across a coffee-table for an hour on a summer morning. She seemed to have known them all her life. And she felt that they in their turn felt like that about her. They really were glad to see her again. They remembered things and asked about them, referred to things she had said, and generally behaved as if she not only was of importance in their scheme of things, but was actually part of that scheme. And Lucy, used to the gushing indifference of literary parties, felt her heart warm afresh to them.

Innes left them together and went away to get ready for the gymnastic display that would open the afternoon's programme, and Lucy walked over to the gymnasium with them.

'Mary is looking very ill,' her mother said. 'Is there anything wrong?'

Lucy hesitated, wondering how much Innes had told them.

'She has told us about the accident, and about falling

197

heir to Arlinghurst. I don't suppose she is very happy at profiting by another student's bad luck, but it can't be just that.'

Lucy thought that the more they understood about the affair the better it would be if—well, the better it would be anyhow.

'Everyone took it for granted that she would get the appointment in the first place. I think it was a shock to her when she didn't.'

'I see. Yes,' said Mrs Innes, slowly; and Lucy felt that more explanation was not necessary; the whole tale of Innes's suffering and fortitude was clear to her mother in that moment.

'I think she might not approve of my having told you that, so——'

'No, we will not mention it,' said Innes's mother. 'How lovely the garden is looking. Gervase and I struggle along with our patch, but only his bits look like the illustration; mine always turn out to be something else. Just look at those little yellow roses.'

And so they came to the gymnasium door, and Lucy showed them up the stairs and introduced them to The Abhorrence—with pricking thoughts of a little metal rosette—and they found their seats in the gallery, and the afternoon had begun.

Lucy had a seat at the end of the front row. From there she looked down with affection on the grave young faces waiting, with such tense resolution, Fröken's word of command. 'Don't worry,' she had heard a Senior say, 'Fröken will see us through,' and one could see the faith in their eyes. This was their ordeal, and they came to it shaken, but Fröken would see them through.

She understood now the love that had filled Henrietta's eyes when she had watched with her on that other occasion. Less than a fortnight ago, that was, and already she had a proprietorial interest and pride in them. When the autumn came the very map of England would look different to her because of these two weeks at Leys. Manchester would be the place where the Disciples were, Aberystwyth the place where Thomas was trying to stay awake, Ling the place where Dakers was being good with the babies, and so on. If she felt like that about them after a matter of days, it was not much wonder that Henrietta, who had seen them come untried into their new life, who had watched them grow and improve, struggle, fail, and succeed—not much wonder that she looked on them as daughters. Successful daughters.

They had got through their preliminaries, and a little of the strain had gone from their faces; they were beginning to settle down. The applause that marked the end of their free-standing work broke the silence and warmed them and made the affair more human.

'What a charming collection,' said a dowager with lorgnettes who was sitting next her (now who owned that? she couldn't be a parent) and turning to her confidentially asked: 'Tell me, are they hand-picked?'

'I don't understand,' murmured Lucy.

'I mean, are these all the Seniors there are?'

'You mean, are these just the best? Oh, no; that is the whole set.'

'Really? Quite wonderful. So attractive, too. Quite amazingly attractive.'

Did she think we had given the spotty ones half a crown to take themselves off for the afternoon? wondered Lucy.

But of course the dowager was right. Except for a string of two-year-olds in training, Lucy could think of nothing more attractive to mind and eye than that set of burnished and controlled young creatures busy dragging out the booms below her. The ropes rushed down from their looped position near the roof, the window-ladder came to vertical, and over all three pieces of apparatus the Seniors swarmed in easy mastery. The applause as they put ropes and ladder away and turned the booms for balance was real and loud; the spectacular had its appeal.

Very different the place looked from that mysterious vault of greenish shadows that she had visited this morning. It was golden, and matter-of-fact, and alive; the reflected light from the sunlit roof showering down on the pale wood and making it glow. Seeing once more in her mind's eye that dim empty space with the single waiting boom, she turned to see whose lot it might be to perform her balance on the spot where Rouse had been found. Who had the inner end of the right-hand front boom?

It was Innes.

'Go!' said Fröken; and eight young bodies somersaulted up on to the high booms. They sat there for a moment, and then rose in unison to a standing position, one foot in front of the other, facing each other in pairs at opposite ends of each boom.

Lucy hoped frantically that Innes was not going to faint. She was not merely pale; she was green. Her opposite number, Stewart, made a tentative beginning, but, seeing that Innes was not ready, waited for her. But Innes stood motionless, apparently unable to move a muscle. Stewart cast her a glance of wild appeal. Innes remained paralysed. Some wordless message passed between them, and Stewart went on with her exercise; achieving a perfection very commendable in the circumstances. All Innes's faculties were concentrated on keeping her standing position on the boom long enough to be able to return to the floor with the rest, and not to ruin the whole exercise by collapsing, or by jumping off. The dead silence and the concentration of interest made her failure painfully obvious; and a puzzled sympathy settled on her as she stood there. Poor dear, they thought, she was feeling ill. Excitement, no doubt. Positively green, she was. Poor dear, poor dear.

Stewart had finished, and now waited, looking at Innes. Slowly they sank together to the boom, and sat down on it; turned together to lean face-forward on it; and somersaulted forward on to the ground.

And a great burst of applause greeted them. As always, the English were moved by a gallant failure where an easy success left them merely polite. They were expressing at once their sympathy and their admiration. They had understood the strength of purpose that had kept her on the boom, paralysed as she was.

But the sympathy had not touched Innes. Lucy doubted if she actually heard the applause. She was living in some tortured world of her own, far beyond the reach of human consolation. Lucy could hardly bear to look at her.

The bustle of the following items covered up her failure and put an end to drama. Innes took her place with the others and performed with mechanical perfection. When the final vaulting came, indeed, her performance was so remarkable that Lucy wondered if she were trying to break her neck publicly. The same idea, to judge by her expression, had crossed Fröken's mind; but as long as what Innes did was controlled and perfect there was nothing she could do. And everything that Innes did, however breath-taking, was perfect and controlled. Because she seemed not to care, the wildest flights were possible to her. And when the students had finished their final go-as-you-please and stood breathless and beaming, a single file on an empty floor as they had begun, their guests stood up as one man and cheered.

Lucy, being at the end of the row and next the door, was first to leave the hall, and so was in time to see Innes's apology to Fröken.

Fröken paused, and then moved on as if not interested, or not willing to listen.

But as she went she lifted a casual arm and gave Innes a light friendly pat on the shoulder.

18

As the guests moved out to the garden and the basket-chairs round the lawn, Lucy went with them, and while she was waiting to see if sufficient chairs had been provided before taking one for herself, she was seized upon by Beau, who said: 'Miss Pym! There you are! I've been hunting for you. I want you to meet my people.'

She turned to a couple who were just sitting down and said: 'Look, I've found Miss Pym at last.'

Beau's mother was a very lovely woman; as lovely as the best beauty parlours and the most expensive hair-dressers could make her—and they had good foundation to work on since when Mrs Nash was twenty she must have looked very like Beau. Even now, in the bright sunlight, she looked no older than thirty-five. She had a good dressmaker too, and bore herself with the easy friendly confidence of a woman who has been a beauty all her life; so used to the effect she had on people that she did not have to consider it at all and so her mind was free to devote itself to the person she happened to be meeting.

Mr Nash was obviously what is called an executive. A fine clear skin, a good tailor, a well-soaped look, and a general aura of mahogany tables with rows of clean blotters round them.

'I should be changing. I must fly,' said Beau, and disappeared.

As they sat down together Mrs Nash looked quizzically at Lucy and said: 'Well, now that you are here in the flesh, Miss Pym, we can ask you something we are dying to know. We want to know *how you do it?*'

'Do what?'

'Impress Pamela.'

'Yes,' said Mr Nash, 'that is just what we should like to know. All our lives we have been trying to make some impression on Pamela, but we remain just a couple of dear people who happen to be responsible for her existence and have to be humoured now and then.'

'Now *you*, it seems, are quite literally something to write home about,' Mrs Nash said, and raised an eyebrow and laughed.

'If it is any consolation to you,' Lucy offered, 'I am greatly impressed by your daughter.'

'Pam *is* nice,' her mother said. 'We love her very much; but I wish we impressed her more. Until you turned up no one has made any impression on Pamela since a Nanny she had at the age of four.'

'And that impression was a physical one,' Mr Nash volunteered.

'Yes. The only time in her life that she was spanked.'

'What happened?' Lucy asked.

'We had to get rid of the Nanny!'

'Didn't you approve of spanking?'

'Oh yes, but Pamela didn't.'

'Pam engineered the first sit-down strike in history,' Mr Nash said.

'She kept it up for seven days,' Mrs Nash said. 'Short of going on dressing and forcibly feeding her for the rest of her life, there was nothing to do but get rid of Nanny. A first-rate woman she was, too. We were devastated to lose her.'

The music began, and in front of the high screen of the rhododendron thicket appeared the bright colours of the Junior's Swedish folk dresses. Folk-dancing had begun. Lucy sat back and thought, not of Beau's childish aberrations, but of Innes, and the way a black cloud of doubt and foreboding was making a mockery of the bright sunlight.

It was because her mind was so full of Innes that she was startled when she heard Mrs Nash say: 'Mary, darling. There you are. How nice to see you again,' and turned to see Innes behind them. She was wearing boy's things; the doublet and hose of the fifteenth century; and the hood that hid all her hair and fitted close round her face accentuated the bony structure that was so individual. Now that the eyes were shadowed and sunk a little in their always-deep sockets, the face had something it had not had before: a forbidding look. It was—what was the word?—a 'fatal' face. Lucy remembered her very first impression that it was round faces like that that history was built.

'You have been overworking, Mary,' Mr Nash said, eyeing her.

'They all have,' Lucy said, to take their attention from her.

'Not Pamela,' her mother said. 'Pam has never worked hard in her life.'

No. Everything had been served to Beau on a plate. It was miraculous that she had turned out so charming.

'Did you see me make a fool of myself on the boom?' Innes asked, in a pleasant conversational tone. This surprised Lucy, somehow; she had expected Innes to avoid the subject.

'My dear, we sweated for you,' Mrs Nash said. 'What happened? Did you turn dizzy?'

'No,' said Beau, coming up behind them and slipping an arm into Innes's, 'that is just Innes's way of stealing publicity. It is not inferior physical powers, but superior brains the girl has. None of us has the wit to think up a stunt like that.'

Beau gave the arm she was holding a small reassuring squeeze. She too was in boy's clothes, and looked radiant; even the quenching of her bright hair had not diminished the glow and vivacity of her beauty.

'That is the last of the Junior's efforts—don't they look gay against that green background?—and now Innes and I and the rest of our put-upon set will entertain you with some English antics, and then you shall have tea to sustain you against the real dancing to come.'

And they went away together.

'Ah, well,' said Mrs Nash, watching her daughter go, 'I suppose it is better than being seized with a desire to reform natives in Darkest Africa or something. But I wish she would have just stayed at home and been one's daughter.'

Lucy thought that it was to Mrs Nash's credit that, looking as young as she did, she wanted a daughter at home.

'Pam was always mad on gym. and games,' Mr Nash said. 'There was no holding her. There never was any holding her, come to that.'

'Miss Pym,' said The Nut Tart, appearing at Lucy's elbow, 'do you mind if Rick sits with you while I go through this rigmarole with the Seniors?' She indicated Gillespie, who was standing behind her clutching a chair, and wearing his habitual expression of grave amusement.

The wide flat hat planked slightly to the back of her head on top of her wimple—Wife of Bath fashion—gave her an air of innocent astonishment that was delightful. Lucy and Rick exchanged a glance of mutual appreciation, and he smiled at her as he sat down on her other side.

'Isn't she lovely in that get-up,' he said, watching Desterro disappear behind the rhododendrons.

'I take it that a rigmarole doesn't count as dancing.'

'Is she good?'

'I don't know. I have never seen her, but I understand she is.'

'I've never even danced ballroom stuff with her. Odd, isn't it. I didn't even know she existed until last Easter. It maddens me to think she has been a whole year in

England and I didn't know about it. Three months of odd moments isn't very long to make any effect on a person like Teresa.'

'Do you want to make an effect?'

'Yes.' The monosyllable was sufficient.

The Seniors, in the guise of the English Middle Ages, ran out on to the lawn, and conversation lapsed. Lucy tried to find distraction in identifying legs and in marvelling over the energy with which those legs ran about after an hour of strenuous exercise. She said to herself: 'Look, you have to go to Henrietta with the little rosette tonight. All right. That is settled. There is nothing you can do, either about the going or the result of the going. So put it out of your mind. This is the afternoon you have been looking forward to. It is a lovely sunny day, and everyone is pleased to see you, and you should be having a grand time. So relax. Even if—if anything awful happens about the rosette, it has nothing to do with you. A fortnight ago you didn't know any of these people, and after you go away you will never see any of them again. It can't matter to you what happens or does not happen to them.'

All of which excellent advice left her just where she was before. When she saw Miss Joliffe and the maids busy about the tea-table in the rear she was glad to get up and find some use for her hands and some occupation for her mind.

Rick, unexpectedly, came with her. 'I'm a push-over for passing plates. It must be the gigolo in me.'

Lucy said that he ought to be watching his lady-love's rigmaroles.

'It is the last dance. And if I know anything of my Teresa, her appetite will take more appeasing than her vanity, considerable as it is.'

He seemed to know his Teresa very well, Lucy thought.

'Are you worried about something, Miss Pym?'

The question took her by surprise.

'Why should you think that?'

'I don't know. I just got the impression. Is there anything I can do?'

Lucy remembered how on Sunday evening when she had nearly cried into the Bidlington rarebit he had known about her tiredness and tacitly helped her. She wished that she had met someone as understanding and as young and as beautiful as The Nut Tart's follower when she was twenty, instead of Alan and his Adam's apple and his holey socks.

'I have to do something that is right,' she said slowly, 'and I'm afraid of the consequences.'

'Consequences to you?'

'No. To other people.'

'Never mind; do it.'

Miss Pym put plates of cakes on a tray. 'You see, the proper thing is not necessarily the right thing. Or do I mean the opposite?'

'I'm not sure that I know what you mean at all.'

'Well—there are those awful dilemmas about whom would you save. You know. If you knew that by saving a person from the top of a snow slide you would start an avalanche that would destroy a village, would you do it? That sort of thing.'

'Of course I would do it.'

'You would?'

'The avalanche might bury a village without killing a cat—shall I put some sandwiches on that tray?—so you would be one life to the good.'

'You would always do the right thing, and let the consequences take care of themselves?'

'That's about it.'

'It is certainly the simplest. In fact I think it's too simple.'

'Unless you plan to play God, one has to take the simple way.'

'Play God? You've got two lots of tongue sandwiches there, do you know?'

'Unless you are clever enough to "see before and after" like the Deity, it's best to stick to the rules. Wow! The music has stopped and here comes my young woman like a hunting leopard.' He watched Desterro come with a smile in his eyes. 'Isn't that hat a knock-out!' He looked down at Lucy for a moment. 'Do the obvious right thing, Miss Pym, and let God dispose.'

'Weren't you watching, Rick?' she heard Desterro ask, and then she and Rick and The Nut Tart were overwhelmed by a wave of Juniors come to do their duty and serve tea. Lucy extricated herself from the crush of white caps and Swedish embroidery, and found herself face to face with Edward Adrian, alone and looking forlorn.

'Miss Pym! You are just the person I wanted to see. Have you heard that——'

A Junior thrust a cup of tea into his hand, and he gave her one of his best smiles which she did not wait to see. At the same moment little Miss Morris, faithful even in the throes of a Dem., came up with tea and a tray of cakes for Lucy.

'Let us sit down, shall we?' Lucy said.

'Have you heard of the frightful thing that has happened?'

'Yes. It isn't very often, I understand, that a serious accident happens. It is just bad luck that it should be Demonstration Day.'

'Oh, the accident, yes. But do you know that Catherine says she can't come to Larborough tonight? This has upset things, she says. She must stay here. But that is absurd. Did you ever hear anything more absurd? If there has been some kind of upset that is all the more reason why she should be taken out of herself for a little. I have arranged everything. I even got special flowers for our table tonight. *And* a birthday cake. It's her birthday next Wednesday.'

Lucy wondered if any other person within the bounds of Leys knew when Catherine Lux's birthday was.

Lucy did her best to sympathise, but said gently that she saw Miss Lux's point of view. After all, the girl was seriously injured, and it was all very worrying, and it would no doubt seem to her a little callous to go merry-making in Larborough.

'But it isn't merrymaking! It is just a quiet supper with an old friend. I really can't see why because some student has had an accident she should desert an old friend. You talk to her, Miss Pym. You make her see reason.'

Lucy said she would do her best but could offer no hope of success since she rather shared Miss Lux's ideas on the subject.

'You too! Oh, my God!'

'I know it isn't reasonable. It's even absurd. But neither of us would be happy and the evening would be a dis-appointment and you don't want that to happen? Couldn't you have us tomorrow night instead?'

'No, I'm catching a train directly the evening per-formance is over. And of course, it being Saturday, I have a matinée. And anyhow, I'm playing Romeo at night and that wouldn't please Cath at all. It takes her all her time to stand me in *Richard III*. Oh dear, the whole thing is absurd.'

'Cheer up,' Lucy said. 'It stops short of tragedy. You will be coming to Larborough again, and you can meet as often as you like now that you know she is here.'

'I shall never get Catherine in that pliant mood again. Never. It was partly your doing, you know. She didn't want to appear too much of a Gorgon in front of you. She was even going to come to see me act. Something she has never done before. I'll never get her back to that point if she doesn't come tonight. Do persuade her, Miss Pym.'

Lucy promised to try. 'How are you enjoying your afternoon, apart from broken appointments?'

Mr Adrian was enjoying himself vastly, it appeared. He was not sure which to admire most: the students' good looks or their efficiency.

'They have charming manners, too. I have not been asked for an autograph once, all the afternoon.'

Lucy looked to see if he was being ironic. But no; the remark was 'straight'. He really could not conceive any reason for the lack of autograph hunters other than that of good manners. Poor silly baby, she thought, walking all his life through a world he knew nothing about. She wondered if all actors were like that. Perambulating spheres of atmosphere with a little actor safely cocooned at the heart of each. How nice it must be, so cushioned and safe from harsh reality. They weren't really born at all; they were still floating in some pre-natal fluid.

'Who is the girl who fluffed at the balance exercise?'

Was she not going to get away from Innes for two minutes together?

'Her name is Mary Innes. Why?'

'What a wonderful face. Pure Borgia.'

'Oh, no!' Lucy said, sharply.

'I've been wondering all the afternoon what she reminded me of. I think it is a portrait of a young man by Giorgione, but which of his young men I wouldn't know. I should have to see them again. Anyhow, it's a wonderful face, so delicate and so strong, so good and so bad. Quite fantastically beautiful. I can't imagine what anything so dramatic is doing at a girls' Physical Training College in the twentieth century.'

Well, at least she had the consolation of knowing that someone else saw Innes as she did; exceptional, oddly fine, out of her century, and potentially tragic. She remembered that to Henrietta she was merely a tiresome girl who looked down her nose at people less well endowed with brains.

Lucy wondered what to offer Edward Adrian by way of distraction. She saw coming down the path a floppy satin bow-tie against a dazzling collar and recognised Mr Robb, the elocution master; the only member of the visiting Staff, apart from Dr Knight, that she knew. Mr Robb had been a dashing young actor forty years ago— the most brilliant Lancelot Gobbo of his generation, one understood—and she felt that to hoist Mr Adrian with his own petard would be rather pleasant. But being Lucy her heart softened at the thought of the wasted preparations he had made—the flowers, the cake, the plans for showing off—and she decided to be merciful. She saw O'Donnell, gazing from a discreet distance at her one-time hero, and she beckoned to her. Edward Adrian should have a real, authentic, dyed-in-the-wool fan to cheer him; and he need never know that she was the only one in College.

'Mr Adrian,' she said, 'this is Eileen O'Donnell, one of your most devoted admirers.'

'Oh, Mr Adrian——' she heard O'Donnell begin.

And she left them to it.

19

WHEN tea was over (and Lucy had been introduced to at least twenty different sets of parents) the drift back from the garden began, and Lucy overtook Miss Lux on the way to the house.

'I'm afraid that I am going to cry off tonight,' she said. 'I feel a migraine coming.'

'That is a pity,' Lux said without emotion. 'I have cried off too.'

'Oh, why?'

'I'm very tired, and upset about Rouse, and I don't feel like going junketing in town.'

'You surprise me.'

'I surprise you? In what way?'

'I never thought I should live to see Catherine Lux being dishonest with herself.'

'Oh. And what am I fooling myself about?'

'If you have a look at your mind you'll find that that's not why you're staying at home.'

'No? Why, then?'

'Because you get such pleasure out of telling Edward Adrian where he gets off.'

'A deplorable expression.'

'Descriptive, though. You simply jumped at the chance of being high and mighty with him, didn't you?'

'I own that breaking the engagement was no effort.'

'And a little unkind?'

'A deplorable piece of self-indulgence by a shrew. That's what you're trying to say, isn't it?'

'He is looking forward so much to having you. I can't think why.'

'Thanks. I can tell you why. So that he can cry all over me and tell me how he hates acting—which is the breath of life to him.'

'Even if he bores you——'

'If! My God!'

'——you can surely put up with him for an hour or so, and not use Rouse's accident as a sort of ace from your sleeve.'

'Are you trying to make an honest woman of me, Lucy Pym?'

'That is the general idea. I feel so sorry for him, being left——'

'My—good—woman,' Lux said, stabbing a forefinger at Lucy with each word, '*never* be sorry for Edward Adrian. Women spend the best years of their lives being sorry for him, and end by being sorry for it. Of all the self-indulgent, self-deceiving——'

'But he *has* got a Johannisberger.'

Lux stopped, and smiled at her.

'I could do with a drink, at that,' she said reflectively. She walked on a little.

'Are you really leaving Teddy high and dry?' she asked.

'Yes.'

'All right. You win. I was just being a beast. I'll go. And every time he trots out that line about: "Oh, Catherine, how weary I am of this artificial life" I shall think with malice: That Pym woman got me into this.'

'I can bear it,' Lucy said. 'Has anyone heard how Rouse is?'

'Miss Hodge has just been on the telephone. She is still unconscious.'

Lucy, seeing Henrietta's head through the window of her office—it was known as the office but was in reality the little sitting-room to the left of the front door—went in

to compliment her on the success of the afternoon and so
take her mind for at least a moment or two off the thing
that oppressed it, and Miss Lux walked on. Henrietta
seemed glad to see her, and even glad to have repeated to
her the platitudes she had been listening to all the afternoon, and Lucy stayed talking to her for some time; so
that the gallery was almost filled again when she took her
seat to watch the dancing.

Seeing Edward Adrian in one of the gangway seats she
paused and said:

'Catherine is coming.'

'And you?' he said, looking up.

'No, alas; I am having a migraine at six-thirty sharp.'

Whereupon he said: 'Miss Pym, I adore you,' and
kissed her hand.

His next-door neighbour looked startled, and someone
behind tittered, but Lucy liked having her hand kissed.
What was the good of putting rose-water and glycerine on
every night if you didn't have a little return now and then?

She went back to her seat at the end of the front row,
and found that the dowager with the lorgnettes had not
waited for the dancing; the seat was empty. But just before
the lights went down—the hall was curtained and arti-
ficially lit—Rick appeared from behind and said: 'If you
are not keeping that seat for anyone, may I sit there?'

And as he sat down the first dancers appeared.

After the fourth or fifth item Lucy was conscious of a
slow disappointment. Used to the technical standards of
international ballet, she had not allowed in her mind for
the inevitable amateurism of dancing in this *milieu*. In
everything she had seen the students do so far they had
been the best of their line in the business; professionals.
But it was obviously not possible to give to other subjects
the time and energy that they did and still reach a high
standard as dancers. Dancing was a wholetime job.

What they did was good, but it was uninspired. On the

best amateur level, or a little above. So far the programme had consisted of tne national and period dances beloved of all dancing mistresses, and they had been performed with a conscientious accuracy that was admirable but not diverting. Perhaps the need for keeping their minds on the altered track took some of the spontaneity from their work. But on the whole Lucy thought that it was that neither training nor temperament were sufficient. Their audience too lacked spontaneity; the eagerness with which they had watched the gymnastics was lacking. Perhaps they had had too much tea; or perhaps it was that the cinema had brought to their remotest doors a standard of achievement that made them critical. Anyhow their applause was polite rather than enthusiastic.

A piece of Russian bravura roused them for a moment, and they waited hopefully for what might come next. The curtains parted to reveal Desterro, alone. Her arms raised above her head and one slim hip turned to the audience. She was wearing some sort of native dress from her own hemisphere, and the 'spot' made the bright colours and the barbaric jewels glitter so that she looked like one of the brilliant birds from her Brazilian forests. Her little feet in their high-heeled shoes tapped impatiently under the full skirt. She began to dance; slowly, almost absent-mindedly, as if she were putting in time. Then it became evident that she was waiting for her lover and that he was late. What his lateness meant to her also became rapidly apparent. By this time the audience were sitting up. From some empty space she conjured a lover. One could almost see the hang-dog look on his swarthy face. She dealt with him: faithfully. By this time the audience were sitting on the edge of their seats. Then, having dealt with him, she began to show off to him; but did he not realise his luck in having a girl like her, a girl who had a waist, an eye, a hip, a mouth, an ankle, a total grace like hers? Was he a boor that he could not see? She therefore showed him;

with a wit in every movement that brought smiles to every face in the audience. Lucy turned to look at them; in another minute they would be cooing. It was magic. By the time she began to relent and let her lover have a word in, they were her slaves. And when she walked away with that still invisible, but undoubtedly subdued, young man, they cheered like children at a Wild West matinée.

Watching her as she took her bow, Lucy remembered how The Nut Tart had chosen Leys because for the proper dancing schools 'one must have a *métier*'.

'She was modest about her dancing after all,' she said aloud. 'She could have been a professional.'

'I am glad she didn't,' Rick said. 'Coming here she has learned to love the English countryside. If she had trained in town she would have met only the international riff-raff that hang around ballet.'

And Lucy thought that he was probably right.

There was a distinct drop in temperature when the conscientious students reappeared to continue their numbers. Stewart had a Celtic verve that was refreshing, and Innes had grace and moments of fire, but the moment Desterro came among them even Lucy forgot Innes and all the others. Desterro was enchanting.

At the end she had an ovation all to herself.

And Miss Pym, catching the look on Rick's face, felt a small pang.

It was not enough to have one's hand kissed.

'Nobody told me that Desterro could dance like that,' she said to Miss Wragg as they went over to supper together when the guests had at last taken their departures with much starting up of engines and shouted good-byes.

'Oh, she is Madame's little pet,' Wragg said in the unenthusiastic voice of Madame's follower speaking of a creature so far gone in sin that she did not play games. 'I think she is stagey, myself. Out of place here, somehow. I honestly think that first dance wasn't quite nice. Did you think that?'

'I thought it delightful.'

'Oh, well,' Wragg said resignedly; and added: 'She must be good, or Madame wouldn't be so keen on her.'

Supper was a quiet meal. Exhaustion, anticlimax, and the recollection (now that they were idle) of this morning's accident, all served to damp the students' spirits and clog their tongues. The Staff, too, were tired after their shocks, exertions, social efforts, and anxieties. Lucy felt that the occasion called for a glass of good wine, and thought with a passing regret of the Johannisberger that Lux was drinking at that moment. Her heart had begun to thud in a horrid way when she thought that in a few moments she must take that little rosette into the office, and tell Henrietta where she found it.

She had still not taken it out of the drawer where she had left it, and after supper she was on the way up to fetch it, when she was overtaken by Beau, who slid an arm into hers and said:

'Miss Pym, we are brewing cocoa in the Common Room, the whole shoot of us. Do come and cheer us up. You don't want to go and sit in that morgue upstairs'—the morgue was presumably the drawing-room—'do you? Come and cheer us up.'

'I don't feel particularly cheerful myself,' Lucy said, thinking with loathing of the cocoa, 'but if you put up with my gloom I shall put up with yours.'

As they turned towards the common-room a great wind out of nowhere swept down the corridor through all the wide-open windows, dashing the green branches of the trees outside against one another and tearing the leaves upward so that their backs showed. 'The end of the good weather,' Lucy said, pausing to listen. She had always hated that restless destroying wind that put paid to the golden times.

'Yes; it's cold too,' Beau said. 'We've lit a wood fire.'

The common-room was part of the 'old house' and had an old brick fireplace; and it certainly looked cheerful with the flame and crackle of a freshly lit fire, the rattle of crockery, the bright dresses of the students lying about in exhausted heaps, and their still brighter bedroom slippers. It was not only O'Donnell who had had recourse to odd footwear tonight; practically everyone was wearing undress shoes of some sort or another. In fact Dakers was lying on a settee with her bare bandaged toes higher than her head. She waved a cheerful hand at Miss Pym, and indicated her feet.

'Haemostosis!' she said. 'I bled into my *best* ballet shoes. I suppose no one would like to *buy* a pair of ballet shoes, slightly soiled? No, I was afraid not.'

'There's a chair over by the fire, Miss Pym,' Beau said, and went to pour out the cocoa. Innes, who was sitting curled up on the hearth superintending a Junior's efforts with a bellows, patted the chair and made her welcome in her usual unsmiling fashion.

'I've cadged the rest of the tea stuff from Miss Joliffe,' Hasselt said, coming in with a large plate of mixed leftovers.

'How did you do that?' they asked. 'Miss Joliffe never gives away even a smell.'

'I promised to send her some peach jam when I go back to South Africa. There isn't really very much though it looks a plateful. The maids had most of it after tea. Hullo, Miss Pym. What did you think of us?'

'I thought you were all wonderful,' Lucy said.

'Just like London policemen,' Beau said. 'Well, you bought that, Hasselt.'

Lucy apologised for the cliché, and sought by going into further detail to convince them of her enthusiasm.

'Desterro ran away with the evening, didn't she, though?' they said; and glanced with friendly envy at

219

the composed figure in the bright wrap sitting upright in the ingle-nook.

'Me, I do only one thing. It is easy to do just one thing well.'

And Lucy, like the rest of them, could not decide if the cool little remark was meant to be humble or reproving. On the whole she thought humble.

'That's enough, March, it's going beautifully,' Innes said to the Junior, and moved to take the bellows from her. As she moved her feet came out from under her and Lucy saw that she was wearing black pumps.

And the little metal ornament that should have been on the left one was not there.

Oh, *no*, said Lucy's mind. No. No. No.

'That is your cup, Miss Pym, and here is yours, Innes. Have a rather tired macaroon, Miss Pym.'

'No, I have some chocolate biscuits for Miss Pym.'

'No, she is going to have some Ayrshire shortbread, out of a tin, and *fresh*. None of your pawed-over victuals.'

The babble went on round her. She took something off a plate. She answered what was said to her. She even took a sip of the stuff in the cup.

Oh, no. No.

Now that the thing was here—the thing she had been afraid of, so afraid that she would not even formulate it in her mind—now that it was here, made concrete and manifest, she was appalled. It had all suddenly become a nightmare: the bright noisy room with the blackening sky outside where the storm was rushing up, and the missing object. One of those nightmares where something small and irrelevant has a terrifying importance. Where something immediate and urgent must be done about it but one can't think what or why.

Presently she must get up and make polite leave-taking and go to Henrietta with her story and end by saying: 'And I know whose shoe it came from. Mary Innes's.'

Innes was sitting at her feet, not eating, but drinking cocoa thirstily. She had curled her feet under her again, but Lucy had no need for further inspection. Even her faint hopes that someone else might be wearing pumps had gone overboard. There was a fine colourful variety of footgear present but not a second pair of pumps.

In any case, no one else had a motive for being in the gymnasium at six o'clock this morning.

'Have some more cocoa,' Innes said presently, turning to look at her. But Miss Pym had hardly touched hers.

'Then I must have some more,' Innes said, and began to get up.

A very tall thin Junior called Farthing, but known even to the Staff as Tuppence-Ha'penny, came in.

'You're late, Tuppence,' someone said. 'Come and have a bun.' But Farthing stood there, uncertainly.

'What is the matter, Tuppence?' they asked, puzzled by her shocked expression.

'I went to put the flowers in Fröken's room,' she said slowly.

'Don't tell us there were some there already?' someone said; and there was a general laugh.

'I heard the Staff talking about Rouse.'

'Well, what about her? Is she better?'

'She's dead.'

The cup Innes was holding crashed on the hearth. Beau crossed over to her to pick up the pieces.

'Oh, nonsense,' they said. 'You heard wrong, young Tuppence.'

'No, I didn't. They were talking on the landing. She died half an hour ago.'

This was succeeded by a dismayed silence.

'I *did* put up the wall end,' O'Donnell said loudly, into the silence.

'Of course you did, Don,' Stewart said, going to her. 'We all know that.'

Lucy put down her cup and thought that she had better go upstairs. They let her go with murmured regrets, their happy party in pieces round them.

Upstairs, Lucy found that Miss Hodge had gone to the hospital to receive Rouse's people when they arrived, and that it was she who had telephoned the news. Rouse's people had come, and had taken the blow unemotionally, it seemed.

'I never liked her, God forgive me,' said Madame, stretched at full length on the hard sofa; her plea to the Deity for forgiveness had a genuine sound.

'Oh, she was all right,' Wragg said, 'quite nice when you knew her. And the most marvellous centre-half. This is frightful, isn't it! Now it will be a matter of inquiry, and we'll have police, an inquest, and appalling publicity. and everything.'

Yes, police and everything.

She could not do anything about the little rosette to-night. And anyhow she wanted to think about it.

She wanted to get away by herself and think about it.

20

Bong! Bong! The clock in that far-away steeple struck again.

Two o'clock.

She lay staring into the dark, while the cold rain beat on the ground outside and wild gusts rose every now and then and rioted in anarchy, flinging her curtains out into the room so that they flapped like sails and everything was uncertainty and turmoil.

The rain wept with steady persistence, and her heart wept with it. And in her mind was a turmoil greater than the wind's.

'Do the obvious right thing, and let God dispose,' Rick had said. And it had seemed a sensible ruling.

But that was when it had been a hypothetical affair of 'causing grievous bodily harm' (that was the phrase, wasn't it?) and now it had ceased to be hypothesis and it wasn't any longer mere bodily harm. It was—was *this*.

It wouldn't be God who would dispose this, in spite of all the comforting tags. It would be the Law. Something written with ink in a statute book. And once that was invoked God Himself could not save a score of innocent persons being crushed under the Juggernaut wheels of its progress.

An eye for an eye and a tooth for a tooth, said the old Mosaic law. And it sounded simple. It sounded just. One saw it against a desert background, as if it involved two people only. It was quite different when one put it in modern words and called it 'being hanged by the neck until you are dead'.

If she went to Henrietta in the——

If?

Oh, all right, of course she was going.

When she went to Henrietta in the morning, she would be putting in motion a power over which neither she nor anyone else had control; a power that once released would catch up this, that, and the next one from the innocent security of their peaceful lives and fling them into chaos.

She thought of Mrs Innes, happily asleep somewhere in Larborough; bound home tomorrow to wait for the return of the daughter in whom she had her life. But her daughter would not come home—ever.

Neither will Rouse, a voice pointed out.

No, of course not, and Innes must somehow pay for that. She must not be allowed to profit by her crime. But surely, surely there was some way in which payment could be made without making the innocent pay even more bitterly.

What was justice?

To break a woman's heart; to bring ruin and shame on Henrietta and the destruction of all she had built up; to rub out for ever the radiance of Beau, the Beau who was unconditioned to grief. Was that a life for a life? That was three—no, four lives for one.

And one not worth——

Oh, no. That she could not judge. For that one had to 'see before and after', as Rick said. A curiously sober mind, Rick had, for a person with a play-boy's face and a Latin lover's charm.

There was Innes moving about again next-door. As far as Lucy knew she had not slept yet either. She was very quiet, but every now and then one heard a movement or the tap in her room ran. Lucy wondered whether the water was to satisfy a thirst or to cool temples that must be throbbing. If she, Lucy, was lying awake with her thoughts running round and round inside her skull like trapped mice, what must Innes be going through?

Humourless she might be, unenamoured of the human species she probably was, but insensitive she most certainly was not. Whether it was thwarted ambition, or sheer anger and hate, that had driven her down to the gymnasium through the misty morning, she was not the sort to be able to do what she had done with impunity. It might well be, indeed, that given her temperament it was herself she had destroyed when she tampered with that boom. In the case-histories of crime there were instances of women so callous that they had come to a fresh blooming once the obstacle to their desires was out of the way. But they were not built like Mary Innes. Innes belonged to that other, and rarer, class who found too late that they could not live with themselves any more. The price they had paid was too high.

Perhaps Innes would provide her own punishment.

That, now she came to think of it, was how she had first thought of Innes, on that Sunday afternoon under the cedar. The stake or nothing. A self-destroyer.

That she had destroyed a life that stood in her way was almost incidental.

It had not, in any case, been intended as destruction; Lucy was quite sure of that. That is what made this business of starting the machine so repellent, so unthinkable. All that the insecure pin was meant to achieve was a temporary incapacity. An assurance that Rouse would not go to Arlinghurst in September—and that *she* would.

Had she had that in mind, Lucy wondered, when she refused the appointment at the Wycherley Orthopaedic Hospital? No, surely not. She was not a planner in cold blood. The thing had been done at the very last moment, in desperation.

At least, it had been *achieved* at the very last moment.

It was possible that its lateness was due to lack of previous opportunity. The way to the gymnasium might never have been clear before; or Rouse may have got there first.

'A Borgia face,' Edward Adrian had said, delightedly.

And Teresa's great-grandmother's grandmother, whom she resembled, *she* had planned. And had lived a long, secure, and successful life as a widow, administering rich estates and bringing up a son, without apparently any signs of spiritual suicide.

The wind flung itself into the room, and Innes's window began to rattle. She heard Innes cross the room to it, and presently it stopped.

She wished she could go next-door, now, at this minute, and put her hand down. Show Innes the ace she held and didn't want to play. Together they could work something out.

Together? With the girl who loosened that pin under the boom?

No. With the girl she had talked to in the corridor last Saturday afternoon, so radiant, so full of dignity and wisdom. With the girl who could not sleep tonight. With her mother's daughter.

Whatever she had done, even if she had planned it, the result had been something she had neither planned nor foreseen. The result was catastrophe for her.

And who in the first place had brought about that catastrophe?

Henrietta. Henrietta with her mule-like preference for her inferior favourite.

She wondered if Henrietta was sharing Innes's vigil. Henrietta who had come back from West Larborough so strangely thin and old-looking. As if the frame she was strung on had collapsed and the stuffing had shifted. Like a badly stuffed toy after a month in the nursery. That is what Henrietta had looked like.

She had been truly sorry for her friend, bereft of some-one she had—loved? Yes, loved, she supposed. Only love

226

could have blinded her to Rouse's defects. Bereft; and afraid for her beloved Leys. She had been truly moved by her suffering. But she could not help the thought that but for Henrietta's own action none of this would have happened.

The operative cause was Innes's vulnerability. But the button that had set the whole tragedy in motion was pressed by Henrietta.

And now she, Lucy, was waiting to press another button which would set in motion machinery even more monstrous. Machinery that would catch up in its gears and meshes, and maim and destroy, the innocent with the guilty. Henrietta perhaps had bought her punishment, but what had the Inneses done to have this horror unloaded on them? This unnameable horror.

Or *had* they contributed? How much had Innes's upbringing been responsible for her lack of resilience? Given that she had been born without 'oil on her feathers', had they tried to condition her to the lack? Who could ever say where first causes lay?

Perhaps after all, even through the Law, it was the Deity who disposed. If you were a Christian you took that for granted, of course. You took for granted that nothing ever happened that there was no cause for. That everyone who would be tortured incidentally by Innes's trial for murder had in some way 'bought' their punishment. It was a fine comfortable theory, and Lucy wished that she could subscribe to it. But she found it difficult to believe that any deficiency on the part of parents as responsible and as devoted as the Inneses could warrant the bringing down on their heads of a tragedy so unspeakable.

Or perhaps——

She sat up, to consider this new thought.

If God did dispose—as undoubtedly He did in the latter end—then perhaps the disposing was already at work. Had begun to work when it was she and not someone else who found the little rosette. It had not been found by a strong-minded person who would go straight to Henrietta with it as soon as she smelt a rat, and so set the machinery of man-made Law in motion. No. It had been found by a feeble waverer like herself, who could never see less than three sides to any question. Perhaps that made sense.

But she wished very heartily that the Deity had found another instrument. She had always hated responsibility; and a responsibility of this magnitude was something that she could not deal with at all. She wished that she could throw away the little rosette—toss it out of the window now and pretend that she had never seen it. But of course she could not do that. However rabbity and inadequate she was by nature, there was always her other half—the Laetitia half—which stood watching her with critical eyes. She could never get away from that other half of herself. It had sent her into fights with her knees knocking, it had made her speak when she wanted to hold her tongue, it had kept her from lying down when she was too tired to stand up. It would keep her from washing her hands now.

She got up and leaned out into the wet, lashing, noisy night. There was a puddle of rainwater on the wood floor inside the window. The cold shock of it on her bare feet was somehow grateful; a physical and understandable discomfort. At least she did not have to mop it up, or wonder about a carpet. All the elements came into this place at their will and everyone took it for granted. One of Innes's few volunteered remarks had been how lovely it had been one morning to waken and find her pillow crusted with snow. That had happened only once, she said, but you could always tell the season by what you found on your pillow in the morning: spiders in the autumn and sycamore seeds in June.

She stayed so long cooling her burning head that her feet grew cold, and she had to wrap them in a jersey to warm them when she got back into bed. That completes it, she thought: cold feet mentally and physically. You're a poor thing, Lucy Pym.

About three o'clock when she was growing sleepy at last, she was shot wide awake by the realisation of what she was proposing to do. She was seriously considering keeping back evidence in a capital charge. Becoming an accessory after the fact. A criminal.

She, respectable, law-abiding Lucy Pym.

How had she got to that point? What could she have been thinking of?

Of course she had no choice in the matter at all. Who disposed or did not dispose was no concern of hers. This was a matter of public inquiry, and she had a duty to do. A duty to civilisation, to the State, to herself. Her private emotions had nothing to do with it. Her views on justice had nothing to do with it. However unequal and wrong-headed the Law might be, she could not suppress evidence.

How in the name of all that was crazy had she ever thought that she could?

Rick was right: she would do the obvious right thing, and let God dispose.

About half-past four she really did fall asleep.

21

THE morning was bleary and sodden, and Lucy regarded it with distaste. The waking-bell had sounded as usual at five-thirty, although on the morning after the Demonstration there were no classes before breakfast. College might make concessions, but it did not discard its habits. She tried to fall asleep again, but reality had come with the daylight, and what had been feverish theory in the dark hours was now chill fact. In an hour or two she would have pressed that button, and altered beyond computing lives of whose existence she was not even aware. Her heart began to thud again.

Oh, dear, why had she ever come to this place!

It was when she had finished dressing and was sticking a few invisible hairpins into appropriate places that she realised that she could not go to Henrietta about the rosette without first going to Innes. She was not sure whether this was a remnant of some childish conception of 'playing fair' or whether she was just trying to find a way of breaking the matter that would make her own personal responsibility less absolute.

She went to Innes's door, quickly before the impulse to action should evaporate, and knocked. She had heard Innes come back from her bath and reckoned that by now she must be dressed.

The Innes who opened the door looked tired and heavy-eyed but composed. Now that she was face to face with her Lucy found it difficult to identify her with the Innes of her disturbed thoughts last night.

'Do you mind coming into my room for a moment?' she asked.

Innes hesitated, looked uncertain for a second, and then recovered herself. 'Yes, of course,' she said; and followed Lucy.

'What a night of rain it was,' she said brightly.

It was unlike Innes to bother with remarks about the weather. And it was exceedingly unlike Innes to be bright.

Lucy took the little silver rosette out of her drawer and held it out on her palm for Innes to see.

'Do you know what that is?' she asked.

In a second the brightness had disappeared and Innes's face was hard and wary.

'Where did you get that?' she snapped.

It was only then that Lucy realised how, deep down, she had counted on Innes's reaction being different. How, unconsciously, she had expected Innes to say: 'It looks like something off a dancing pump; lots of us have them.' Her heart stopped thudding and sank into her stomach.

'I found it on the gymnasium floor very early yesterday morning,' she said.

The hard wariness melted into a slow despair.

'And why do you show it to me?' Innes said dully.

'Because I understand that there is only one pair of those old-fashioned pumps in College.'

There was silence. Lucy laid the little object down on the table and waited.

'Am I wrong?' she asked at last.

'No.'

There was another silence.

'You don't understand, Miss Pym,' she said in a burst, it wasn't meant to be——. I know you'll think I'm just trying to whitewash it, but it was never meant to be—to be the way it turned out. It was because I was so sick about missing Arlinghurst—I practically lost my reason over that for a time—I behaved like an idiot. It got so

231

that I couldn't think of anything in the world but Arling-hurst. And this was just to be a way of—of letting me have a second chance at it. It was never meant to be more than that. You must believe that. You must——'

'But of course I believe it. If I didn't I don't suppose I should be sharing the knowledge of this with you.' She indicated the rosette.

After a moment Innes said: 'What are you going to do?'

'Oh, dear God, I don't know,' said poor Lucy, helpless now that she was face to face with reality. All the crimes she had met with were in slick detective stories where the heroine, however questionable, was invariably innocent, or in case-histories where the crime was safely over with and put away and a matter only for the scalpel. All those subjects of case-history record had had friends and rela-tions whose stunned disbelief must have been very like her own, but the knowledge was neither comfort nor guide to her. This was the kind of thing that happened to other people—happened daily if one could believe the Press—but could not possibly happen to oneself.

How *could* one believe that someone one had laughed and talked with, liked and admired, shared a communal life with, could be responsible for another's death?

She found herself beginning to tell Innes of her sleepless night, of her theories about 'disposing', of her reluctance to destroy half a dozen lives because of one person's crime. She was too absorbed in her own problem to notice the dawning hope in Innes's eyes. It was only when she heard herself saying: 'Of course you cannot possibly be allowed to profit by Rouse's death,' that she realised how far she had already come along the road that she had had no intention of travelling.

But Innes pounced on this. 'Oh, but I won't, Miss Pym. And it has nothing to do with your finding the little ornament. I knew last night when I heard that she was dead that I couldn't go to Arlinghurst. I was going to tell

Miss Hodge this morning. I was awake too last night. Facing a lot of things. Not only my responsibility for Rouse's death—my inability to take defeat and like it. But—oh, well, a lot of things that wouldn't interest you.' She paused a moment, considering Lucy. 'Look, Miss Pym, if I were to spend the rest of my life atoning for yesterday morning will you—would you——' She could not put so brazen a suggestion into words, even after Lucy's dissertation on justice.

'Become an accessory after the fact?'

The cold legality of the phrase discouraged Innes.

'No. I suppose it is too much to expect anyone to do. But I *would* atone, you know. It wouldn't be any half-hearted affair. It would be my life for—hers. I would do it gladly.'

'I believe you, of course. But how do you plan to atone?'

'I thought of that last night. I began with leper colonies and things like that, but they were rather unreal and didn't make much sense in connection with a Leys training. I have a better idea. I decided that I would work alongside my father. I hadn't planned to do medical work, but I am good at it and there is no orthopaedic clinic in our home town.'

'It sounds admirable,' Lucy said, 'but where is the penance?'

'My one ambition since I was a little girl has been to get away from living in a little market town; coming to Leys was my passport to freedom.'

'I see.'

'Believe me, Miss Pym, it would be penance. But it wouldn't be a barren one. It wouldn't be just personal flagellation. I would be doing something useful with my life, something that would—would make it good value for exchange.'

'Yes, I see.'

There was another long silence.

The five-minute bell rang, but for the first time since she came to Leys Lucy was unconscious of a bell.

'Of course you have nothing but my word for it——'

'I would accept your word.'

'Thank you.'

It seemed too easy a way out, she was thinking. If Innes was to be punished, the living of a dull and useful life hardly seemed a sufficient exaction. She had forfeited Arlinghurst of course; that would cost her something. But would it pay for a death?

What, in any case, would pay for a death? Except a death.

And Innes was offering what she obviously considered a living death. Perhaps after all it was not so poor an exchange.

What she, Lucy, was faced with was the fact that all her deliberations, her self-communing and comparing of arguments, fused at this moment into one single and simple issue: Was she going to condemn to death the girl who was standing in front of her?

It was, after all, as simple as that. If she took that little rosette to Henrietta this morning, Innes would die before the first students came back to Leys in the autumn. If she did not die she would spend her twenties in a living death that would indeed be 'barren'.

Let her spend her years in the prison of her choice, where she could be useful to her fellows.

Certainly she, Lucy Pym, was quite unequal to the task of condemning her.

And that was that.

'I am entirely in your hands,' she said slowly to Innes, 'because I am quite incapable of sending anyone to the gallows. I know what my plain duty is and I can't do it.' Odd, she thought, that I should be in her reverence rather than she in mine.

Innes stared at her, doubtfully.

'You mean——' Her tongue came out and ran along her dry lips. 'You mean that you won't tell about the rosette?'

'No. I shall never tell anyone.'

Innes went suddenly white.

So white that Lucy realised that this was a phenomenon that she had read about but never seen. 'White as a sheet', they said. Well, it was perhaps an unbleached sheet, but it certainly was 'going white'.

Innes put her hand out to the chair by the dressing-table and sat down abruptly. Seeing Lucy's anxious expression she said: 'It's all right, I'm not going to faint. I've never fainted in my life. I'll be all right in a minute.'

Lucy, who had been antagonised by her self-possession, her ready bargaining—Innes had been far too lucid on the subject, she felt—was seized with something like compunction. Innes had not after all been self-possessed. It had been the old story of emotion clamped down and taking a mean revenge when it found escape.

'Would you like a drink of water?' Lucy said, moving to the wash-basin.

'No, thank you, I'm all right. It's just that for the last twenty-four hours I've been so afraid, and seeing that silver thing on your hand was the last straw, and then suddenly it is all over, you've let me buy a reprieve, and—and——'

Sobs came up in her throat and choked the words. Great rending sobs without a single tear. She put her hands over her mouth to stop them, but they burst through and she covered her face and struggled for composure. It was no use. She put both arms on the desk with her head between them and sobbed her heart out.

And Lucy, looking at her, thought: Another girl would have begun with this. Would have used it as a weapon, a bid for my sympathy. But not Innes. Innes comes self-contained and aloof, offering hostages. Without the breakdown no one would have guessed that she was suffering. Her present abandonment was the measure of her previous torture.

The first low murmur of the gong began in a slow crescendo.

Innes heard it and struggled to her feet. 'If you'll forgive me,' she said, 'I'll go and dash some cold water on myself. That will stop it.'

Lucy thought it remarkable that a girl so racked with sobs that she could hardly speak should prescribe for herself with such detachment; as if she were another person from this hysterical individual who had taken possession of her and was making such an exhibition of herself.

'Yes, do,' Lucy said.

Innes paused with her hand on the door-knob.

'Some day I'll be able to thank you properly,' she said, and disappeared.

Lucy dropped the little silver rosette into her pocket and went down to breakfast.

22

IT was a horrible week-end.

The rain poured down. Henrietta went about looking as though she had had a major operation that had not proved a success. Madame was at her worst and not at all helpful, either actually or verbally. Fröken was furious that such a thing should have happened in 'her' gymnasium. Wragg was an ever-present Cassandra scattering depressing truisms. Lux was quiet and tired.

Lux had come back from Larborough bearing a small pink candle wrapped in pale green tissue paper. 'Teddy said I was to give you this,' she said. 'I can't think why.'

'Oh? From a cake?'

'Yes. It's my birthday about now.'

'How nice of him to remember.'

'Oh, he keeps a birthday diary. It's part of his publicity. It is his secretary's duty to send telegrams to all the appropriate people on the appropriate days.'

'Don't you ever give him credit for anything?' Lucy asked.

'Teddy? Not for a real emotion, I don't. I've known him since he was ten, don't forget. He can't fool me for more than five seconds together.'

'My hairdresser,' Lucy said, 'who lectures to me while he is doing my hair, says that one should allow everyone three faults. If one makes that allowance, one finds that the rest is surprisingly nice, he says.'

'When you allow for Teddy's three faults there is nothing left, unfortunately.'

'Why?'

'Because his three faults are vanity, selfishness, and self-pity. And any one of the three is totally destructive.'

'Whew!' said Lucy. 'I give up.'

But she stuck the silly little candle on her dressing-table, and thought kindly of Edward Adrian.

She wished she could think as kindly of her beloved Beau, who was making things as difficult as possible by being furious with Innes for giving up Arlinghurst. In fact Lucy understood that things had come as near a quarrel between them as was possible between two people so mutually devoted.

'Says she wouldn't be happy in dead men's shoes,' said Beau, positively giving off sparks with wrath. 'Can you imagine anything more ridiculous? Turning down Arlinghurst as if it were a cup of tea. After nearly dying of chagrin because she didn't get it in the first place. For God's sake, Miss Pym, you talk to her and make her see sense before it is too late. It isn't just Arlinghurst, it's her whole future. Beginning at Arlinghurst means beginning at the top. You talk to her, will you? Talk her out of this absurd notion!'

It seemed to Lucy that she was always being implored to 'talk to' people. When she wasn't being a dose of soothing syrup she was being a shot of adrenalin, and when she wasn't being that she was being just a spoonful of alkaline powder for general consumption.

When she wasn't being a *deus ex machina*; a perverter of justice. But she tried not to think of that.

There was nothing she could say to Innes, of course, but other people had said it. Miss Hodge had wrought with her long and faithfully; dismayed by the defection of the girl she had not wanted to appoint in the first place. Now she had no one to send to Arlinghurst; she must write and tell them so and see the appointment go elsewhere. Perhaps when the news of the fatal accident leaked round the academic world Arlinghurst would decide to look elsewhere next time they wanted a gymnast. Accidents shouldn't happen in well conducted gymnasiums; not fatal accidents, anyhow.

That, too, was the police point of view. They had been very nice, the police, very considerate. Very willing to consider the harm that undesirable publicity would do the establishment. But there had to be an inquest, of course. And inquests were painfully public and open to misconstruction. Henrietta's lawyer had seen the local Press and they had promised to play down the affair, but who knew when a clipping might catch the eye of a sub-editor at a temporary loss for a sensation? And then what?

Lucy had wanted to go away before the inquest, to get away from the perpetual reminders of her guilt in the eyes of the Law, but Henrietta had begged her to stay. She had never been able to say no to Henrietta, and this pathetic aged Henrietta was someone whom she could not refuse. So Lucy stayed; doing odd jobs for Henrietta and generally leaving her free to deal with the crowd of extraneous duties that the accident had saddled her with.

But to the inquest she would not go.

She could not sit there with all her load of knowledge and not at some point be tempted to stand up and tell the truth and have the responsibility off her soul.

Who knew what rat the police might smell out? They had come and viewed the gymnasium, and measured things, and reckoned the weight of the boom, and interviewed all and sundry, and consulted the various experts on the subject, and listened and said nothing. They had taken away the pin that had been so fatally insecure; and that may have been mere routine, but who could tell; Who could tell what suspicions they might be entertaining in their large calm breasts and behind their polite expressionless faces?

But as it turned out, a quite unexpected saviour appeared at the inquest. A saviour in the person of Arthur

Middleham, tea importer, of 59 West Larborough Road; that is to say, a resident in one of the villas which lined the highroad between West Larborough and the gates of Leys. Mr Middleham knew nothing about College except that it was there, and that the scantily attired young women who flew about the district on bicycles belong to it. But he had heard about the accident. And it had struck him as odd that a pin in the gymnasium at Leys had moved out of place on the same morning, and presumably about the same time, as a pane of glass had been shaken out of his drawing-room window by a passing convoy of tanks from the works at South Larborough. His theory was, in fact, the same as Miss Lux's; vibration. Only Miss Lux's had been a hit in the dark and of no value. Mr Middleham's was reasonable and backed by three-dimensional evidence: a pane of broken glass.

And as always when someone has given a lead, there were gratuitous followers. (If someone invented a story and wrote to the Press that they had seen a green lion in the sky at 5.30 the previous evening, at least six people would have seen it retrospectively.) An excited woman, hearing Mr Middleham's evidence, got up from the body of the hall and said that her ginger jar that she had had for years had dropped off the little table in her window of its own accord at the same time.

'Where do you live, madam?' the coroner asked, when he had winkled her out of the crowd and installed her as evidence.

She lived in the cottages between Leys and Bidlington, she said. On the highroad? Oh, yes, much too much on the highroad; in the summer the dust was a fair sickener, and when the traffic was them there tanks——. No, she had no cat. No, there had been no one in the room. She had just come in after breakfast and found it on the floor It had never happened before.

Poor O'Donnell, very nervous but clear and decided,

gave evidence that she had put up the end by the wall and that Rouse had attended to the middle end. 'Putting it up' meant hoisting the boom by the pulley rope and pushing the pin under it to keep it up. It was also kept up, to a certain extent, by the rope, the hanging end of which was given a turn round a cleat on the upright. No, they had not tested the apparatus before going.

Fröken, asked about the rope which had not proved a substitute for the pin, said that it had not been wound tightly enough to prevent sagging when the pin was removed. The twisting of the rope round the cleat was an automatic gesture, and no student thought of it as a precautionary measure. It was that, in fact, of course. The metal of the pin might break through some fault, and the rope in that case took the strain. Yes, it was possible that a rope, unaccustomed to a greater strain than the weight of a boom, had stretched under the sudden addition of a ten-stone burden, but she thought not. Gymnasium ropes were highly tested and guaranteed. It was much more likely that the twist Miss Rouse gave it had been inadequate.

And that seemed to be all. It was an unfortunate accident. The pin the police had abstracted had been used by all and sundry during the Demonstration, and was no evidence of anything.

It was obviously Death By Misadventure.

Well, that was the end of it, Lucy thought, when she heard the news. She had waited in the drawing-room, looking out at the rainy garden, not able to believe that something would not go wrong. No crime was ever committed without a slip-up somewhere; she had read enough case-histories to know that.

There had been one slip-up already, when that little ornament came loose from a shoe. Who knew what else the police might have unearthed? And now it was over, and Innes was safe. And she knew now that it was for Innes that she had put herself in the Law's reverence. She had thought it was for Innes's mother, for Henrietta, for absolute justice. But in the latter end it was because whatever Innes had done she had not deserved what the Law would do to her. She had been highly tried, and her breaking-point was lower than normal. She lacked some alloy, some good coarse reinforcing stuff, that would have helped her to stand tension without giving way. But she was too fine to throw away.

Lucy noticed with interest the quality of the cheer that greeted her as she went up to receive her diploma on Wednesday morning. The cheers for the various Seniors varied not only in intensity but in quality. There was laughter, for instance, and affection in the reception they gave Dakers. And Beau got a Head Senior's tribute; the congratulations of her inferiors to a highly popular Senior. But there was something in the cheer that they gave Innes that was remarkable; a warmth of admiration, a sympathy, and a well-wishing, that was accorded to no one else. Lucy wondered if it was merely that her inability to take the Arlinghurst appointment had moved them. Henrietta had said, during that conversation about Rouse and her examination tactics, that Innes was not popular. But there was something more in that cheer than mere popularity. They admired her. It was their tribute to quality.

The giving of diplomas, postponed from Tuesday to Wednesday because of the inquest, was the last event of Lucy's stay at Leys. She had arranged to catch the twelve o'clock train to London. She had been touched during the last few days to receive an endless string of small presents, which were left in her room with written messages attached. She hardly ever returned to her room without finding a new one there. Very few people had given Lucy presents since she grew up, and she still had a child's pleasure in being given something, however small. And these gifts had a spontaneity that was heart-warming; it was no concerted effort, no affair of putting the hat round; they had each given her something as it occurred to them. The Disciples' offering was a large white card which said:

THIS WILL ADMIT

Miss Lucy Pym

TO THE FOUR DISCIPLES CLINIC

AT MANCHESTER

and will provide

A COURSE OF TREATMENTS

Of any kind whatever

At any time whatever.

Dakers had contributed a small untidy parcel, labelled: 'To remind you every morning of our first meeting!' which on being opened proved to be one of those flat loofahs for back-scrubbing. It was surely in some other life that she had been peered at over the bathroom partition by that waggish pony's-face. It was certainly not this Lucy Pym who had sat in the bath.

The devoted Miss Morris had made her a little felt purse—Heaven alone knew when the child had found time to fabricate it—and at the other end of the scale of worldly magnificence was Beau's pigskin case, which bore the message: 'You will have so many parting gifts that you will need something to put them in,' and was stamped with her initials. Even Giddy, with whom she had spent odd half hours talking about rheumatism and rats, had sent up a plant in a pot. She had no idea what it was—it looked fleshy and faintly obscene—but was relieved that it was small. Travelling with a pot plant was not her idea of what was fitting.

Beau had come in between breakfast and Diploma-giving to help her pack, but all the serious packing was done. Whether anything would close once everything was in was another matter.

'I'll come back and sit on them for you before morning clinic,' Beau said. 'We are free until then. Except for clinic there is nothing much to do until we go home on Friday.'

'You'll be sorry to finish at Leys?'

'Dreadfully. I've had a wonderful time. However, summer holidays are a great consolation.'

'Innes told me some time ago that you were going to Norway together.'

'Yes, we were,' Beau said, 'but we're not any more.'

'Oh.'

'Innes has other plans.'

It was evident that this relationship was not what it had been.

'Well, I'd better go and see that the Juniors haven't hogged all the best seats at the Diploma Do,' she said, and went.

But there was one relationship that showed satisfactory progress.

The Nut Tart knocked at her door and said that she had come to give dear Miss Pym a luck-piece. She came in, looked at the piled cases, and said with her customary frankness: 'You are not a very good packer, are you? Neither am I. It is a pedestrian talent.'

Lucy, whose luck-pieces in the last few days had ranged from a Woolworth monkey-on-a-stick to a South African halfpenny, waited with some curiosity to see what The Nut Tart's idea of the thing might be.

It was a blue bead.

'It was dug up in Central America a hundred years ago and it is almost as old as the world. It is very lucky.'

'But I can't take that from you,' Lucy protested.

'Oh, I have a little bracelet of them. It was the bracelet that was dug up. But I have taken out one of the beads for you. There are five left and that is plenty. And I have a piece of news for you. I am not going back to Brazil.'

'No?'

'I am going to stay in England and marry Rick.'

Lucy said that she was delighted to hear it.

'We shall be married in London in October, and you will be there and you will come to the wedding, no?'

Yes, Lucy would come to the wedding with pleasure.

'I am so glad about it,' she said. She needed some contact with happiness after the last few days.

'Yes, it is all very satisfactory. We are cousins but not too near, and it is sensible to keep it in the family. I always thought I should like to marry an Englishman; and of course Rick is a parti. He is senior partner although he is so young. My parents are very pleased. And my grandmother, of course.'

'And I take it that you yourself are pleased?' Lucy said, a shade dashed by this matter-of-fact catalogue.

'Oh yes. Rick is the only person in the world except my grandmother who can make me do things I don't want to do. That will be very good for me.'

She looked at Lucy's doubtful face, and her great eyes sparkled.

'And of course I like him very much,' she said.

When the diplomas had been presented, Lucy had mid-morning coffee with the Staff and said good-bye to them. Since she was leaving in the middle of the morning no one was free to come to the station with her. Henrietta thanked her, with undoubted tears in her eyes this time, for the help she had been. (But not in her wildest imaginings would Henrietta guess how much the help amounted to.) Lucy was to consider Leys as her home any time she wanted to come and stay, or if she ever wanted a lecturers' job again, or if—or if——

And Lucy had to hide the fact that Leys, where she had been so happy, was the one place in the world that she would never come back to. A place that she was going, if her conscience and the shade of Rouse would let her, to blot out of her mind.

The Staff went to their various duties and Lucy went back to her room to finish packing. She had not spoken to Innes since that so-incredible conversation on Saturday morning; had hardly seen her, indeed, except for the moment when she had taken her diploma from Miss Hodge's hands.

Was Innes going to let her go without a word?

But when she came back to her room she found that word on her table. A written word. She opened the envelope and read:

Dear Miss Pym,

Here it is in writing. For the rest of my life I shall atone for the thing I can't undo. I pay forfeit gladly. My life for hers.

I am sorry that this has spoiled Leys for you. And I hope that you will not be unhappy about what you have done for me. I promise to make it worth while.

Perhaps, ten years from today, you will come to the West Country and see what I have done with my life. That would give me a date to look forward to. A landmark in a world without them.

Meanwhile, and always, my gratitude—my unspeakable gratitude.

Mary Innes

'What time did you order the taxi for?' Beau asked, coming in on top of her knock.

'Half-past eleven.'

'It's practically that now. Have you everything in that is going in? Hot-water bottle? You hadn't one. Umbrella downstairs? You don't possess one. What do you do? Wait in doorways till it's over, or steal the nearest one? I had an aunt who always bought the cheapest she could find and discarded it in the nearest waste-paper bin when the rain stopped. More money than sense, as my nanny used to say. Well, now. Is that all? Consider well, because once we get those ~ases shut we'll never get them open again. Nothing left in the drawers? People always leave things stuck at the back of drawers.' She opened the small drawers of the table and ran her hands into the back of them. 'Half the divorces in the Western Hemisphere start through the subsequent revelations.'

She withdrew her right hand, and Lucy saw that she was holding the little silver rosette; left lying at the back of the drawer because Lucy had not been able to make up her mind what to do with it.

Beau turned it over in her fingers.

'That looks like the little button thing off my shoe,' she said.

'*Your* shoe?'

'Yes. Those black pump things that one wore at dancing class. I hung on to them because they are so lovely when one's feet are tired. Like gloves. I can still wear the shoes I wore when I was fourteen. I always had enormous feet for my age, and believe me it was no consolation to be told that you were going to be tall.' Her attention went back to the thing she was holding. 'So *this* is where I lost it,' she said. 'You know, I wondered quite a lot about that.' She dropped it into her pocket. 'You'll have to sit on this case, I'm afraid. You sit on it and I'll wrestle with the locks.'

Automatically Lucy sat on it.

She wondered why she had never noticed before how cold those blue eyes were. Brilliant and cold and shallow.

The bright hair fell over her lap as Beau wrestled with the locks. The locks would do what she wanted, of course. Everything and everyone, always, since the day she was born, had done what she wanted. If they hadn't, she took steps to see that they did. At the age of four, Lucy remembered, she had defeated a whole adult world because her will to have things her way was greater than all the wills combined against her. She had never known frustration.

She could not visualise the possibility of frustration.

If *her* friend had the obvious right to Arlinghurst, then to Arlinghurst she should go.

'There! That's done it. Stand by to sit on the other if I can't manage it. I see Giddy's given you one of his loathsome little plants. What a bore for you. Perhaps you can exchange it for a bowl at the back door one day.'

How soon, Lucy wondered, had Innes begun to suspect? Almost at once? Certainly before the afternoon, when she had turned green on the spot where it had happened.

But she had not been sure until she saw the silver rosette on Lucy's palm, and learned where it had been found.

Poor Innes. Poor Innes, who was paying forfeit.

'*Tax-i!*' yelled a voice along the corridor.

'There's your cab. I'll take your things. No, they're quite light; you forget the training I've had. I wish you weren't going, Miss Pym. We shall miss you so much.'

Lucy heard herself saying the obvious things. She even heard herself promising Beau that she might come to them for Christmas, when Beau would be home for her first 'working' holidays.

Beau put her into the cab, took a tender farewell of her, and said: 'The station' to the driver, and the taxi slid into motion and Beau's face smiled a moment beyond the window, and was gone.

The driver pushed back the glass panel and asked: 'London train, lady?' Yes, Lucy said, to London.

And in London she would stay. In London was her own, safe, nice, calm, collected existence, and in future she would be content with it. She would even give up lecturing on psychology.

What did she know about psychology anyhow?

As a psychologist she was a first-rate teacher of French.

She could write a book about character as betrayed by facial characteristics. At least she had been right about that. Mostly.

Eyebrows that sent people to the stake.

Yes, she would write a book about face-reading.

Under another name, of course. Face-reading was not well seen among the intelligentsia.

A Shilling for Candles

Josephine Tey

Beneath the sea cliffs of the south coast, suicides are a sad but common fact of life. Yet even the hardened coastguard knows something is wrong when a beautiful film actress is found lying dead on the beach one summer's morning. Inspector Grant has to take a more professional attitude: death by suicide, however common, has to have a motive – just like murder . . .

'Josephine Tey has always been absolutely reliable in producing original and mysterious plots with interesting characters and unguessable endings'
Spectator

'Witty, ingenious, and makes one regret more than ever that there will be no more from the same pen'
Vernon Fame, *Sphere*

arrow books

ALSO AVAILABLE IN ARROW

The Daughter of Time
Josephine Tey

Inspector Alan Grant of Scotland Yard, recuperating from a broken leg, becomes fascinated with a contemporary portrait of Richard III that bears no resemblance to the Wicked Uncle of history. Could such a sensitive, noble face actually belong to one of the world's most heinous villains – a venomous hunchback who may have killed his brother's children to make his crown secure? Or could Richard have been the victim, turned into a monster by the usurpers of England's throne?

Grant determines to find out once and for all, with the help of the British Museum and an American scholar, what kind of man Richard Plantagenet really was and who killed the Princes in the Tower.

'A detective story with a considerable difference. Ingenious, stimulating and very enjoyable'
Sunday Times

'Most people will find *The Daughter of Time* as interesting and enjoyable a book as they will meet in a month of Sundays'
Observer

arrow books

Brat Farrar

Josephine Tey

A stranger enters the inner sanctum of the Ashby family posing as Patrick Ashby, the heir to the family's sizeable fortune. The stranger, Brat Farrar, has been carefully coached on Patrick's mannerisms, appearance and every significant detail of Patrick's early life, up to this thirteenth year when he disappeared and was thought to have drowned himself.

It seems as if Brat is going to pull off this most incredible deception until old secrets emerge that threaten to jeopardise the imposter's plan and his very life . . .

'Ingenious, stimulating and very enjoyable' *Sunday Times*

arrow books